Luxembourg & The Jenisch Connection

By the same author

An Expat's Life, Luxembourg & The White Rose
ISBN: 0-595-31485-6

See **www.diadembooks.com/luxembourg.htm**

Luxembourg & The Jenisch Connection

A Novel

David Robinson

iUniverse, Inc.

New York Lincoln Shanghai

Luxembourg & The Jenisch Connection
A Novel

iUniverse books may be ordered through booksellers or by contacting:

iUniverse
2021 Pine Lake Road, Suite 100
Lincoln, NE 68512
www.iuniverse.com
1-800-Authors (1-800-288-4677)

ISBN: 0-595-34840-8

Printed in the United States of America

For my mother

Author's Note

I hope you will enjoy Luxembourg & The Jenisch Connection. It is my first fiction novel following my debut reality book: *An Expat's Life, Luxembourg & The White Rose.*

Currently I am living in Bratislava, Slovakia, where I am writing a second reality book—about Bratislava!

A sequel to this novel is planned.

To contact me with your comments—good, bad or indifferent—you can reach me through my email

expat@internet.lu

or visit www.expat.lu

David Robinson

CHAPTER 1

▼

August 2003
Luxembourg

It was an unusually warm summer, the hottest in fifty years according to the papers. Everyone was dressed down, the guys in shorts and T-shirts, the girls wearing even less. Strains of urban rock followed by a techno mix troubled the turgid air while the barmaids changed shifts and played their own choices. To the punters outside The Red Rose it was music.

Jason Evans was relaxed as he knocked back his beer. He was on holiday, having left England earlier that afternoon from London City airport. His brother had recently moved to Luxembourg after securing himself a job as a translator. Shaun had invited him to go over for a week to catch up with the joys of Luxembourg. Having discovered The Red Rose, he had quickly settled into the expat evening routine of downing a few pints with his new friends.

As Shaun came back from the bar with another round of drinks he said, "Jason, as it's your first night I'd like to take you to one of my favourite restaurants."

"Okay," he replied.

"Oh, which one?" asked Carmen, Shaun's stunningly beautiful Spanish girlfriend.

"That Portuguese one we went to last week."

"Yes, it's nice there," she agreed.

"Is that all right for you, Maria?"

"Fine," Maria smiled languidly. She was Carmen's Portuguese girlfriend and equally attractive.

Shaun raised his glass. "Let the weekend commence! Cheers. May I suggest we walk there? It's such a fine evening."

The others agreed.

"Is it far?" asked Jason.

"No, not really. It's a short stroll, maybe fifteen minutes. There's no rush."

They finished their drinks and Shaun settled the tab, leaving a tip as he did so. "Are you fit?" he asked as he returned from the bar.

"No, I'm Jason," his brother smirked.

The girls laughed and the group set off at a leisurely rate up the Avenue de la Liberté. The trees gave the party some shade as the group strolled towards the city centre.

The conversation varied in language between French, Spanish and back to English. They discussed their jobs, how long they had been in Luxembourg and where they came from.

Jason was twenty-five, was Welsh, but had grown up in Romford, Essex, making him feel more of an Essex man. He had time on his hands, having recently been made redundant.

Maria de Santos Rodriguez was a beautiful, longhaired brunette, twenty-four, born in Luxembourg and working at one of the banks in town. She had become friends with Carmen after meeting her in a salsa bar in the city.

Carmen Chávez Fernández was a stunning brunette, also with long hair, twenty-five and was born in Barcelona. She worked as a translator at Eurolangue, a company serving the European Union. She spoke Spanish, French and English and had been in Luxembourg for three months.

Twenty-seven year old Shaun, Essex born, was also a translator but with the European Union. He had applied for one of the competitions anyone could take who wished to work there, realising he could utilize his language skills if he could get in. Having taken various tests, he had eventually been lucky enough to land a job in Luxembourg. Thus far he had been there two months and had met Carmen during his first week.

There was laughter in the air as they approached the Adolphe Bridge. Jason felt his trip to Luxembourg could turn into something pleasant, especially if he continued his friendship with Maria.

The group crossed the zebra crossing in the Place du Metz and walked onto the right hand side of the Adolphe Bridge, admiring the panoramic view.

"That's the Place de la Constitution," Shaun said, pointing. "The statue in the centre is the Golden Lady, which, I think, commemorates the Great War. The old fort on your left is Bastion Beck and down below is the Pétrusse valley and river."

"You'd make a good tour guide!" Jason laughed.

Jason captured the moment by photographing the valley with the old town below. Using his new digital zoom camera, he was able to get a close up of the Golden Lady herself. Swinging round, he took a couple more shots of buildings they had walked past. A nearby clock tower looked magnificent in the evening sunlight, Jason's photo recording the moment at 7.48 p.m.

"Those buildings are actually a bank," said Shaun.

"Luxembourg might be a small country but these views are great," Jason said, taking some pictures of the group on the bridge.

It was whilst they were mucking around swapping places that the brothers noticed the blonde that hovered on the other side of the bridge, further back from where they were. She strolled towards the centre of the bridge from the Boulevard Royal side. Jason and Shaun paid no particular attention but were aware of her, for she was stunning. Jason took some more pictures of the valley, then more of the girls with the Avenue de la Liberté in the background. They were enjoying the moment—but something was odd.

The blonde, it seemed, was trying to catch their eye. It was almost as if she was trying to tell them something. Was she trying to talk to them, or was it someone else, as there were other people around? Without warning she got up onto the stone wall of the bridge and started to walk along it. She halted and appeared to be dithering, almost looking for something, as she stood there motionless for a moment or two.

She seemed to find what she was looking for. She looked around her before glancing over at the lads, then stepped forward and disappeared over the side.

The two brothers were standing with their backs to the Boulevard Royal. Jason had just taken another photo of the girls. Shaun was next to him. Both had witnessed the girl jumping but thought she was larking around.

At first, they simply looked at each other. Each appeared to freeze in the moment. Neither quite believed what they had witnessed. When the girls saw the look of horror on their faces they too realised that something awful had happened.

Rushing across the bridge Jason thought at first that it was some form of stunt taking place. They looked over the bridge. The body of the girl lay in the Pétrusse valley. Other people had seen the girl jump and were looking over the side of the bridge. Shaun reached for his mobile phone to call the emergency services.

He called 118 and, speaking in French, requested an ambulance. He gave the location of the incident and his name. At the same time, the girls looked over the bridge, staring in disbelief at the body below.

Jason meanwhile was peering along the bridge towards Boulevard Royal when something nearby caught his eye. It was a small crumpled pink piece of paper. In the confusion of everyone looking over the side and with his brother on the phone, he walked over, reached down and put it in his pocket.

Ernie Meyer woke up to the joys of another day in Luxembourg. The bedroom felt like a furnace even though the window was open and the blind down. In fact, every window in his flat was open. There was no wind and he felt stifled.

He wandered across to the bathroom and put the radio on en route. It was set to Future FM, a local Luxembourgish station, which he listened to most of the time. Finishing in the bathroom he returned to the bedroom where he quickly dressed in T-shirt and shorts—it was too hot for anything else. He crossed to the kitchen and put the kettle on, and whilst making himself a coffee, lit a cigarette, sucking in the smoke to savour the moment before blowing it out. He opened the window to let the smoke drift out.

Cigarettes he enjoyed. They released the pressures off life. He looked out of the window to see what if anything was going on, standing there for a moment thinking about his life.

Ernie Meyer was a forty-four year old Luxembourger. He was a second generation French Italian but was proud to be a Luxembourger. He spoke fluent Luxembourgish, French, German, Italian and reasonably good English. He was divorced, with three grown up kids from his previously long marriage to an Italian. In his free time he liked to socialize with his friends, his local bar being an Italian Portuguese bar called La Cité on the Place de Paris. These day's he mostly worked nights, not out of choice but because of the nature of his job. For the moment that suited him.

Ernie Meyer was a Detective working for the Police Grand-Ducale. He currently worked undercover in the division of the state secret police. Their speciality was to investigate individuals and to find out more about them. Detective Meyer had been posted to a late night surveillance team. His job for the present was to listen in to conversations in the bars to find out what was going on and to pick up snippets of conversation, which might prove interesting, often meeting up with regular informers. If there were anything hot happening, they would text him and he would follow it up. The reports he wrote were used by other officers who would investigate further.

The job could be incredibly boring but a career change or promotion was out of the window after his mistake a few years ago on a case. His wife had run off with another guy and he was not able to concentrate on the job. The result cost him his career. He was offered an alternative but the job was more like a punishment.

His instructions came from above. Occasionally he followed individuals. New people arrived in the country daily—it had always been like that. Some were investigated.

The Luxembourg secret police were rumoured to be one of the most ruthless in Europe although they were currently understaffed. Detective Meyer was aware the state knew everything about its citizens and if they stepped out of line, they could always control them. It was easy—it always had been. That's how Luxembourg was run. The state was ruthless, and he knew it.

Most people loved the place but if a foreigner upset the authorities, their job was to harass or deport them over the border where they became the French, Belgium or the Germans' problem. He knew that was done on more than one occasion. Mind you, in similar situations these countries sent their throw-outs across the border. These days with open borders, it was easy.

Detective Meyer drank his coffee, making himself another as he ate a salami sandwich. Switching on the TV, he hoped the sport would be interesting. Realising it was too hot to stay in the flat he grabbed his wallet, keys and cigarettes and went out for a stroll.

He walked down the Montée de la Pétrusse to the park in the Pétrusse valley spending half an hour sunbathing and collecting his thoughts before returning to the flat. He was due to start work at six, which was earlier than normal and was in-between shifts on account of colleagues on summer vacations. He had been available when asked to do a spot of overtime until his regular beat kicked in later.

Detective Meyer reported for duty at Police Grand-Ducale headquarters a few minutes before six. He changed into uniform and grabbed a soft drink from the machine on the way to his office. He sat at his desk and drank it, sweating in the uniform. Lighting a cigarette, he started his paperwork. He was on standby and if anything happened, he would go out and investigate. The first couple of hours were quiet. He hoped his main duties later would be more productive.

At seven fifty-three the communications room housing the emergency calls at the Gendarmerie headquarters in rue Marie et Pierre Curie received a 118 call. The operator took the details from the caller who spoke in French.

The caller urgently requested an ambulance in the Pétrusse Valley under the Adolphe Bridge. A woman had just committed suicide.

"Could I have your name?" the female operator asked.

"Shaun Evans."

Regular procedures were immediately actioned. The ambulance station was alerted and details fed through. Likewise, the police investigation unit was immediately scrambled to investigate, the operator using 'Code S', meaning a suspected suicide had been reported.

Detective Meyer was one of those beeped for action. Leaping up from his chair, he grabbed his jacket and rushed down to the police cars designated for emergency response.

CHAPTER 2

▼

Within minutes of his call Shaun Evans heard the sound of sirens. From the direction of the main town and driving down the Boulevard Royal was an ambulance and backup vehicle. From the other direction of the Boulevard de la Pétrusse came the sound of police sirens.

On the corner of Boulevard Royal, the ambulance and backup vehicle veered a sharp right, driving down a small, narrow winding road into the valley below. The crew knew where to go, having been updated over their communication radios en route. They reached the spot under the bridge where the girl lay, checking her for life. But she was already dead.

Seconds later three police vehicles arrived at the scene. Two of them stopped at one end of the bridge. The traffic was momentarily disrupted. The first police car continued across it, following the same route as the ambulance into the Pétrusse valley below.

Detective Meyer got out of one of the police cars that had stopped. He looked over the bridge at the events now taking place below him. A small crowd had gathered. He and his colleagues started to move people off the side where the girl had jumped.

In the valley below, four police officers surveyed the scene. They searched the immediate area looking for clues, chatting briefly with the ambulance crew.

"Do you think this will take long?" asked an ambulance man.

"It depends," replied one officer.

"Let us know when you want us to move her."

On the nearby footpath, some runners glanced across as they ran past. A woman walking her dog also surveyed the scene.

The police began their tests after putting a tent around the body. They also sealed off the surrounding area with some red and white stripped tape to isolate the scene. Inside an officer conducted his business of looking for any obvious clues including the girl's identity. Fingerprint swabs were taken in case they matched with any previously held.

On the bridge, two police officers walked up to where Jason and Shaun were standing with Carmen and Maria.

Shaun said in French: "I'm Shaun Evans. I was the one who called."

The police officer replied, "I'm Detective Meyer. Could you tell me what happened?"

Shaun briefly explained what they had witnessed. The Detective took down some notes before remarking, "It would be better if you accompany me down to the police station to make a full statement of what you saw."

The meal was now on hold. Having witnessed the suicide, they knew they would have to follow it through, the brothers being two key witnesses.

The question everyone had on their minds was why did she jump? None knew the answer. They had never seen her before. No one else on the bridge came forward to speak to the officers. As the foursome walked to a waiting police car Jason said, "So much for the night out."

"Well, you did say you wanted to do something different." Shaun smiled grimly.

"Yeah, but not that different, not like this," Jason added, rather peed off about the turn of events.

Detective Meyer drove off with the foursome towards police headquarters. Everyone was upset, their faces glum. Meyer's colleague remained with the other officers, supervising events on top of the bridge.

On the face of it the incident certainly appeared to be another suicide from the Adolphe Bridge and was nothing new to the police. The bridge was forty-two meters above the Pétrusse valley and had become a mecca for people to take their own lives after the alterations on the City's Red bridge—alterations that had effectively stopped suicide attempts there.

In the valley, when the police officers were satisfied with the findings of their tests, they signalled to the waiting ambulance crew to take the body away. The police took down the tent and barrier tape before returning to their police car and heading back to base.

The police car with the Evans brothers and the girls pulled up at Police Grand-Ducale headquarters. Detective Meyer got out and ushered them to a reception area inside. "Please wait here and you'll be attended to," he said. After a moment, a round jolly looking police officer appeared and took them to a police waiting room on the second floor. As the group sat totally fed up, he said, "Someone will see you shortly."

Meanwhile, Detective Meyer reported the details to his superior Inspector Bruns who, due to lack of cover, asked him, "Can you and Gendarme Henckels take some statements from the four witnesses, please?"

Detective Meyer called into a nearby office where she was seated. "Tammy, it's urgent," he said. "I've got four witnesses in upper reception waiting for statements to be taken and the boss wants us to deal with it." She stopped what she had been doing and together they went down to the reception area.

Entering the room Detective Meyer said, "Would you follow me?"

The four were conducted to an interview room with a large table surrounded by seats. On the right was a police cell, open, the black bars standing out, and beyond it a toilet.

"Please take a seat," Detective Meyer said to the group who sat silently around the table. He hoped it wouldn't take long as he fancied an easy night. Gendarme Henckels handed everyone a statement pad and pen. Detective Meyer reintroduced himself and his colleague, and asked, "Could you tell me your name, address and telephone number? Also, do you have any identity cards on you?"

Shaun, Maria and Carmen produced their IDs, passing them over to Gendarme Henckels who took down the details. Jason Evans produced a photocopy of his passport that was in his wallet.

"Could you describe to me the events leading up to the incident, the incident itself and what happened afterwards?"

The four explained what had occurred on the bridge. The girls and Shaun spoke in French, Jason in English. Gendarme Henckels struggled to understand the English as it wasn't her strongest subject. However, being on the side of the law meant that she couldn't say anything. She kept her mouth shut and kept writing. She certainly understood more English than she could speak.

Detective Meyer said, "Can you write down what you have mentioned, so we have a written statement?"

The girls were remarkably composed in light of the situation but were clearly upset by the event. The brothers remained resilient, thinking more about the time lost on a good night out with the girls than being stuck in a police station giving interviews to an officer whose English was less than perfect. Carmen's French was better at times than the officers' English. Shaun found it surprising as every Luxembourger spoke four languages fluently, or so he thought.

Water was offered to everyone, as it was extremely hot in the room. Shaun wondered if the air-conditioning had been deliberately turned off to make things more uncomfortable. He couldn't be sure as he sat there, the sweat forming on everyone's brow.

Time was ticking on. Food was on everyone's mind, though after recent events no one felt really hungry. A look of horror formed on their faces when they realised how long this would take. Eventually, having finished their statements, Detective Meyer spoke with Gendarme Henckels in Luxembourgish to confer the situation.

"Have you got everything written down that we'll need?"

She nodded.

Maria, who spoke Luxembourgish, understood exactly what was going on.

Detective Meyer went through everything again in English, asking at the end, "Have you left anything out?"

Everyone replied, "No"

He paused for a moment, adding, "Do you have anything more you may wish to add?"

The four shook their heads. They wanted to leave and enjoy their night.

Detective Meyer concluded, "Thank you—you can go now."

The group departed the room, headed down the stairs to the reception desk and escaped into the street outside.

For Detective Meyer and Gendarme Henckels it meant another hour of form filling. Neither could work out why the blonde had jumped. To them, also, it didn't make sense. None of it made sense. The on-the-spot report had revealed no drugs or needles on her. He thought it a tragedy and such a waste of life. The whole thing nagged him.

Once the officers had concluded, they adjourned to the police canteen where they discussed the incident. At that time of night it was practically deserted. Gendarme Henckels was clocking off. Detective

Meyer still had a night's work ahead of him. After their meal, each lit a cigarette.

Before departing she said, "I'm off now, Ernie. See you tomorrow. *Äddi.*"

Detective Meyer puffed at his cigarette and began to think, remembering a case he had worked on eighteen months previously that involved the death of a twenty-year-old youth. He was a drug addict who had nearly taken his Chinese girlfriend with him as he went over. Thankfully, the girl had held back at the last moment and had since become a completely different person. The youth's death had put the fear of God up her and she had now quit the drug scene.

He remembered the time when the Red Bridge used to have a suicide every week. That had only stopped some years back when the government had insisted on a protective barrier each side of the bridge being erected. He shook his head, thinking, 'It didn't solve the problem of people taking their own lives. They simply chose another bridge!' He took a last drag on his cigarette, stubbed it in the ashtray and got up and walked out. He made his way to a changing room where he donned his civvies uniform, ready for another night in town.

Outside on the steps of the police station the group of four discussed food.

Shaun said, "I was going to take you to a Portuguese restaurant, but in the circumstances…"

"I don't feel like it," replied Carmen.

It was getting late so Jason suggested, "Let's go for a McDonalds?"

"Good Idea," said Maria.

"There's one nearby," added Carmen.

The group set off. It was now almost dark, yet the city wasn't busy at all. At the restaurant they piled through the door that Shaun held open. The others were now ahead of him and had formed an untidy queue. They ordered their choices and found a table. When their orders arrived they all wolfed their food, washed down with the drinks. Suddenly they had regained their appetites.

After the meal Shaun said, "I needed that."

"So did I," replied Jason.

The foursome discussed sport, food and holidays. Carmen and Shaun swapped stories about living in Spain, while Maria wanted to know about life in Romford. The one subject everyone finally returned to was the blonde who had jumped—and why?

Feeling the moment was right, Jason said, "Let's go back to The Red Rose."

"Good idea," said Maria.

The others agreed and they walked the short distance.

Inside the Red Rose, it was busy. However, for the Evans brothers, Carmen and Maria the merriment of earlier was gone. As Shaun bought a round, Suzanne the barmaid said to him, "You don't look too happy."

He briefly explained why.

"I see," she replied, slightly shocked, quickly sorting the round before serving another customer propping up the bar.

Meanwhile the lads desperately wanted the night to be a success but everyone knew it would be difficult. Still, the girls were making an effort.

It was Friday night, the weekend, so a few drinks were drunk with some of Shaun's friends. Joining the group round the table was Helmut, an Austrian, and Eberhardt, a German.

The story of what happened was retold.

"That's the third suicide this week," said Helmut.

"You're joking," added Jason.

"No, I'm not. The other two were off the viaduct."

"I never hear anything on the radio," added Shaun.

"That's because the state doesn't want it advertised. Did you know that Luxembourg is the suicide capital of Europe?"

"No," said Jason.

Eberhardt added, "The Catholic Church doesn't want any bad news and as the state is controlled by them the news is blacked out."

"You mean it's censored?"

"Yes."

Franck, a Luxembourg resident, was also in the group. He interjected, "I think you'll find that the state doesn't put these suicides on the radio as it doesn't want to encourage anyone else to do the same thing."

"That's a good comment," said Shaun.

"You know what?" said Eberhardt, continuing, "Last week my mother was visiting me. One afternoon we walked in the park. When we got to the viaduct, I showed her the spot where someone had landed only a few days before. You could still see the dent and the red mark on the ground. We continued our walk when suddenly there was a thud. Naturally, we looked round but knew instinctively what it was. A man had jumped! If we had been a minute earlier, he would have landed on us. It was terrible. Imagine how my mother felt. I can tell you it spoilt the day."

"It must have been awful," said Carmen.

"Yes, and you know what? When I was walking across the viaduct only two weeks before all this, I saw a man try to commit suicide. He was in his early thirties, beefy looking with strong-arm muscles. He didn't look a drug addict. It took several of us to stop him jumping. The police were called and somehow they managed to calm him down and take him away. I tell you it was scary."

"Do you think we could change the subject?" said Maria.

"Good idea," said Carmen who had come back from the toilet.

The conversation moved on, some darts were played and finally everyone had a good time.

On this particular night, Detective Meyer started his patrol of Luxembourg City with his colleague Muriel Weber in an unmarked black Volkswagen Golf. They wore tiny headphones with a mouthpiece, so if anything occurred it could be relayed.

It was a quiet night, two drunken Americans, a Luxembourg drug addict and a German prostitute along with the regular French wide boys up from Thionville.

They drove from the gare to Rue Wenceslas, the red light area of the city where a string of black women from Brussels stood on the corner looking for business. The officers knew they would be on the early morning train back to Brussels; no known troublemakers were around so they continued on their patrol round the city.

At twelve thirty, they returned to base where they split up, Detective Meyer making his way on foot towards the first of his regular Friday night joints.

Because of the terrible events earlier in the night Carmen and Maria chose to leave The Red Rose early. The lads, not wishing to miss a moment, decided to escort them back to their respective flats.

A taxi was called and the girls were dropped off one after the other. Before they left the taxi, the group agreed to meet the following evening in The Red Rose to go for the meal that everyone should have enjoyed that night.

Detective Meyer entered The Trafalgar in Rue Dicks. The regulars were propping up the bar; two Brazilians sat in a corner, a Thai and Japanese girl at a fruit machine, the Brazilian barmaid speaking with her latest boyfriend.

He sat at the bar watching what was going on, ordering himself a small beer. Lighting a cigarette he watched the smoke rise up as he blew it from his mouth. As it was nearly closing time, he decided to move round to the games machines. He liked to spend time on them—it was a good place to 'ear wig'.

A couple of Filipinos came in, as did a Frenchwoman with a toy boy who came over to the machine next to his and started to play. Detective Meyer listened. Nothing untoward was happening so he returned to the bar, ordered another beer, paid the barmaid and went back to the machine. Nothing. His time was up—he had done his three quarters of an hour. He left and headed for his next bar.

The brothers took the lift up to Shaun's flat where they drank a few beers. Neither was drunk. Jason went to the bathroom and as he washed his hands sneezed loudly. Putting his hand in his pocket for a tissue, he felt the small crunched up bit of paper. Looking at it, he discovered a telephone number, which he read to himself.

"021 419 969."

Returning to the lounge he said, "I forgot to mention I found this on the bridge just after the girl jumped."

"It's a Luxembourg mobile number," said Shaun.

"Maybe there's a connection between it and the girl? After all, she did appear to be trying to tell us something."

They talked for what seemed like hours about the incident, going over it again and again. Why would a stunningly beautiful blonde want to take her own life? It didn't make sense. Eventually, the brothers went to bed.

Both slept. Jason dreamt of whose phone number he had, Shaun of Carmen, grateful it wasn't her who had jumped.

Detective Meyer's next call was The Red Rose. Going into the packed bar he said hello to the barmaid and ordered a small beer. Lighting a cigarette, he sat at the end of the bar and listened.

No one talked to him. The regulars ignored him. They knew his business, knowing he would drink his two beers and leave. It was the same routine every time.

At that time of night, the drink did the talking. It always did. It was amazing what one could find out about all sorts of people. The best bit was that the person didn't have to be in the pub. Their friends always discussed them once they were gone. This was called backstabbing.

He could always find out what his regular foreign friends were up to simply by sitting there listening. No one would ask him his job and if they did, he would lie. That was what undercover cops did. They lied, invented stories to cover their backs to get out of difficult situations. Only as a last resort would he show them his ID.

Detective Meyer finished his beer and ordered another. As he sat there, he thought, 'Thank God I don't have to do this every night; otherwise I'd turn into an alcoholic.' He lit another cigarette. He was certainly addicted to those.

Some lively Scottish guys came into the pub. At one of the tables sat some Finnish people, at another some English. Whilst sitting there listening for anything unusual his ears picked up on the barmaid talking to one of the English crowd.

"Did you hear about the blonde committing suicide on the Bridge earlier?" she said.

He knew her name, knew all about her, how many boyfriends she had had, what she did before she worked in the pub. He knew it all. None of it was exciting. All run of the mill stuff that foreigners get up to whilst in Luxembourg.

Finishing his beer, Detective Meyer looked at his watch. He had been in The Red Rose for exactly three quarters of an hour. It was time to move on to his final place of spying.

He walked up the avenue de la Liberté towards the Honey nightclub. The other pubs had closed except for those with a special licence, which included The Red Rose. That left Eastern Delight, the other nightclub, and South Pacific, the famous late night drinking den in the immediate area. His colleagues tonight would cover those joints together with other bars around the station.

At the entrance, the doorman recognised him and let him in. He knew there were some new girls who had arrived from Moscow that week. They seemed to come in small groups and stay for three months before heading off somewhere new.

Going over to the bar, he ordered himself a beer. He was glad he got the money back on expenses. A Russian woman who was older than the cabaret girls served him. He knew she'd been around. As he lit another cigarette a new girl he'd not seen before came up to him and said romantically, "What's your name? My name's Natasha."

"I'm Paulo."

He lied, knowing what was coming next.

Natasha asked, "Where do you come from?"

"Rome."

Her eyes lit up when he mentioned this. She fancied Italian men, thinking they were all Romeos.

"I come from Moscow," she said in a Russian accent.

She did look quite nice. Some of them didn't. Still, he was on duty so he played it straight.

The third question came as it always did, in a seductive tone: "Do you want some company?"

To which he replied, "Not tonight."

Eventually, the girl left, only to be told by one of the other girls who he was.

She vowed, "I won't make that mistake again."

The girls loved playing nasty tricks on each other and this was one of them.

Natasha had only arrived by plane on the Monday so was still getting used to the new country. 'Her friends' were showing her the ropes. She had a room upstairs so was happy enough.

After that Detective Meyer was left alone. He smoked another cigarette and watched a couple of floorshows, ordering himself another beer whilst doing so. He quite enjoyed the shows but never admitted it to anyone.

When Natasha came on later to do her show, he thought she looked particularly fit. As he sat there watching her dance he noticed her supple breasts were in the right proportions to her body. It was a pity he was on duty!

He made a mental note of the clients. Two in particular interested him who were English. One fattish man with a ponytail came from Manchester, while the other who had a bushy moustache came from Cornwall. Detective Meyer thought he was shifty and resolved to find out more about him in the next day or so.

The men were enjoying themselves, spending a few euros on ladies' drinks. Each had a girl sitting with them.

"Mugs," he thought.

Finishing his cigarette, he stubbed it in the nearby ashtray, finished his beer and called it a night. The bouncer let him out and he made his way home.

It was now early morning. Detective Meyer was tired and decided to write his reports on his next shift.

Arriving at his flat, he switched on the TV to catch some late night sport before dragging himself off to bed. Daylight was peeking in at the shutters.

Another day in Luxembourg was at an end.

CHAPTER 3

▼

Jason Evans woke up late having not slept well. His brother's snoring had disturbed him in the night—he had forgotten how bad it could get.

Getting up for the bathroom, he looked at the clock on the table—nine thirty. Jason was surprised. The brothers had obviously slept in but he still felt tired. He was thinking about the blonde as opposed to Maria who for the moment seemed to have gone out of his mind.

Wandering over to the kitchen, he put the kettle on to make a cup of tea, found himself a clean mug and located the tea bags.

'Where's the bloody sugar?' he thought.

"I'll have one as well," a voice murmured from the bedroom.

His brother had woken with the sound of the toilet flushing.

Jason located another mug and popped another teabag in followed by two sugars. The kettle boiled and he poured the water into the mugs, stirred them around and found some milk in the nearby fridge. Taking the tea into the lounge, he put both mugs on the table.

Shaun got up and joined him. After a chat about nothing in particular they drank their tea and put the TV on. Jason found BBC World before channel flicking, eventually, sticking on CNN. It was all the same news as before. Another three Americans killed in Iraq, the David Kelly inquiry in England, the fires in Portugal, and another killing in Afghanistan. Jason wondered if the world would ever be without wars? Would the Americans quit Iraq?

Each visited the bathroom and dressed. Shaun made breakfast, preparing bacon sandwiches using the packet Jason had brought over from the UK.

Originally, he had thought about going to Vianden for the day, but was wavering. He said, "I'm not sure we should go now after last night."

"Why not?" replied Jason

"Well…" Shaun didn't have an answer.

The pink piece of paper lay on the table in front of them. Jason was still thinking about it. After finishing his tea he said, "Let's go to Vianden. I need a day out to take my mind off things."

His brother replied, "Yeh, don't let it spoil your trip."

"Well that's settled then. Are you ready?"

"I was ready before you!"

"Right, let's go. Anyway, we don't wanna waste the car hire?"

Shaun knew Jason had a point. He had yet to get himself a car, using the bus to get to work, as they were regular. He had hired an Opel Corsa for a week so they could get about.

Leaving the flat, they located the car parked down the street and set off with Shaun driving.

The brothers drove north on the motorway passing through Mersch and Ettelbruck.

"This is the life!" yelled Shaun.

Jason smiled. It was all new to him. The wooded hills and green valleys he thought looked splendid.

"This is where the real Luxembourgers live," added Shaun.

"What do you mean?" replied Jason.

"Most of the natives live up north or in the countryside. They leave the city to the foreigners…"

Putting his foot on the accelerator, they sped onwards, through Diekirch, following signs to Vianden. Jason loved the scenery; the forests covering the rolling hills and the streams and fields, which were rather dry due to the long heatwave the country was going through.

The Evans brothers arrived in Vianden just after twelve thirty. Parking the car, they walked down an old cobbled narrow street that led down to a river. After pausing on a bridge to look at the view Jason noticed a chairlift that crossed the river further up. He said, "Can we go on that?"

"If you want," replied Shaun.

They walked to where the chairlift started its ascent and bought a return ticket from the attendant. Taking their place in the queue, the brothers were soon able to leap onto the chairlift.

As it made its climb, the two of them sat in silence admiring the views en route to the top. Eventually it was Jason who spoke. "This reminds me of my skiing holidays."

Shaun responded, "Well, they do some form of skiing somewhere in this region, cross country I think."

Their journey continued in silence. At the top they leapt off and climbed some steps. Discovering a restaurant Jason said, "Why don't we have lunch here? I'm starving."

"Yeah, me too, why not?" replied his brother.

Sitting at a table with a stunning view of the valley and town below, they watched the people coming up on the chairlift and looked down at the river. Even the tents in a field further down from the bridge were visible. Beyond that on the top of the hills were wind turbines that sat virtually idle due to the lack of wind.

After their meal Jason said, "I've been thinking."

"What about?" replied his brother.

"Last night,"

"And?"

"Well, that number, its bugging me. When we get back I'm going to ring it." He added, "I've got a funny feeling about all this."

"I agree. It's an unusual situation, but the police are dealing with it." Shaun continued, "If they want to find out more they'll investigate it further. The police officer did say other people jump off that bridge when you asked him."

"I know," said Jason. "But I didn't tell them about that bit of paper as I forgot."

"And?" said Shaun, nodding his head.

"Well, just say she was trying to tell us something? That number could be the answer."

"Look, Jason, it could have been dropped by anyone. It might not be hers. Let's face it, there's only a slim chance she might have dropped it."

"True."

"But even if it was hers," Shaun said sarcastically, "it could be her boyfriend's telephone number, or her hairdresser's, or the Grand Duke himself!"

"Or it could be something more," said Jason curiously. "Anyway, I've decided to ring it when we get back and see if we get an answer."

"That's up to you, Jason."

"She looked a bit like a model."

"Maybe, but she could be a secretary, or a translator. There's a few blonde translators where I work."

"She could have been a tourist."

"I doubt it."

They finished their drink, called the waitress over and paid the bill before making their way back to the chairlift, taking a leisurely trip back down.

Crossing the river and after an uphill climb, they located the chateau, spending the rest of the afternoon strolling around it.

At Police Grand-Ducale headquarters, Detective Meyer sat in his boss's office. Inspector Bruns said, "I've read your report. The girl's suicide doesn't make sense. She wasn't on drugs or anything like that. We're waiting on the lab report. First impressions tell us she did have a few bruises on her, but nothing other than those caused by the fall."

"So what do you think?" asked Detective Meyer.

"Well, since your report and while you've been sleeping we've found out more about her. I got Andre and his team to do a bit of investigating."

"And?"

"They trawled through the list of all the cabaret girls in town, checked their IDs and came up trumps. She's a cabaret girl like we thought. Her name is Nadia Ponomariov. She arrived here a month ago, from Ukraine."

"Don't they all!" interjected Detective Meyer.

"Well, not always. She had a work permit and initially was working in the Honey nightclub, then moved on to Eastern Delight. That we do know."

"I've not seen her in either."

"That's because you were on your two weeks holiday when she was working there."

"You mean she moved onto another club?"

"Normally that's what they do, right, but in her case we need to find out more. Can you check it out further and let me know?"

"Yes, no problem."

"This is your case, Ernie; call it a secondment. See what you can find out. If you need assistance, let me know. This could be your passport to redemption."

Detective Meyer was surprised and said, "You mean a green card?"

"Well, you don't want to be stuck on surveillance forever, do you?"

Detective Meyer didn't respond. He was lucky to have a job after he messed up a case a couple of years back.

"Instead of your surveillance tonight, check out the last place she was at. Go in uniform and see what you can find out. Go with Gendarme Henckels. I've assigned her to help you with the case."

It was early Saturday evening when the Evans brothers arrived back in Luxembourg City after their day out. During the day both had received SMS messages on their mobiles from the girls. The rendezvous was still on for seven o' clock at The Red Rose. Arriving at the entrance to the flat both legged it up the stairs as they had less than an hour to get ready. Shaun put the TV on and Jason made a cup of tea. They watched a bit of sport while they got ready.

Jason decided he had to find out if the telephone number on the pink piece of paper had anything to do with the girl who had jumped. Leaning over from his chair he picked it up, found his mobile and dialled 021 419 969.

At first, the call kept ringing. He tried again. After his third attempt, it went to an answer phone. A girl's voice could be heard saying something in what Jason believed to be Russian. It said something like 'Leave a message', but since he didn't speak the language, he couldn't be sure.

He rang off and five minutes later decided to try again. A man with a Russian accent answered. Certainly, the language was Russian—of that, Jason was sure. He listened to see what happened.

The man at the other end of the phone, sensing no one was responding, hung up.

Shaun came out of the bathroom and went into the bedroom. As he dressed, Jason told him about the calls he had made. "It must have been the girl."

"So who was the guy?" asked Shaun.

"Perhaps he's the boyfriend."

"Or some mafia type."

They ran through several options.

"Perhaps he's the Russian President."

They both laughed.

"Perhaps he's the head of the KGB," suggested Shaun.

"It could always be her brother," said Jason.

He was fascinated and felt compelled to find out more. The question of *why* still haunted him.

Back in his office Detective Meyer sat at his desk and smoked a cigarette, thinking for a moment about what his boss had said.

"A passport to redemption."

He knew the police were short staffed as it was the holiday season, but this was good news for him as it could improve his situation. Not many opportunities arose in the Luxembourg police force, and for his boss to offer him a way forward was gratifying.

Detective Meyer was middle-aged and aware of the difference of attitudes between his older and younger colleagues. He stayed out of the politics but knew that the careers of many of his younger officers were, like him, going nowhere. He knew his superiors hung onto their jobs purely for their pension, making it virtually impossible to progress up the career ladder.

Returning to the situation in hand, he stubbed his cigarette in the nearby ashtray and picked up the phone. "Gendarme Henckels, please." He waited a few moments. "Gendarme Henckels, it's

Detective Meyer. I've been to see Inspector Bruns who's read the report I prepared last night. He's assigned me to investigate the case. He assigned you to assist me and I've got whatever resources I need." He briefly updated her, adding, "He wants us to go to the Eastern Delight nightclub tonight. I suggest we rendezvous at my office about ten thirty. Is that okay? Great, see you later."

Having been called in early meant Detective Meyer hadn't eaten. His stomach demanded attention. Picking up his jacket, mobile and cigarettes, he went to the canteen.

At seven Jason and Shaun Evans arrived at The Red Rose. Carmen and Maria were late and very apologetic with their excuses.

Shaun said to his brother, "But that's women for you. Still, I don't mind. We've got plenty of time."

"You said that last night and look what happened," replied Jason.

They enjoyed a couple of drinks before Shaun called a taxi. Within minutes, it arrived and they jumped in. "The old town, *s'il vous plaît*," Shaun said to the Italian driver.

Returning from the canteen Detective Meyer spent the next two and a half hours doing his paperwork. He wrote up the previous night's surveillance findings—not one of his favourite tasks but it had to be done. Meyer was anxious to get on with his new assignment, allowing himself plenty of time to work on his new case. A search of the LPCCP database on Nadia Ponomariov revealed that there wasn't much on her. Printing it out anyway, Meyer added it to the file he had started the previous night.

The information did reveal the maiden name of her mother and, more importantly, her home address of Kiev in Ukraine. He checked the database for the contact address, telephone numbers and email address of the Kiev main police station before preparing and sending the necessary documentation to them of her death.

Detective Meyer knew his Ukrainian police colleagues would act immediately, informing Nadia's parents. They would liaise via him and would arrange flights to Luxembourg so they could identify and collect the body of their daughter. The detective looked up the address, telephone and fax number of the Ukrainian Embassy in Luxembourg after which he sent them a fax informing them of events, asking them to contact him on Monday morning.

After half an hour, the first response came back from Kiev. Meyer sent them a further email that gave more information about the suicide. He also sent two visa waver forms that the police used in circumstances like this. In-between he collated and read the information sent in from the communications room together with the ambulance report. Meyer also sent an email to the morgue, saying that he'd be down on Monday morning to discuss their findings, then checked the airlines flight schedules, including both domestic and cargo schedules to find the easiest way to transport the body back to Kiev. Meyer was intent on getting as much done as possible before his visit to the nightclub.

On arrival in the old town, Shaun Evans paid the driver while the other three waited. Jason looked around him, fascinated by the area, saying to Maria, "It's pretty old round here."

"It's one of the oldest parts of the city," she said.

The foursome walked round a corner where Shaun located the Portuguese restaurant, the one he had originally wanted to go to previously. Joking and laughing, they went in, down some stone steps where at the bottom a waiter greeted them, leading them to a table. The youngsters dined on gambas and steaks, drinking Maria's favourite red Portuguese wine.

During the meal, they discussed the telephone call Jason had made earlier. None of them knew much, if any, Russian. A lively debate took place as to whether the voice on the answer phone was the girl who had jumped? Moreover, was the man with the Russian accent her brother or a Russian spy?

"The police are investigating so they'll find the answer," said Maria.

Jason responded: "Sure, but they don't know about the pink bit of paper or about the Russian guy."

"They'll find out," added Shaun, refilling their glasses.

"If we tell them," said Jason, rather glad in a way he had forgotten. He felt it gave him an edge on the situation.

"If they want anything more they'll ask," said Shaun, wishing the conversation to move on.

The meal continued without further reference to the incident. However, Jason kept it at the back of his mind.

Gendarme Henckels arrived at Detective Meyer's office just before ten thirty where he updating her about the situation. Shortly after, they left for the nightclub.

CHAPTER 4

▼

Just after eleven, Detective Meyer and Gendarme Henckels arrived at the Eastern Delight where the doorman greeted them.

Detective Meyer said, "Good evening. We'd like to speak to the boss?"

The surprised doorman replied, "Certainly, would you follow me please."

They went in and he led them upstairs, past a bouncer who stood outside a door. The doorman knocked and a voice said, "Come in."

The police officers entered. A man got up from his desk, went over to them and said, "Good Evening, I'm Boris Tarovsky, owner of the club. Please, take a seat."

Word had already reached Boris that the police were in the building.

"How can I help you?" asked Boris.

"Nadia Ponomariov?"

"Yes," said a cautious Boris.

"She works for you?"

"Well, yes, she does."

Detective Meyer knew she worked there as his computer had told him.

"I afraid we've some bad news for you," he responded.

"Oh?" said Boris cautiously.

"Last night she committed suicide off the Adolphe Bridge."

"Oh my God, this is terrible news," he said, shocked and speechless.

"Yes, I'm sorry to break it to you."

Boris didn't like the police asking too many questions and a suicide was the last thing he needed.

Detective Meyer wanted some background information.

"I have some questions to ask you. To begin with, what can you tell us about her?"

"Well, she arrived about a month ago from the Ukraine and started work in The Honey. Straight away, she transferred here, living upstairs. However, Nadia only worked here a week before quitting the bar, going to live with a guy."

Detective Meyer knew they didn't allow anyone to leave without some kind of backhander.

"Who was this guy?" he asked. "What can you tell me about him?"

"I gather he was German. He did what they normally do, bought the girl lots of champagne, met her again in the club and again outside, whilst at the same time showering her with gifts. All these girls want a western husband."

"What was this man's name?"

"I afraid I don't know. I'll have to ask the girls."

"Did she have many friends here?"

"She had a few, but because Nadia wasn't in the club long she wasn't well known."

Gendarme Henckels was busy writing down the facts.

Boris continued, "I'll call some of the girls up and you can ask them about her, if that's any good to you." He added, "You can use this office."

"Thank you," Detective Meyer said. "First, I would suggest we break the bad news to everyone. After that, we'll talk to those who knew her."

"No problem," said Boris who got up, went, and spoke to the bouncer outside. "Call everyone who is not entertaining clients to this office immediately. Also instruct Mikhail not to let in any new customers for the next twenty minutes."

"Yes boss." The bouncer went downstairs to inform everyone. There were only two customers in the bar, so he left two of the girls with them. While Mikhail remained on the door, the other girls went upstairs where they squeezed in the room.

When all had gathered, Boris said in Russian, "I'm sorry to interrupt your evening but the police have asked me to give you an important announcement." Looking at Detective Meyer, he added in English, "In Russian?"

Detective Meyer nodded.

Boris stood up and said, "I'm afraid I have some bad news to tell you. Last night a girl committed suicide off the Adolphe Bridge. I'm sorry to advise it was Nadia Ponomariov."

There was a shocked silence, followed by a few of the girls bursting into tears. Some instinctively cried on each other's shoulders. It was an instant reaction. Everyone was stunned. More weeping followed and tissues were passed round. No one could believe what they had just heard.

Boris said in English, "May I say a few words of comfort to everyone in Russian?"

Detective Meyer nodded.

Boris continued, "Please take a few seconds to pray for Nadia." He paused for ten seconds, then added, "Those of you who knew her, could you wait outside as the police would like to ask you some questions about her. The others may go now."

The girls filtered out of the room upset, making their way down-stairs.

Speaking in Russian, Boris said to the waiting bouncer, "Would you send in the girls who are waiting one by one."

"Okay boss."

The bouncer left the room.

The first girl entered looking a little nervous but Boris quickly reassured her in Russian saying, "Please, sit down."

She sat opposite Boris and next to the two police officers. Speaking in English she said, "My name is Olga Baryshnikov."

Detective Meyer asked her in English, "Where are you from?"

"St Petersburg"

"What languages do you speak?"

"Russian and English," she replied.

He continued in English. "What can you tell me about Nadia Ponomariov?"

The girl replied, a little upset and uneasily, "I don't know much about her. She was working here a short time. Nadia was pleasant and interesting to talk to." Olga didn't say much because she knew Nadia was living away from the bar. She continued, "Nadia was friends with another girl here called Olga."

"Olga who?" asked Detective Meyer.

"Olga Yeltsin," replied Olga, adding, "She met this man, a German who liked her—bought her lots of Champagne. She was living with him, I think."

Olga didn't offer any more information so Detective Meyer thanked her and moved on. The second girl couldn't help their enquiries, nor the third. The fourth girl came in.

Boris spoke to her in Russian. "Could you give the officer your name please—in English?"

"My name is Olga Yeltsin."

"Ah, I'm Detective Meyer." He was relieved he had at last found a lead. "I'd like to ask you some questions about Nadia Ponomariov. I understand you were her best friend here?"

"Yes," said a nervous Olga.

"What can you tell us about her?"

Olga explained. "She went off to live with a guy she met."

Detective Meyer knew that already from earlier conversations. "What was his name?"

"Klaus someone—er—I forget his last name, I'm sorry."

Gendarme Henckels wrote the information down.

"Do you know where he lived?" asked Detective Meyer.

"Yes, in Limpertsberg."

She told him the address, which they would check later.

Detective Meyer asked, "What can you tell me about him?"

"He's a diplomat working at the German Embassy. He met her in the cabaret and after a week went to live with him in his apartment. I went there once—it's nice."

"What does he look like?"

"Well, let's see. He's quite old, maybe fifty, got curly brown hair and smokes."

"I see," said Detective Meyer, pausing. "Do you know why Nadia might have killed herself?"

"No."

"When did you last see her?"

"I saw her last week; we had a coffee in a bar on the Place de Paris in the afternoon."

"Was she okay?"

"Fine,"

"You met her working here, I gather?"

"Yes, we shared a room together upstairs but after a week she left. Nadia and I kept in touch. We would text each other but met up when we could. Yesterday I rang her but her phone was off. I thought something was wrong but I didn't know what. I was worried, as I hadn't heard from Nadia. Her battery could have been on recharge. I thought she might have gone on holiday with the guy and left her mobile behind. We had an arrangement to contact each other and I was concerned. I wish I had done something before now. I should have mentioned it to someone but you don't like to think the worst, do you?"

Detective Meyer didn't comment but added, "Would you come down to the station tomorrow with your mobile so we can check your text messages in case there is anything in them that might help us see why she committed suicide?"

"No problem," replied Olga. "What time?"

"Six o' clock"

"Where do I go?"

Detective Meyer gave directions to the police station, adding, "Thank you for your assistance. You can go now."

Olga got up and left the room.

Detective Meyer had what he wanted, so turning to Boris, said, "Thank you for your help and cooperation. It will greatly assist our investigation. Will you thank your girls? "

"My pleasure," replied Boris.

The officers stood up and made their way down the stairs through the bar area, nodding at the girls as they went. The doorman opened the door. Outside they walked up the street back to headquarters.

Boris also went downstairs, crossed the bar to where Olga Yeltsin sat and said, "Are you okay?"

Wiping a tear, she replied, "Oh, I'm fine, thanks."

"That's good in the circumstances; anyway, the police have got the information they needed. Just be careful what you say about the club. You know what I mean. If they need any more answers, I'm sure they'll be back. Thanks for your help. I know it wasn't easy for you."

She was surprised by this comment, but Boris was a nice guy with the girls and was also upset about the suicide. It was via his contacts that Nadia had got the job in the first place.

Sometimes Boris went out of his way to help people so he decided to treat the girls to a drink. Signalling to Sandra, the chief barmaid, to come over, he said to her, "Can you prepare a tray of vodka shots for everyone and bring it over to the corner with the girls who are not entertaining."

They gathered around him a bit surprised. Giving each a glass, he said in Russian, "Nadia's death is a tragic loss, and I realise some of you will be upset. It will be difficult for all of us. We will miss her. To Nadia, an absent comrade and friend."

"Nadia," they replied, knocking back their shots.

He couldn't think of anything better to say.

For the two brothers and the girls the evening turned into a great night compared with the previous one. Once the meal had finished they walked round to the Double Time bar in the old town. Outside it was packed, full of French girls and wide boys from Thionville in France, up for a Saturday night out in Luxembourg.

Maria bought the round and they stood outside, enjoying the moment.

"I must show you the Danish bar underneath," said Shaun to his brother.

When it came to the next round, they went down some narrow stone steps into The Copenhagen.

"Oh, sorry, you're too young," said Shaun to Jason as they descended the stairs.

"Cheeky sod," replied Jason.

The sign on the wall read 'Over 21's only.'

They went in. Inside was an underground cave. After Shaun had bought a round of drinks from an Egyptian French girl, he said to his brother, "There's more," leading them into a larger cave.

"Down there," said Shaun to the girls.

Walking down some steps Jason said, "Dungeons!" The place he thought certainly had atmosphere. He added, "It's quite unusual."

"Not full of tourists, just locals," said Shaun.

The group stayed a short time before going outside to an old cobbled area where Maria said, "It was so hot in there."

"As hot as Spain," joked Carmen, wishing right now she were on some exotic beach with Shaun.

The night continued with much merriment before the bars finally closed after one in the morning, the foursome managing to find a waiting taxi to take them to their flats. It had been a fun night. Jason was getting to like Luxembourg.

Detective Meyer and Gendarme Henckels arrived back at Police Grand-Ducale headquarters, stopping at the coffee machine.

"We need to investigate the German Nadia lived with. He will know more about her, for sure," said Detective Meyer.

"But why hadn't he reported her missing?" Gendarme Henckels replied.

"Does he know she's dead?"

The conversation was interrupted by another colleague. After a brief chat, they returned to Detective Meyer's office where they wrote up their report.

After a while he joked, "We haven't got much to work on but something tells me we've got a long way to go!"

"Yes Ernie!" replied Gendarme Henckels.

Staring at his computer, he typed in 'Olga Yeltsin'. Nothing much came up, most of which he knew already. It was only what the staff at the Bierger-Center had entered. This was the place where all new arrivals in the country registered.

Detective Meyer typed in Klaus and the address in Limpertsberg he now had. Within seconds, he had the answer he was looking for. Nadia's boyfriend was called Klaus von Muller.

According to the screen, Klaus von Muller had lived in Luxembourg for two years. Before that he lived in Morocco. He was a German Diplomat in Luxembourg, which is what the cabaret girls had said about him.

Detective Meyer noticed his parents were Erich and Ellie von Muller. His mother's maiden name was Pitt, which he recognised as a Luxembourg name but knew also that it was German.

The police records showed they were already keeping an eye on him, as they did with all foreigners. Detective Meyer discovered a large note on the file that said, 'Diplomatic Immunity.'

'Typical,' he thought, 'Another D.I. case.'

Delving a little deeper he discovered that Klaus von Muller had previously worked at the German embassy in Rabat, Morocco, for four years.

Reading the file a little more, the officers discovered that during his four years in Morocco, Muller was shadowed by the authorities who had become suspicious after he had undertaken some property dealings in Marrakech. They had noted he had done several deals, which, for a diplomat, they thought odd. As Muller hadn't done anything wrong they were powerless to act but had nevertheless passed their information onto Europol and Interpol.

He printed out the information on the screen and added it to his file. Detective Meyer thought it made fascinating reading. Nevertheless, it didn't answer the immediate question regarding the girl's suicide.

Speaking to Gendarme Henckels, he said, "The thing I find intriguing is why this Klaus von Muller hasn't rung up and reported her missing?' Looking at his papers, he located Muller's phone number. "Let's ring him," he said. Meyer dialled the number he had. There was no reply.

"Perhaps he's away for the weekend so he might not know she's dead?" said Gendarme Henckels helpfully.

All these thoughts went through Meyer's mind. He tried again but still got nothing. Finally, he said to Gendarme Henckels, "Let's check him out further."

Detective Meyer and Gendarme Henckels took a police car round to Klaus von Muller's address in Limpertsberg. They found the flat but as it was the middle of the night decided to return later that day.

It was unclear which floor he lived on, but the post box had both his name and that of Nadia Ponomariov on it. That, it would seem, confirmed she had lived there. Returning to the station, they called it a night.

CHAPTER 5

▼

The two lads had a lie in. It was Sunday and the only day Shaun would get a chance. They rose late, washed, dressed and drank a cup of tea. Jason was still curious about the telephone number on the pink piece of paper. After a further cup of tea together with a bacon sandwich, he sat down and decided to call it again, using Shaun's mobile. This time a girl answered. Again, it was in Russian.

"Hello, do you speak English?" said a delighted Jason.

"Yes, I speak English," the girl replied in a strong Russian accent.

"Ah, good," said a relieved Jason. "Sorry to trouble you, but I'm trying to find whose number this is?"

The girl at the other end at once sounded suspicious.

"Who wants to know?" she said.

"I do. I'm Jason Evans," he replied.

"So what do you want?" she said more bluntly.

He didn't really know what to say but continued, "Well, I found this pink piece of paper and on it had a number..."

Before he could continue, the girl interrupted.

"I'll call you back," she said and with that hung up.

That was a bit strange, he thought. Still, at least he had some form of contact.

Half an hour later Shaun's mobile rang. Answering it, he said, "It's for you," and he handed his brother the phone.

"Hello," said Jason

"Hello," said the voice at the other end.

He recognised it instantly as the girl who had said she'd ring back. He wondered how she could, as she hadn't given him time to give her his number.

"My name's Olga. Sorry about earlier, I had company."

"Oh, that's okay," replied Jason. "Say, how did you get this number?"

"Well, I pressed the save button following your call, so it was easy," she replied.

Jason was impressed. Why hadn't he thought of that?

Olga continued, "You mentioned something about a phone number on a pink piece of paper?"

"Well, yes actually, I found it on the pavement."

"You found a pink piece of paper on the pavement with a telephone number on and you decided to call it. What are you, some type of a pervert, or what?" The girl sounded angry.

"Well no, I found it on the Adolphe Bridge."

There was silence at the other end of the phone.

"Hello," said Jason

"Tell me more," Olga said in a sharp tone.

"Well, I was on the bridge on Friday evening and I saw a girl jump off…"

"Stop!" said the girl. "Can you meet me to discuss this?"

Surprised, Jason replied, "Well—er—yes, when?"

They agreed to meet at le St Tropez Bar on the Place de Paris at 4 p.m. Jason informed his brother of events and, getting quite excited about it, asked, "Where is this bar?"

Shaun told him before phoning Carmen to ask, "Is it okay to pop round shortly?"

"Sure," she replied.

After reporting for duty, Detective Meyer left Police Grand-Ducale headquarters in a patrol car with Gendarme Henckels. They parked outside Klaus von Muller's flat and walked up to his apartment. They rang the bell and there was again no reply.

"We'll have to come back later," said Meyer.

They rang a few of the other bells. A girl with an Irish accent responded.

"Hello?"

"Police."

"Oh, just a minute."

He waited for the girl to appear at the door.

Sensing she spoke English, he said, "We're looking for Klaus von Muller. Have you seen him recently?"

She shrugged her shoulders. "No, hardly ever," she replied.

"Do you know where he is?"

"No, I'm sorry, I don't."

"Okay, sorry for troubling you." Meyer wasn't going to divulge anything at this stage.

"Not at all," said the girl, closing the door behind her.

The police officers returned to their car. As they got in Detective Meyer said to Gendarme Henckels, "We'll have to come back tomorrow. If we don't get an answer we'll have to take it further."

They returned to police headquarters.

Shaun Evans dropped his brother off at the Place de Paris en route to Carmen's flat. It was still hot so Jason decided to sit under a canopy on the terrace. Many others were doing the same, making the most of the good weather. He ordered a beer and waited. He was early. The meeting sounded as if it could be interesting.

Just after four, he noticed a tall good-looking brunette of East European origin walk into the bar. He looked around, thinking it must be another girl, when suddenly she reappeared and wandered over.

Jason looked at her and stood up. "Excuse me, are you Olga?"

"Are you Jason?" she replied with a strong Russian accent.

Nodding, he added, "Yes."

She recognised the voice, smiled and sat down opposite him. The waitress came over and she ordered a coke. Taking a cigarette from her handbag she lit it and said, "So, you saw a girl jump off a bridge and you find a piece of paper with a number on it and decide to call it."

"Strange, but yes. Let me explain."

Jason ran through the events of Friday night. He also told her his own situation. Olga listened as she smoked her cigarette. When he had finished she said, raising her eyebrows, "Very interesting."

She in turn explained her situation. "I come from Russia and have been in Luxembourg for one month working in a cabaret bar. I'm twenty-one. Before that I lived in Moscow."

"What brought you to Luxembourg?"

She laughed, then said, "Well, when I left school, I looked for a job. At the same time, I found myself a boyfriend. He introduced me to working in a cabaret bar. One thing led to another, and now I find myself in Luxembourg working in another cabaret bar."

"Which one?" asked an intrigued Jason.

"Eastern Delight," she replied.

Jason was surprised. "Actually, I drink in the bar next door but one—The Red Rose."

He ordered another beer and coke and the conversation resumed.

"I take it you know this girl?" he asked.

"Yes I do, she was my best friend here in Luxembourg. She also worked in the cabaret."

"What was her name?"

"Her real name was Nadia Ponomariov."

"Her real name—what other name did she use?"

"Oh, it's not what you think," replied Olga, laughing. "She was called 'Naddy' by her friends."

Well, that was a good start, thought Jason. At least he had her name now. "How old was she?"

"She was also twenty-one."

"Twenty-one!" He was amazed and shocked. "Why would a girl of twenty-one want to kill herself? It's such a waste of a life."

"I agree," said Olga.

"Where did she come from?" thinking Olga would say Moscow.

"Ukraine," said Olga.

"Ukraine!" repeated Jason "So how do you know her?"

"We met a month ago, shortly after I arrived in Luxembourg. Nadia was my flatmate. Not long after she started work, she met a German guy who lives in Luxembourg. A diplomat, I think. He wined and dined her and a week later she was living with him."

Jason listened, fascinated. "What was his name?"

"Ah, that's a good question. His first name was Klaus. I forget his last name."

"Well, that helps."

Olga continued: "Nadia still had to go to work because of her work permit, but her boyfriend managed to get her to stop as he didn't like her going off with other men."

"But that's no reason to jump?"

"I agree," said Olga, sipping her drink. "I do know she was worried about him."

"Oh, why's that?" said Jason, thinking it all a bit strange.

"He's not just a diplomat," replied Olga in a hushed tone, looking around her as she said it, her accent very Russian.

"What do you mean?"

"Well, he was into other things which Nadia wouldn't say. She was scared of him. He used to beat her up."

"Didn't she go to the police?"

"No, because she was afraid she would be sent home. They're bastards at times."

Jason listened, getting more intrigued as the conversation developed. Certainly the two of them after their false start seemed to hit it off. Both he and Olga were relaxed in their conversation with each other, at times talking frankly.

"The thing I don't understand is why would she jump? Also, this pink bit of paper I found. It turned out to be your number on it and if you don't mind me asking, who was the Russian guy on your phone?"

Olga responded, "He's my ex-boyfriend, and I'd just broken up with him. You caught us having a—how do you say it in English? A row?"

"Ah yes," replied Jason, laughing.

"And just at that moment he grabbed my mobile and answered it. He was a bastard."

"I see," said Jason.

"Nadia, she was my best friend here. We carried each other's phone number, not just on our mobiles but separately as well, just in case. In fact, our secret code was the number on a pink piece of paper. That's why I was so interested and wanted to meet you." She continued: "If we didn't call each other every forty-eight hours we would know there was a problem; you know, girl talk and all that. In my job, it can be dangerous. At times you can get beaten up."

"She took her life," replied Jason.

"Yes," added Olga, pausing. "Normally she has her mobile on her, which was turned off on Friday. It's still off now."

"Well, she's dead."

"Yes, but the police could have turned it on."

Jason hadn't thought of that. He said, "I'd like to get to the bottom of this, as something clearly isn't right."

Olga replied, "Be careful because this German guy is dangerous. I don't know why, but he gives me the creeps."

"Maybe we could find out more?"

"You can. For me it's too dangerous. You don't know how it works."

"What do you mean?"

"I work in a cabaret bar. If I get in any trouble I get kicked out of the country. I've got a baby in Moscow that my mother looks after and I have to save what I can to send home to support my child and family. We are poor and life is not as easy, compared to here in the west."

Jason was silent as he listened throughout, fascinated.

Olga leaned over the table. Her low cut top revealed her cleavage that drew Jason's eyes.

"There's something I must tell you," she said softly.

"Oh, what's that?"

"Last night the club had a visit by the police. There were two officers, a man and a woman."

Intrigued, Jason cut in: "What were their names?"

"Oh dear, I'm not very good with names. Was it Meyer and..."

"Detective Meyer? That's the guy who interviewed us. Did the woman have ginger hair?"

Olga nodded.

"That's his sidekick. Wait. Let me think. Ah yes, Gendarme Henckels. Anyway, you were saying?"

"Well, they were asking questions about Nadia."

"So what happened?"

"They went up to the office and spoke to our boss; then all of us had to go up there and he told us about Nadia's suicide. It was not very nice. I was very upset, as you can imagine. A few of us were questioned, including me."

"What did he ask?"

Olga explained what she had said, adding, "I've got to go to the police station this evening at six with my mobile so they can check the messages on it."

"Why do they want to do that?"

"To see if there are any clues in her messages."

"Oh, I see,"

"Are you going?"

"Yes, of course," she nodded. "I want to find out myself why she jumped."

Changing the subject, they chatted about life, Luxembourg and their own countries. Finally, Olga added, "Actually, if you hadn't called I had several things I was going to do before I go to work."

"Well, thanks for coming," said Jason. "Can I meet you again?"

"Yes, why not?" Olga smiled. "We can meet here; it's safe in the afternoon. All the girls meet on the terraces of the Place de Paris in the afternoon before they start work in the evening. We all get up around two and spend some of our free time here."

Jason gave her his number.

"That's not the number I called," said Olga in a worried tone.

"No, that's because I used my brother's phone. He's got a Luxembourg number. Mine is English. It might be an idea to use his to contact me—it's cheaper. He'll pass the message on and I'll call you."

"Thank you, that's thoughtful of you."

Jason continued: "Look, I'm on holiday for a week and I'm not currently working. I could stay for another week. I'm in no rush."

They finished their drinks and he paid the waitress. As they were leaving he realised he hadn't asked the obvious question and as they left their table said, "Can you give me Nadia's address, please?"

Olga got a piece of paper out from her handbag, wrote it down and gave it to him.

"Limpertsberg," he said, reading the name as they carried on walking.

"She lived in a new flat up there. It's nice—about a year old. I went there a couple of times."

"Well, thanks for the information. When I know something I'll call you."

"Yes, please do, or meet me in Eastern Delight. You'll like it there." She smiled. "There are many beautiful girls, including me!"

Something told Jason he would be visiting this nightclub. Why hadn't he been there when he had first arrived? It sounded interesting.

"Listen, I'd better go now," said Olga.

"Yeah, me too," added Jason.

She leant forward and kissed him twice on the cheek before departing. Both were glad of the meeting.

Detective Meyer had his head down typing some emails when Inspector Bruns walked in the room.

"Ah, Ernie, how's it going?"

He looked up from his screen and said, "Fine sir. I'm in the middle of some emails to the Kiev police. They've managed to contact the girl's parents and break the news to them."

"I take it you've sent the visa waiver forms through?" the Inspector said.

"Last night."

"What about the Ukrainian embassy?"

"I sent them a fax. I don't expect to hear from them until tomorrow."

"Good man. When are the parents flying over?"

"Well, the Kiev police only managed to contact them this afternoon. In the meantime they contacted various airlines and managed to book them onto a flight that leaves Kiev tomorrow morning."

"What airline are they flying?"

"Aeroschrott."

"Aeroschrott!"

"It's the best one in the circumstances. They'll fly to Moscow, then onto Frankfurt. After that, they're on an AirLux connecting flight to Luxembourg. It's a bit of a long way round, but what with the time difference, it'll get them here reasonably quickly."

"I take it you'll meet them at the airport?"

"Yes, the plane gets in around three thirty."

"What about accommodation?"

"I'll get Gendarme Henckels to organise that shortly."

"How long are they here for?"

"Three nights, the standard time with normal procedures kicking in. They're booked to fly out on the same airlines on Thursday morning. Oh, and I'll hopefully take them to the Ukrainian embassy on Tuesday."

"What about the body? Is that going on Aeroschrott or can you get it on LuxCargo?"

"Unfortunately they don't fly to Kiev otherwise it would have been easy. I didn't ask Aeroschrott directly as I managed to get Ardennes International Cargo to take the body. They've got a plane that leaves directly for Kiev on Friday night so I've booked the body onto that flight subject to the lab reports being okay at the morgue. However, we won't know that until Monday at the earliest."

"Excellent."

"Oh, and I've contacted translation department to request a Russian translator to be available at all times to be with the parents of the girl. Hopefully we'll get Tatiana as she's quite good."

"Well done, Ernie. Nevertheless, don't forget your days off. I know what you're your like when you're on a case, but you're still entitled to them."

"Well, I did have Tuesday and Wednesday booked, but that'll have to change because of Nadia's parents being here."

"Why don't you and Tammy take Wednesday off? I take it your schedule gives them that day to look round and relax?"

"Yes. That's what I had planned."

"Good, do that and perhaps take one day at the weekend. We're not going to solve this case straight away. It'll all take time."

"Yes sir."

"Now, how did last night at the nightclub go?"

Detective Meyer updated him of the events at the end of which Inspector Bruns said, "Good work, thanks for the latest. I'll leave you to it."

The Inspector left the room and Meyer resumed his emails to Kiev.

After a short walk round town Jason Evans headed over to The Red Rose where he had arranged to meet his brother. Ordering a pint at the bar, he went outside, picked up a paper from the window ledge, sat down at a table and read it over his pint.

Olga Yeltsin walked into Police Grand-Ducale headquarters. She was a couple of minutes late and was worried because of it. Arriving at reception, she gave her name to the receptionist and the name of the person who she was there to see.

The receptionist told her to take the lift to the second floor and wait in the reception area. She followed his instructions and waited in the room. A few minutes later Detective Meyer came in and said, "Good afternoon Madame Yeltsin, could you come with me please?"

They went round to an interview room where, sitting at a desk, he asked, "Did you bring your mobile with you?"

"Yes, I did, and it is on." She handed it over to him.

"What is the telephone number please, and also, may I have the pin number?"

She gave him the numbers, which he tested. The phone rang and he could hear himself.

"I'll need it for twenty four hours so we can check the contents," he said.

"No problem."

"Thank you, we'll return it tomorrow night. You can pick it up at the reception desk downstairs from six. Is there anything else you can tell us about Nadia?"

"Nothing more than I mentioned last night," she added.

"Well, that's fine. Thank you for coming in."

Olga made her way out and walked up the street.

Several pints and newspapers later, Jason Evans got a call from his brother.

"Where are you?" Shaun asked at the other end of the line.

"I'm in The Red Rose."

"Okay, I'll be there in ten minutes."

Bang on time, he rolled up having parked nearby, ordered a drink and joined his brother. "How did you get on?" he asked.

Jason updated him. Shaun was equally fascinated. There was definitely more to be found out, but somehow he didn't share his brother's keenness. His interest was centred on Carmen.

"How's the girlfriend?" Jason asked his brother.

"She's fine."

They sat and passed the time of day, reading the Sunday papers over a drink. Later they went to the cinema, taking potluck on what was showing.

After a short meal break, Detective Meyer returned to his office, picked up his phone and rang a colleague. "Hello Jacques, its Meyer. Listen, I've got the number and mobile phone of Olga Yeltsin, the suicide girl's friend. I'll drop it in shortly and leave you to do the necessary. No, no, she'll pick it up tomorrow night at reception from six. *Merci, Äddi.*"

At that moment, Gendarme Henckels walked into his office. Looking up, Meyer said, "Ah Tammy, just the person I need to see."

"I bumped into Inspector Bruns in the corridor. He said you had something to tell me."

"I do, but take a seat first!"

She sat opposite him and he updated her on recent events. As he did so, an email arrived. Checking it, he said, "Ah, that's a response from the translation department. Tatiana Cooper will be joining us for the next few days to translate. We'll pick her up on the way to the airport." He cleared his throat. "I'd like you to organise three nights accommodation for Nadia's parents. Is that okay?"

"I'll get it sorted right away. Shall I put them in the usual, up at Kirchberg?"

"That's fine," he nodded. "We've got to meet Nadia's parents' tomorrow afternoon at three thirty at the airport. I'll need you to liaise with them during their time in Luxembourg. I guess the mother will need a female shoulder to cry on, if you get me."

Gendarme Henckels nodded. It was all part of a day's work for her. She asked, "So what do you plan to do about Muller?"

"We'll go and see him tomorrow, but before that..." Meyer looked at his on-screen diary. "We've got to go down to the morgue in the morning. I'll rendezvous with you, say about ten?"

"Fine. Are you still taking Tuesday and Wednesday off?"

Meyer laughed. "Ah yes, I knew there was something I had to tell you. Inspector Bruns wants us to take Wednesday off; also a day at the weekend, subject to what happens on this investigation, if you see what I mean. Any preferences?"

"I'd prefer Saturday—then I can do a bit of shopping."

"Right, we'll do that. Look, I'd better drop Olga Yeltsin's mobile off to Jacques so I'll catch you later. It's going to be a long day tomorrow. But thanks, Tammy, for your assistance so far."

She smiled and they got up and departed his office, each going in opposite directions.

Meyer popped his head round the door of Jacques' office. "Hello Jacques," he said.

Jacques was on the phone but placed a hand over it. Whispering loudly, Meyer quickly said, "Here's the phone I promised you." He left it on his desk.

"*Merci*, Ernie," replied Jacques before returning to his call.

After a quick cigarette, Meyer returned to his desk to check his emails. Gendarme Henckels had sent him one confirming the accommodation for Nadia's parents.

'Well done Tammy,' thought Meyer. He responded with a 'thanks,' before deciding to call it a night.

CHAPTER 6

▼

Early the next morning Jason Evans left his brother's apartment and walked towards the Adolphe Bridge. There wasn't much traffic about at that time of day. He had borrowing a city map, which he looked at on the bridge. Finding Limpertsberg on it, he set off and a short time later arrived in the street where Nadia had lived.

He checked the numbers on the doors and flats. There were more flats than houses. He noticed that each block of flats had a number. The names of the tenants were on the post-boxes and doorbells. Before long he located the address that Olga had given him and searched for Nadia's name. He couldn't find it, not on the post-box or the doorbell. He thought that a bit odd. On the post-boxes were a real mixture of nationalities—French, Irish, Portuguese, English and Italian. One name did stand out—'Klaus von Muller.' Jason thought this must be the German Nadia had lived with. The strange thing was why her name wasn't on the doorbell or post-box with his? He made a note of the tenants in case it might come in useful.

On closer inspection he realised the label of Klaus von Muller looked rather new compared with the others. He retraced his steps and returned to his brother's flat.

Detective Meyer and Gendarme Henckels arrived just after eleven at the morgue to see the body. At the reception desk he said, "Good morning, Detective Meyer to see Doctor Jennings."

"Good morning, Detective Meyer," the receptionist replied. "Would you follow me please?"

She took them into the autopsy room, which had white rectangular tiles on the walls. There were several body cabinets on one side of the room. At the far end a body was laid out on a steel table and covered with a white sheet. Standing next to it was Doctor Jennings. On seeing them, he said, "Ah Ernie, good to see you."

"Doctor Jennings, we meet once again," Meyer said. "This is Gendarme Tammy Henckels." They shook hands and he continued: "Tell me, what have you found."

The Doctor pulled back the sheet to show the face of the girl. "Nothing suspicious, you'll be pleased to hear," he said formally. "It looks like a straight suicide, like you said."

Pulling the sheet a little further, he revealed more of the body.

"The girl died instantly so she didn't suffer," the Doctor continued. "The bruises and breakages are in line with the distance fallen. However, there were several more bruises on her which indicate to me she was beaten by someone in the days before this suicide. You can see this here—and here." He pointed to the marks. "The girl has some body piercing and several tattoos, some in the most intimate of places. Most don't give any clues. However, one tattoo is new." The doctor turned the body over to show the girl's back. "See, look at this. There are still some small scabs indicating the skin is in recovery mode. I'd say this is no more than a week old."

The tattoo was of a dragon.

"Very oriental, don't you think! It seems to be the latest trend. Mind you, I've not seen this design before."

Enshrined in the design were some letters and numbers.

They read *UB44138JS.*

He continued, "Now that's a bit odd, don't you think?"

"Yes, it is. It's hardly a love tattoo, or is it?" replied Meyer, making a note of it. "Could you get me a photo of this please, so I can look at it further?"

"I thought you'd ask me, so I took some photos on the lab's digital camera. I'll send you them via email shortly."

"Thanks. When will the body be ready for release?"

"I can have it ready by tomorrow."

"Oh, that's fine, except we've provisionally booked a cargo flight for Friday night, subject to your findings."

"That will be good. By the way, which airline is she flying on?"

"Ardennes International Cargo."

"What time is the flight?"

"It leaves Findel at nine thirty in the evening. It's a direct flight to Kiev. I gather it's a weekly service."

"Do you want me to sort out the arrangements, Ernie?"

"I'd appreciate it, Doctor Jennings."

"No problem. Leave it with me."

"Good, I'll contact the airline, confirm the booking and tell them you'll be in touch."

"Fine."

"Is there anything more?"

"No, that's it."

Meyer added, "Well, thanks for your investigation, doctor. By the way, we're still trying to get in touch with the deceased's boyfriend. When we do, I'll bring the guy down so he can formerly identify her. Here's the ironic thing. He lives up the road in Limpertsberg, yet so far we haven't been able to get in touch with him. However, the girl's parents live in Kiev and we've informed them via our contacts there. They're flying in this afternoon and we're meeting them at the airport. Once they've checked into their hotel we'll bring them here, if that's okay with you?"

"No problem," replied Doctor Jennings.

"Say about six?"

"Fine."

"Oh, and a final thought. Could you have a large photo of this dragon ready for me on my next visit? It may assist us. In the meantime I'll be in touch, *Äddi*."

The police officers left the morgue and returned to their car.

On their way down the street, Meyer's mobile rang.

"Hello," he said listening. "You got the message? Good. Yes, thanks for returning the call. I'll email further details to you shortly. Thanks, goodbye."

"Who was that?" asked Gendarme Henckels.

"That was the Ukrainian Embassy. They got my message and it's taken them till now to contact me." Meyer laughed. "Good job it's not urgent eh!"

When he returned to the flat Jason Evans decided to check Muller out. At first, he looked in a local phone book, but it was a 1999 edition and he guessed it was out of date.

One thing he had learnt was that in Luxembourg, many people stay only a year before moving on. Nevertheless, it had been worthwhile, just in case. He decided to do what his brother had suggested. He logged on to the internet and, following his instructions, found the Luxembourg directory. Suddenly he yelled, "There it is!"

The screen gave Muller's address in Limpertsberg. His telephone number stared him in the face, so he rang it.

A man with a German accent answered. "Muller!"

Jason disconnected the call. He had made contact and could now plan his next move.

Detective Meyer returned to his office to check his emails. One was from Doctor Jennings and had an attachment of various photographs of the girl. Quickly flicking through the images, he stopped to look at one with a dragon. Continuing to the next image, he zoomed in on the inscription. As he did so, he picked up the phone and rang Klaus von Muller.

"Ja," was the reply.

Surprised, Meyer quickly replaced the receiver, grabbed his jacket and left, calling in where Gendarme Henckels was standing talking to a colleague.

"He's there, so let's go," he said to her.

Detective Meyer and Gendarme Henckels arrived in the police car at Klaus von Muller's flat where he rang the bell. It was just after midday.

"Ja?" said the person answering.

"Herr Muller?"

"Ja,"

"Police,"

"Oh! Moment."

Thirty seconds later Klaus von Muller opened the door.

Speaking in an official tone in German, Meyer introduced themselves and added, "May we come in? I have some important information to give you regarding your girlfriend."

"Er—yes, sure," said a surprised Muller.

They followed him to the lift, taking it to his flat on the second floor. Muller opened the door and ushered them in. "Please take a seat." He sounded worried.

Meyer shook his head and remained standing. "We've been trying to contact you, Herr Muller."

"Oh, I'm sorry—I've been in Germany."

"It's about your girlfriend Nadia Ponomariov. I have some bad news to convey to you."

Muller looked at him, surprised. Meyer watched his reaction.

"On Friday night your girlfriend committed suicide."

Muller registered disbelief. "You mean she's, she's...*dead*?"

Meyer nodded. There was a pause while the man sat down abruptly.

"How? When? How did it happen?"

The Detective was surprised by his genuine look of horror. He continued, "She took her own life off the Adolphe Bridge on Friday evening—around ten to eight."

Muller sat in silence and shock.

Meyer continued, "Could you tell us where you were on Friday night?"

"Yes, I was in Germany."

"Where in Germany?"

"I was in Frankfurt, at my flat that I have there."

"And what about Nadia? Why didn't she go with you?"

"She told me she was meeting friends for the weekend, so I decided to go to Frankfurt. I left on Friday afternoon and got back about an hour ago."

"Did you fly or drive?" Meyer asked.

"I drove."

Nodding his head, Meyer watched him carefully. He continued, "Do you know why she might have committed suicide?"

Muller looked up, his face still blank with shock. "Er—no, I mean—I cannot believe it."

"What were you doing in Frankfurt?"

"I've been to my flat; you know, sorting out household bills, cleaning. Nothing special." Muller was thinking aloud. "What will her parents think?"

"They've already been contacted and are travelling over from Ukraine to see her body. They are arriving this afternoon and will be here for the next three days. I'd like them to meet you?"

"Of course. When, where?"

"Tomorrow afternoon, say around four o' clock here?"

He nodded. "Yes, that will be fine."

"When they come over, would it be possible for you to have everything of hers packed and ready to return to them? We can provide you with extra boxes if you need them."

"No, that shouldn't be necessary. She didn't have too much luggage."

Detective Meyer continued. "We would also like you to come down to the Morgue to identify the body."

"When?"

"Right now, if it's convenient."

"No problem."

"Thank you, Herr Muller." Meyer added after a pause: "Okay, shall we go?"

The three of them made their way to the lift. As they left the flats, something caught Meyer's eye. He noticed the sticker on the post-box had altered. It now read 'Klaus von Muller'. They continued to the police car, got in and departed for the Morgue.

Jason Evans ate a quick lunch in the flat watching TV. So far, he was delighted with his progress. The meeting with Olga he felt had been the turning point. Having come to Luxembourg to see his brother, the events of the previous Friday evening had somehow altered his holiday. He had been dragged into something he couldn't have even imagined a week before and now found himself wanting to know more. He didn't know why, but it gave him a sense of excitement. It was something different. Of course his brother had told him, "Forget it, you're on holiday," and, "Don't let it spoil your time in the Grand Duchy." But that was part of the difference between the brothers. Whilst Shaun was more laid back in his thinking, Jason liked to follow things through. Nevertheless they would help each other out when necessary and, like most of the Evans family, were close.

Jason was more business-like, Shaun the drifter. However, Shaun's new job had helped him feel more secure, whereas Jason had the unsettling experience of finding himself another job. Having been through this pleasure only a few years before, he was sick of it all, so the week's holiday with his brother was a good idea. The fact they had witnessed a girl killing herself was unfortunate. The trouble was, the harder he tried to put it to the back of his mind, the more he felt compelled to find out what was going on. Yes, he was well aware the police were doing their own investigation, but after the meeting with Olga, it had only intrigued him further. He felt sorry for her, yet at the same time he had to admit he quite fancied the girl. In truth, she was a stunner. It was a pity she had a baby. Still, he relished the thought of meeting her again. Quite when, he didn't know, but he wanted to see her, even if (according to his brother) it would cost him a bottle of champagne!

Having made contact with Nadia's boyfriend earlier in the morning, Jason began to wonder what this Klaus von Muller looked like. All sorts of images went through his mind. He came to a decision. The only way to find out was to go back to the flat in Limpertsberg and, if possible, take this Muller guy's picture. It sounded daft, but he felt compelled to do it.

He grabbed his camera, map and keys, and headed for Limpertsberg.

At the morgue, after what had been a silent journey in the police car, the two police officers and Klaus von Muller walked over to the reception desk.

"Is Doctor Jennings available?"

The receptionist recognised him immediately. "Just a minute, Detective Meyer." She picked up the phone. "Detective Meyer is here again, Doctor Jennings." She ushered them into the laboratory.

"Detective Meyer, so soon!" Doctor Jennings said. "This is a surprise."

"Hello Doctor, this is Klaus von Muller, the girl's boyfriend."

"Good afternoon," said Muller in German.

Doctor Jennings went to one of the cabinets, pulled the body out and folded the sheet back to show the head of the girl.

Muller nodded and turned away. After composing himself he said, "Yes, it is Nadia." He thought she looked at peace with herself. Taking a tissue, he wiped his eyes. Being a man didn't stop him being emotional at a time like this.

Meyer watched him, saying at a suitable moment, "Herr Muller, Nadia has an unusual tattoo on her back." He nodded at the Doctor who produced the photograph of the dragon. "I wonder if it means anything to you?"

Muller looked at it closely. "It's a tattoo. I know many girls who have similar."

"Do you know when she got it done?"

"No, no, I don't." Muller paused, then blew his nose. "Wait a minute. I think she got one done about a week ago. Sorry, I'm all over the place right now."

"Do you know where?"

"I don't sorry." He wiped the tears from his eyes.

"Thank you, Herr Muller."

Meyer nodded to the doctor who covered the body and added, "And thank *you*, Doctor."

"My pleasure," he replied.

The two police officers and Muller departed. Meyer thought he was okay in the circumstances as he looked genuinely upset—but was it all an act? Speaking to Muller, he said, "Thanks for coming.

We'll need to go to headquarters. I have some belongings of hers from Friday to give you."

"No problem," replied Muller.

On arrival at Police Grand-Ducale headquarters, the two officers and Klaus von Muller alighted from the car, going into the reception area where Meyer said, "If you could wait here, Herr Muller, I'll fetch her belongings for you."

After a couple of minutes he reappeared with a small bag. Inside it was a small amount of Euros. Handing it over, he said, "I'm afraid that's all there is."

"Thank you very much," said a distraught Muller.

"Apparently, she went out with only cash and her mobile phone. We've kept her phone for investigation purposes." Pausing, he added, "One other question, Herr Muller."

"Yes?" he replied.

"Your mailbox. I noticed you've changed it from Klaus von Muller and Nadia Ponomariov to Klaus Muller. Is there a reason for this?"

Muller looked at him and said jokingly, "Well, I can guess what you're thinking, but I put the new label up this morning purely because I noticed the old one had fallen off. It was rather old and weather-beaten. You know these labels don't last long. I don't have any spare sticky ones with Nadia's name but managed to find an old one of my own. If I didn't put something up the post won't get delivered. In fact, I've got to get another label done this afternoon in case she gets any post. That's my next priority."

"Thank you, Herr Muller," Meyer responded, unconvinced.

The two police officers drove Muller back to his flat before returning to Police headquarters.

It took half an hour or so for Jason Evans to walk back to Limpertsberg, through the park with its wonderful flower displays and up across the Glacis car park. It was another glorious summer's day and he wasn't in any rush. Soon he was back in the Avenue de la Falencerie, three hours or so after his first visit.

'All this exercise will make me fit!' he thought.

As he walked past a cinema, a police car went past him going in the same direction. His eyes followed it up the street. Jason had a little way to walk to Nadia's flat that was now less than three hundred metres away. The police car, he noticed, had stopped outside it.

'Hello, what's going on?' Jason thought.

Instinct told him to get out his camera. Luckily for him his new digital lens had a good zoom. That was one reason he had bought it.

The street was relatively quiet.

'I probably stick out like a sore thumb,' he thought to himself.

A man got out of the police car. Jason took a couple of shots of him as he walked from the vehicle into the flats. He had a feeling this could be Klaus von Muller but wasn't sure. Something told him it could be. Luckily, the guy didn't appear to have noticed him taking the photos. The police car pulled away and turned right at the next junction.

Jason walked past the flat. He also turned right and right again at the end of the street, ending back on the Glacis. Crossing it, he made his way back through the park and into the city centre for a look round. He had time, plenty of it, until his brother finished work.

After a light lunch with colleagues in the staff canteen, Detective Meyer and Gendarme Henckels made their way back to his office. They called en route at Inspector Bruns office. The door was open and he was smoking a cigar.

"Hard at it, Inspector?" Meyer said jokingly to his boss.

"Ah, Ernie, Tammy, have a seat. Tell me, what's the latest?"

They updated him after which his boss said, "What's all this about an Olga Yeltsin? Is she the ex-President's daughter?" The Inspector roared with laughter. "It's interesting! This Klaus von Muller played it straight, eh!"

"Yes sir,"

"You'd better check him out. Perhaps he's not the nice guy you met after all. Maybe there's a dark side. Put him on the LPCCP. That'll help you."

"Yes sir."

Meyer knew it would automatically make things easy.

His boss continued: "The dragon image you mentioned. I'd like to see it. Can you forward me a copy?"

"No problem."

The phone went. Inspector Bruns answered it and with the conversation virtually over he said over the covered telephone, "I'll catch you later."

They got the hint, got up and headed to Meyer's office, grabbing a coffee on the way. Something told Meyer that Muller wasn't telling him everything. Arriving in his office, they sat down at his desk where he said, "Tammy, can you ring Boris Tarovsky at the Eastern Delight nightclub and arrange for him and Olga Yeltsin to meet Nadia's parents? It might be an idea to ring her as well. Tell them Nadia's parents want to look round her flat, etc…you know, memories and all that."

"What time shall I say?" asked Gendarme Henckels.

"Say around three."

"And can you contact Ardennes International Cargo and confirm the provisional booking I made for Friday night. Tell them Doctor Jennings will be in touch with regard to the arrival of the body."

"Yes, I'll do that in just a second, Ernie, but first I must visit the ladies."

"Oh, right!" Meyer grinned.

He checked his emails. Finding the photos from the lab that Doctor Jennings had sent, he forwarded them to the Inspector. Picking up the phone, he dialled a number at the Villa Louvigny. "Andre, its Detective Meyer. How are you? How's the view from the top of the tower? Listen, I need a couple of favours. Do you have a pen handy? Good, well here goes. Could you put a tap on the following phone numbers please?" He gave the details. "I'll need the transcripts on a daily basis, probably for the next three months as it's a level nine priority. I'll need a report of all calls made together with the phone numbers he's called from his Frankfurt flat over the last year. Tap into his friend's conversations to see what that might throw up. Finally, check his bank accounts. If there's nothing on him, send the night squad round to check his dustbin. If that doesn't give you anything, do a balaclava operation. In addition, it might be an idea to park the Panda for a few weeks. I'll send you a confirmation email shortly. Great, thanks a lot, Andre."

Meyer sent a few emails, copying his boss in to confirm his phone requests, knowing it would take time to collate the information. He put the receiver down and found his cigarettes. He lit one and watched the smoke drift upwards. It tasted good. It calmed him down. He resumed checking his emails and discovered a reply from the Ukrainian embassy. He sent a second mail to them advising further details of his intended visit the following afternoon.

Gendarme Henckels came back into the room. "I've made the calls you requested. Tomorrow afternoon is sorted."

"Thanks," Meyer nodded.

After a moment Gendarme Henckels said, "Listen, are you ready, Ernie? We'll be late for the flight."

Looking at his watch Meyer realised she was right. "I said I'd pick Tatiana up on the way, so we'd better go."

He grabbed his mobile, cigarettes and jacket and they set off.

After walking round Luxembourg City centre for an hour or so, Jason Evans thought to himself, 'Very continental. I can see why Shaun likes it here.' He located Place d'Armes and found a table under the trees to sit at. Across the square, the band played on the bandstand. He enjoyed the moment, ordering a small beer from the French waitress. Muller was on his mind. The waitress returned with his beer and he drank it in the afternoon sunshine.

Originally, he had thought about going to Germany for the day, but after the two visits to Limpertsberg, he felt compelled to check things out further. Jason pondered. The suicide had given him a mission that he found exciting.

Whilst sitting in the square he took a few photos of the bandstand and town hall. Supping his beer he realised his digital camera still contained Friday's photographs of the bridge. Could one of them have one of the girl who jumped? He began to play with the camera, flicking back past the pictures he had taken that day until he reached the photos.

'Was the girl going to be in any?' he thought.

She was in the background on one of them! Looking closely at a few more, he discovered she was on two more pictures in the background. What surprised him was that in the last photo she was standing on the right of the shot, on the wall of the bridge, looking at him taking the photo of Maria and Carmen. She appeared to be looking at something. The question Jason asked himself was, 'What?'

Having an idea, he finished his drink, got up and crossed Place d'Armes. Abandoning his look round he made his way back to the flat.

CHAPTER 7

▼

Detective Meyer, Gendarme Henckels and Tatiana Cooper stood at the arrivals area at Findel, Luxembourg's main airport. The flight from Frankfurt had landed and its passengers were in the customs hall. The officers were waiting for Vladimir and Anna Ponomariov to come through the gateway.

The Kiev police had emailed a photo of them to Detective Meyer so they knew whom to look for. Shortly after 3.45 p.m. the couple came through the door pushing their baggage trolley. Detective Meyer waved a sign with their name on. Seeing it, the couple walked over to where the three of them were waiting.

Tatiana spoke first, in Russian. "Vladimir and Anna Ponomariov? Good afternoon—I'm Tatiana Cooper. I'm a translator for the Luxembourg police. This is Detective Ernie Meyer and Gendarme Tammy Henckels. Both are investigating your daughter's suicide. We're extremely saddened about the loss of your daughter and give you our condolences. Perhaps you could follow us please? We've got a car outside waiting to take you to your hotel."

Anna was in tears, so Tatiana comforted her before they went outside to the police car. Meyer put the luggage in the boot and when everyone was seated drove off towards the hotel. En route, the officers talked to Nadia's parents via Tatiana making light conversation. He decided to leave the main questioning until later.

Back at the apartment, Jason Evans went to his brother's computer and turned it on. Grabbing some leads, he plugged the camera into the computer and pressed a few buttons to find what he was looking for. In seconds, displayed on the screen were the photos which he saved onto the hard drive, using the zoom to get a closer look at her.

He thought she was a stunner and liked her nickname, asking himself, 'Naddy, why did you jump?' Checking the shot of her looking at something, he yelled, "That's it! She's looking at the pink bit of paper." He was delighted with himself, wondering why he didn't think of it before.

Flicking the film forward, he enlarged the photographs of the man going into the flat. Jason thought he looked typical German, but wondered what typical German was? The man had longish brown tight curly hair, was fat, looked in his late forties and had a moustache. He contemplated what Nadia saw in him, if indeed it was her boyfriend. Deciding to make further copies of the photos, Jason borrowed his brother's printer and printed out the photographs of Nadia and the man.

The police car pulled up outside the ABC Hotel in Kirchberg. The commissionaire, on seeing it, quickly summoned a porter who dashed outside and took the luggage from the boot.

"This way please," he said, beckoning them inside.

The three police officers and Nadia's parents ventured in to the reception desk where Vladimir and Anna Ponomariov checked in.

Using his diplomatic voice, Meyer said to them via Tatiana, "We'll wait here for you while you freshen up. I realise you've had a long journey and you're both tired, but I know you want to see Nadia today. Unfortunately, due to cargo flight schedules, her body can't be flown home until Friday night. It will arrive in Kiev on Saturday morning where you'll be reunited. In the meantime I've arranged we visit the morgue this afternoon once you have settled in."

"Thank you very much," said Vladimir.

Nadia's parents wandered over to the lift and went up to their room.

At Shaun's flat Jason Evans couldn't do a lot more, so closing the computer down, he flicked the TV on, but realised there was nothing on the box that interested him. He looked at his brother's DVDs and decided to ring him. Reaching for the phone, he said, "Hello Shaun, it's Jason."

"Hi, how did you get on?"

Jason updated his brother, adding, "What time are you coming home?"

"I've got to work late so won't be back till after eight."

"You're kidding!"

"Yeah! Sorry."

"Listen—are you a member of any video shops?"

"Yeah, Video Walton."

"Can I borrow your video card?"

"No problem! It's in the top draw in the lounge on the right."

"Thanks! Oh, where is it?"

"Video Walton? It's in Rue Bender."

"Rue what?"

"Rue Bender."

"That's what I thought you said. Is it a gay street?"

"No! Nothing like that. It's actually in another street, but I can't think of the name. You'll find it."

"I will?"

"Yeah, it's easy. Oh, and remember it's zone two, and you'll need the password."

"Which is?"

"Level 42."

"Level 42. That's an eighties band, isn't it?"

"Yeah. Look, I've got to go, see you later."

Shaun hung up and after a quick glass of orange juice, Jason departed for the video shop.

He discovered his brother was right. The video shop was easy to find. Going in, he quickly located the zone two DVDs, stopping en route to look at zone one. Choosing one, he paid for it and returned to the flat where he watched the movie.

The police officers waited in the reception area of the ABC Hotel in Kirchberg whilst Nadia's parents freshened up. Detective Meyer felt a bit impatient, as they seemed to take forever. Eventually her parents reappeared.

Anna Ponomariov said with tears in her eyes, "Sorry we took so long. We wanted to change and take a shower. I want to look my best before I meet my daughter." Bringing a handkerchief to her face, she continued, "I've been dreading this moment since we heard the news, but I'm ready now."

Gendarme Henckels said, "There, there, Madame Ponomariov. It's a short journey to the morgue from here. Shall we go now?"

Tatiana translated.

Anna Ponomariov nodded

Nadia's parents and the officers walked outside. The commissionaire rushed ahead to open the police car doors. Everyone got in and Meyer drove off.

The police car pulled up outside the morgue. Meyer let everyone out before parking in the nearby car park. Gendarme Henckels led everyone to the reception desk where, in Luxembourgish, she said to the receptionist, "*Moïen*, I'm Gendarme Henckels. Detective Meyer is just parking the car and will be with us shortly. We've come to see Doctor Jennings."

"Ah, just a moment," said the receptionist who picked up the phone and dialled a number. "Doctor Jennings. Gendarme Henckels with some others. They want to see you." She replaced the receiver and said, "He'll be with you shortly."

She pointed to some chairs. "Please wait over there."

Meyer walked in. "And?" he said to Gendarme Henckels.

"We're just waiting for the Doctor."

"Fine."

At that moment, the doorway swung open and Doctor Jennings appeared. On seeing them he said, "Ah Ernie, Tammy, good to see you again."

They shook hands and Detective Meyer introduced everyone after which Doctor Jennings said, "Please come this way."

He led them to the autopsy room, going over to a steel door where he pulled Nadia's body out, pulling back the cover to reveal her face. There was a moment of silence before Nadia's mother burst into tears. Tammy comforted her.

Detective Meyer said quietly, "If you don't mind, we need you to confirm this is your daughter."

"It is," replied a distraught Vladimir Ponomariov.

"Thank you, we'll wait outside for you. Please take your time."

The officers left the room and waited in the reception area.

Nadia's parents wept privately and her mother said some prayers before holding her daughter's hand for the last time.

When they were ready she covered the body with the sheet and nodded to the doctor who returned the corpse back to the storage cabinet.

Anna hugged her husband. Both cried for a few moments before they composed themselves and slowly walked arm in arm back to the reception area. Once through the doorway Anna burst into tears again and Gendarme Henckels rushed over to give her another hug.

Tatiana spoke to her in Russian. "Will you be okay, madame Ponomariov?"

"Yes, yes I'm fine. Just give me a few moments."

There was a silence in the air, the sort associated with morgues. When Anna had wiped the tears away Gendarme Henckels put her arm round her and said, "Shall we go back to your hotel? Everything else can wait until the morning, eh?"

Tatiana translated and through her tissue, Anna nodded.

Doctor Jennings appeared through the doorway and Detective Meyer said to him, "Thanks for everything, Doctor Jennings. I'll be in touch."

"Fine, Ernie."

Detective Meyer, sensing the moment was right, tactfully said to everyone, "I'll get the car."

Outside the ABC Hotel in Kirchberg Meyer said to Nadia's parents, "We'll pick you up at ten in the morning as there's a few things we need to do tomorrow. In the meantime, I hope you have a good night's rest. Tatiana, did you want to add anything?"

"No, only if they need anything to ring me."

She translated the conversation into Russian and gave Vladimir her card.

"Thanks very much," he replied.

The Ponomariovs went inside the hotel entrance and Meyer drove back to HQ.

On their return to Police Grand-Ducale headquarters, Meyer said to Tatiana Cooper, "Thanks for your help this afternoon. We'll see you in the morning; say nine forty-five, here?"

"Fine," she replied before departing.

Detective Meyer and Gendarme Henckels grabbed a soft drink and, once in his office, chilled for a moment.

"I've got something to show you," he said to her, going to his computer where he located the email of the photos showing the dragon feature. "What do you make of those?"

Gendarme Henckels looked and said, "Well, I didn't pay much attention this morning, but I must admit it's an interesting tattoo. It's very oriental and erotic. They're the in-thing. I've got a similar one on my back."

"Yes, but not quite the same as that, eh?"

"True," replied Gendarme Henckels.

Detective Meyer continued, "Nor, I doubt, will most people have a number inscribed like that."

"You have a point, Ernie." Looking at it more closely, she added, "Can you zoom in on it please?"

He did. It read *UB44138JS*.

"Well, what do you think, Tammy?"

Studying the image for a moment, she hesitated. "It looks like some sort of coded number."

"Yes, I can see that, but what sort of coded number?"

"Well, it could be anything. Perhaps it's a bank account?"

"Yes, that's what I thought. The question is, if it's a bank account, what bank is it and where is the bank located?"

"I'm only guessing here, but if you take the U and the B and add in the S you get UBS. That's Union Bank of Switzerland. Mind you, that's just a hunch."

"It's a good hunch, but what about the J?"

"I don't know the answer to that, but if you look, there's some form of date in the middle. It looks to me as if it says the 13th August 1944."

Detective Meyer said, "Again, that's what I thought. Assuming you're right, why would a twenty-one year old blonde get herself a tattoo, add a date in it, then kill herself?"

Neither knew the answer.

After a moment Gendarme Henckels said, "This is just another hunch, but what if she had found something out but couldn't tell anyone. I mean, who did she know as friends here in Luxembourg? There's the new boyfriend and the girls at the Eastern Delight nightclub. That's it. They're hardly a trustworthy bunch of people. If she *were* in danger, at least by getting the tattoo done if she was killed the evidence of whatever this is wouldn't have been lost, surely? After all, something must have been bad if she killed herself."

"That's a good point, Tammy. Of course, the meaning of the letters could have another meaning, like United Belgium, but somehow I doubt it. As for J.S., well, that could be anything or anyone."

"I've got an idea, Ernie."

"Oh, what's that?"

"You asked Muller when she got the tattoo done, right?"

"Yes."

"Well, didn't he say in the last week or so? Therefore, she must have had it done in Luxembourg. Why don't we pay a visit to the tattooists to find out which one gave her the tattoo. There's not that many in Luxembourg. They may be able to help us."

"Good thinking, Tammy. We'll do that. Can you get me a list of Tattooists whilst I check my emails? Then we can eat, eh? I don't know about you but I'm starving."

"So am I," she smiled.

As Gendarme Henckels started to look up the addresses of all the tattoo shops in Luxembourg, Meyer interrupted her. "I've got two messages from Jacques. One says he's completed his investigation on Olga Yeltsin's mobile phone. He's included four attachments of telephone numbers called, received and all SMS messages sent and received. He adds she's picked up her phone. The second email says he has completed a similar exercise on Nadia Ponomariov's mobile. I'll forward both of them to you. I'm printing out the attachments for the file as I speak."

They spent the next five minutes studying the printouts on their screens after which Meyer said, "What do you think, Tammy?"

"It appears Nadia went on holiday to Spain with this guy. However, her texts indicate she wasn't happy from about half way through it. Something happened, possibly several things, as her tone changes from bright happy girlie messages to one of 'he's a complete bastard.' Well, just my initial thoughts."

Meyer continued looking at the lists. "Nadia obviously trusted her friend Olga, judging by the messages sent. The thing that puzzles me, are the messages sent by Muller to her? They seem to be very romantic, yet it doesn't feel right. Sure, he's using her as she is him, but when she asks him to take her to Frankfurt, he refuses. He does it in a nice way but it's almost as if he's hiding something from her. I mean, why not let her go there? He could get round the visa problem if he wanted. What's he doing in Frankfurt?"

"He's got a flat there. Muller told you himself he had bills to pay, etc…most people in Luxembourg have a property elsewhere, so it's quite normal to go home, say, once a month."

"Yes, I realise that, but if you look at this message towards the end of the holiday, she tells Muller to 'Stuff your friend and your father.'"

They continued analysing the SMS messages.

Gendarme Henckels continued, "Here's one Olga sent. 'Are you okay Nadia. Do you want to discuss it over a drink?'"

Meyer was reading the messages Nadia had sent. "This one puzzles me. Nadia asks Muller 'Who's the dragon man?' Who indeed is he?"

"And is there a connection between him and the tattoo?"

"That's a good point, Tammy. You see, text messages sometimes shed light on things phone messages miss."

Gendarme Henckels said, "This message is interesting. 'Are you more interested in tunnels than me?'"

"Here's another. 'Never mind Munich what about Majorca?' I get the impression he promised her the world and she got nothing, ending up as his personal sex slave in Luxembourg. It got her out of the cabaret bar but I guess she felt trapped."

"And she found something out he didn't like, so he beat her up."

"It's possible," Meyer said. "And she may have found out a bit too much. To the point where there was no way out."

"Hence she killed herself."

"Exactly. But we've got to prove that."

Meyer looked at his screen and read the rest of his emails.

"I've got one here from the Ukrainian Embassy. They've confirmed the Ambassador will see us tomorrow afternoon at two thirty." Looking at his watch, he said, "Oh, let's go and eat."

"Good idea," replied Gendarme Henckels. "But I haven't finished the list of tattooists yet."

"It can wait. Do it when you've got a moment."

Shutting down their computers, they departed for the canteen.

Soon after eight Shaun Evans returned to the flat. After a quick freshen up he and his brother headed for a small Italian restaurant just off the Place de Paris. During the meal their conversation went over the day's events in more detail. Jason showed Shaun the photos. They reviewed the situation but Shaun was in no mood for spending the whole night discussing it.

Afterwards, the lads adjourned to Le Swede, a Swedish bar for a few pints and a game of darts. Shaun was feeling tired, so it wasn't a late night.

CHAPTER 8

▼

Klaus von Muller was up early. He was still on holiday but decided to go into town at his usual leaving time to visit the bank and get a paper. As he walked out of the flat, he noticed the flat's wheelie bins were missing.

Strange, he thought, where are they?

Walking down the street towards the centre, Muller found them near the cinema entrance. He knew the bins belonged to his flat as they had the number painted on the side.

Muller wondered what they were doing there. Perhaps some kids had done a prank and moved them? Dragging them back to the flat, he returned the bins to their storage space. As he did so, he opened one. Then it struck him.

He realised someone had looked through the rubbish and removed a couple of sacks, carefully replacing everything else. Having put his rubbish out the night before, he realised it was those sacks that were missing. He thought about it as he walked into town. Knowing his girlfriend had killed herself, it was obvious to him the police had raided the bins to check for any useful information he had discarded. Of course, he couldn't prove it.

In the reception of the ABC Hotel in Kirchberg, Detective Meyer, Gendarme Henckels and Tatiana Cooper waited. Just after ten the lift doors opened and Vladimir and Anna Ponomariov appeared.

"Good morning," said Tatiana in Russian to them.

"Good Morning," they replied.

"Did you have a good night's sleep?" Meyer asked.

"Not really, but maybe tonight. Still, the breakfast was very good, wasn't it dear?" replied Anna Ponomariov.

"Oh yes," agreed Vladimir.

Detective Meyer said, "We'd like you to come down to the police station with us so I can ask you some further questions."

Anna Ponomariov looked shocked.

"Don't worry, Madame Ponomariov, it's not what you think!" Meyer added reassuringly. "After that, we'd like to show you the place where she took her life so you can pay your respects. I've arranged lunch in a nice restaurant following which we've arranged a visit to the Ukrainian Embassy, as unfortunately there will be a few papers to sign. After that we'll take you to the club where Nadia worked so you can look around and collect anything she may have left. One of the girls who knew her will show you where she stayed. Later, around four, we'll meet her boyfriend Klaus von Muller. He lives at a flat in Limpertsberg. You can see where she lived and can collect her belongings. We'll take her things back to your hotel room where you can repack them. On Thursday before you go we'll collect them and send them by transport carrier to your address in Kiev. Don't worry about anything as it's all taken care of. Tomorrow you have a free day. Perhaps you might like to see our city. How does that sound?"

Tatiana did a sterling job of translating after which Anna said sadly, "Yes, thank you—it sounds fine."

"Shall we go?" Meyer said.

The five left the hotel and after a commissionaire had administered the doors of the police car, they departed for the police station.

Jason Evans had a lie in. His brother had gone off to work earlier and he had drifted back to sleep. When he did wake up he went into the kitchen in his boxer shorts to make a cup of tea, putting the TV on to watch CNN before getting washed and dressed.

Later he decided to go to Trier but remembered the DVD had to go back. Grabbing his wallet and keys, he walked up the street towards the video shop.

The Ponomariovs found themselves in an interview room on the second floor of Police Grand-Ducale headquarters. At the table they were sitting at were several glasses. Gendarme Henckels emptied a bottle of water into a jug and poured everyone a drink.

Meyer started his questions to the Ponomariovs. "Tell me, did your daughter write to you a lot?"

Via Tatiana, they replied.

Vladimir said, "Yes, we got a letter about once a week. Mind you, she did phone us weekly but we kept the calls short because of the cost."

"Were there any clues in her communications that may have given you an indication why she would take her life?"

"Not really. She tried to keep any bad news away from us. Anna, my wife, doesn't like what she was doing and used to get upset enough as it was. We are old and we don't need bad news, but she was our daughter so we tried to help her when and where we could. However, I do know she didn't tell us everything due to the distance. Anyway, we wouldn't understand. We come from a poor country. Listen, this is our first visit to the west and the lifestyles and cultures here are vastly different to what we're used to."

"I see," Meyer nodded and continued, "We discovered from the autopsy that Nadia was beaten a few days before she took her life. Do you know why this is?"

Both the parents shook their heads.

Vladimir said, "We know she was beaten by her last boyfriend in Kiev. Bit of a gangster, actually. Mafia and all that. We don't get involved except when she asks for help. Nadia was a typical girl who once she had finished school dreamt of living in the west. She wanted a western husband to support her. All the girls in Ukraine want this as it will give them a better life. The trouble is, it's difficult for anyone in Ukraine to live in the west. The easiest way for a girl to work there is in a cabaret bar. Nadia got herself this thug of a boyfriend in Kiev who promised her everything and ended up giving her nothing. Yes, he wined her and dined her, made her feel good. Even put her up in a good flat. He demanded she pay for it and made her sleep with other men to get his money back. It's the oldest trick and she fell for it. She wanted to live in the west and he promised her a friend could get her a job as an au pair. Again, she believed him. When she arrived in your country, she was told to work in one of the cabaret bars. She could either say no and be beaten up or she could do her ninety days and enjoy her life in the west. She decided to do the latter. If she was lucky, I remember her saying; she would meet a nice guy, marry him and live happily ever after. Well, she met this German and from what we know, he did look after her. In fact, we were surprised when she told us that he took her back to his flat to live with him. That was after a week, I think. She said she didn't have to work in the cabaret any more— but we weren't sure about that as she didn't go into detail and we don't ask questions."

"What do you know about Klaus von Muller?" Meyer asked.

"Well, like I say, he looked after her," Vladimir continued. "We thought everything was going well. I think he's twenty-five years older than her, but that's normal in our country. She said she loved him, but I doubt that. You know he even took her on holiday."

"Did he?" said Detective Meyer, knowing anyway. "And where was that?"

"Spain."

"Did she say where in Spain?"

"She did say, but I can't remember. Those Spanish towns all sound the same to us. Costa something."

"Where did she stay? In a villa or a hotel?"

"No, I think she stayed at his flat."

Detective Meyer raised his eyebrows, thinking, another flat! Christ, how many more has this guy got?

"When did she go?"

"Oh, I guess in the third week of her stay here, so what's that? Her second with him. She said she had a lovely time. Nadia even sent us some postcards of the place, which we only got last week. It looked quite nice. After Ukraine anything is good!" Vladimir said this with a wry smile.

"What did she do on her holiday?"

"Well, she went to the beach and on some boat trips. Nadia said she went up into the mountains. Fabulous scenery, I gather."

"Did she do anything unusual when she was there?"

"No, not that we know of. What sort of thing had you in mind?"

"Nothing in particular." Meyer shrugged. "But did she meet anyone when over there."

"Yes, she mentioned a couple of people."

"Anyone in particular?"

"A Spanish girl."

"Do you know her name?"

"I forget. Anna, can you remember the Spanish girl's name Nadia said she'd met?"

"Oh, just a minute," she paused. "Wasn't it Martha?"

"That's it. Martha. Nevertheless, Nadia said she didn't like the girl as she got the feeling she was another girlfriend. I think she was jealous. I mean, why have two girlfriends? Surely, one is enough. Moreover, as for them meeting and Nadia discovering this, I can only guess there was some friction as she detested that sort of thing."

"Did she say that?"

"Not exactly. She said she felt used."

"Is that all she said?"

Vladimir wriggled uncomfortably in his chair. "Used and abused, if I'm being honest with you."

"Was there anyone else she met whilst in Spain?"

"Yes, she said she spent some time with another German man."

"Does he have a name?"

"Again, I'll have to think about that. Wait a minute. Was it Volkert? Yes, that's it. Comes from south Germany, if I remember rightly."

"South Germany?" Meyer's eyebrows rose. "Do you know where in south Germany?"

"It's the place the Nazis used to meet."

"Nuremburg."

"No, no, one of the other places."

"Munich."

"That's it."

"Munich," Meyer said, thinking things through in his mind. "Tell me, Vladimir, did you or your wife know Nadia had a tattoo on her back?"

He shook his head. "No, what sort of tattoo?"

Meyer produced two enlarged photos. One showed the tattooed dragon. The other showed *UB44138JS*.

Both parents looked astonished.

Meyer continued: "The dragon design is quite popular among girls of her age here in the west. However, I think the design is special but as yet I can't prove it. I mention it because it has an unusual marking on it, possibly of no connection to the dragon. I wondered whether it might mean anything to you?"

Nadia's parents looked at it but both shook their heads.

"I'm afraid not," said Vladimir. "Like I said, she didn't mention it."

'Pity,' thought Meyer, who said aloud, "Did she mention when she came to Luxembourg she shared a flat with another girl?"

"Yes, she mentioned a girl called Olga Yeltsin," Anna said. "A nice girl by the sound of it. Same age as Nadia. Comes from Moscow. She's got a baby who lives with her mother."

That was new to the police officers.

"Were they close?" continued Meyer.

Anna said, "Nadia didn't really say, but we got the impression she could share her secrets with her. You know, girl talk."

Gendarme Henckels underlined the point in her notes.

Meyer continued, "What did she say about her boyfriend in Luxembourg?"

"She was delighted to meet him."

"Are you sure?"

"Yes, at first she said she really liked living with him. What was his name?"

"Klaus von Muller."

"That's it. Well, he's a German and we don't like Germans because of the war and all that. It's our age group. Can't do anything about it, I'm afraid. Still, he offered her a better life."

"You mentioned she was happy at first."

"Yes, because it was true. In the first week, her letters and calls reflected this. After she had left the cabaret, which I understand is a good move for the girls who work there, everything was fine. But in her last letter Nadia mentioned a bad experience in Spain."

"What was that?"

"She didn't say. But I know she was glad to get back. I thought it unusual considering what a lovely place it looks."

"What did she do when she got back?"

"Not a lot by the sound of it. We were waiting for her next letter when all this happened."

"I see, so you've no idea why she took her life?"

"No, the only clue we got was that during her holiday in Spain something upset her. The holiday wasn't what it could have been."

"Madame Ponomariov, do you know your daughter well?" Meyer asked.

The mother sighed. "Well, I used to. When she left school at eighteen and moved in with that gangster, she changed. I felt as if I had lost a daughter. I think that maybe she just grew up. Still, she's my child and always will be, even now." She wiped a tear from her eye.

Vladimir added, "The thing is, my daughter was easily led. I think she was very upset a lot of the time yet tried not to show it. She always used to meet the wrong sort of men, who abused her."

"Abused her?"

Vladimir was embarrassed and muttered, "Well, you know, used her for sex."

Meyer nodded. "I'm sorry to ask, but did she have many partners?"

"For a girl who was good looking, at first she didn't. Once she'd met this boyfriend in Kiev she changed. It was too embarrassing so we never talked about it."

"I see," Meyer said.

Gendarme Henckels continued to take notes.

"You are aware of what goes on in a cabaret?"

"Of course, we're not stupid. Only in our country, it's a way of life. You know, a girl earns more by working in one of those places for a short time than most people earn in a year. That's why they're so popular with the girls. After all, why work in a factory earning peanuts when you can enjoy yourself!" Vladimir smiled grimly. He was careful with his words as his wife was sitting next to him.

"Is there anything else you can tell us that may assist our enquiries?"

Vladimir and Anna looked at each other before he said, "She mentioned he went to Frankfurt a lot."

"Frankfurt?" said Meyer, raising his eyebrows. "What's special about Frankfurt?"

"He's got a flat there."

This Meyer already knew but was curious as to what Nadia's parents might tell him. "Did she go with him?"

"No, he didn't let her. Told her the visa didn't allow it, which was probably true."

Meyer made no comment.

Vladimir continued, "Come to think of it, she did say that getting one for Spain was difficult. I think there was a back hander."

"Did Nadia mention what Klaus von Muller did in Frankfurt?"

"Well, from her letters she said he went there to sort his mail, clean the flat, etc…Nadia did offer to clean it for him but he refused. 'She was far too beautiful and intelligent to be cleaning flats' he told her."

"Is there anything else?"

"No, do you have anything, Anna?" asked Vladimir.

"No dear, I don't."

Anna was becoming a little restless. Meyer felt now was a good moment to conclude the meeting. He said, "Thank you for being so helpful. I'm sorry if I asked any embarrassing questions but obviously I need to find some answers as to why she killed herself. Maybe now would be a good time to take a short break. If we meet up, say, in fifteen minutes downstairs at the reception area, that'll give you time for a coffee or whatever before we go up to the bridge. Is that okay?"

"Fine," said Vladimir.

They rose and left the room.

.

CHAPTER 9

▼

Jason Evans walked into the video shop and dropped the DVD over the counter. Everything was in order so he decided to look round. Fascinated by the choice of languages, he thought, 'You don't get this in England.' Further round he discovered the adult section. He was surprised by the choice—from teenage to old grannies, gay sex to group sex, it all looked the same to him. After a glance at the box of chuck outs he came across an area labelled, 'New Releases.' Running his eye along a row of DVDs, one caught his eye. He reached up to look at it and discovered on the cover pictures of several girls. It was the largest picture he looked at closely.

"Bloody Hell! That's Nadia," he said aloud.

On the back of the DVD were more pictures that left little to the imagination. In some, she was naked.

"So, she made a porn movie."

Jason discovered the film was made in Frankfurt, Germany, which he found interesting, as Olga had mentioned Nadia had lived with a German guy. Was he anything to do with the movie? Was she in any more? He searched the shelves but found no others. He never bought porn films but felt compelled to buy this one. He wanted to get to know more about the girl who had jumped. He took the DVD to the counter and bought it, asking for a bag. He left the shop quickly, feeling like a dirty old man.

After the short break, Detective Meyer met Vladimir and Anna Ponomariov in the reception area. Gendarme Henckels and the Russian translator Tatiana Cooper joined him.

"This way, ladies and Gentlemen," said Meyer, leading them out to the waiting car.

Once inside he said to Nadia's parents, "We thought it nice to get you some flowers which you can lay where she fell." He added as an afterthought: "Mind you, if you don't want to it doesn't matter."

"No, that's a lovely gesture," Vladimir replied. "Actually, we thought about it ourselves and were going to do the same tomorrow. We might still do, eh Anna?"

In a short while the police car pulled up in the Place du Metz next to the bridge. Everyone got out with Meyer leading the way.

"What lovely architecture," Anna said with a sad smile, taking in the buildings in the avenue de la Liberté.

They walked onto the bridge where half way across Meyer said, "This, tragically, is where Nadia jumped."

Vladimir and Anna looked over the side. Meyer gave them time to take it all in. Anna started to weep. Gendarme Henckels put a comforting arm around her.

"Were there any witnesses?" asked Vladimir.

"There were two Englishmen," Meyer replied.

"What did they say?" Vladimir wanted to know her final moments.

Meyer was diplomatic. "They informed me she climbed onto the bridge. They thought at first it was a stunt. She seemed to hover and look at them before going over."

"Thank you," said Vladimir, wiping his eyes.

Meyer gave Nadia's parents all the time they needed. When the moment was right he said, "I'd like to take you down into the valley to her final resting place. We can either walk down or we can drive. It's up to you."

"What do you want to do, Anna?" asked Vladimir.

"Let's walk dear," she said.

Detective Meyer said, "Gendarme Henckels, can you and Tatiana escort them into the valley while I take the car down?"

He walked over to the car while the rest walked down the steep hill into the valley below.

Five minutes later, everyone met under the bridge. Detective Meyer produced a bouquet of flowers from the boot of the police car. With everyone present, he handed it to Vladimir. "Your daughter came to rest over there." He led the way, stopping at a point on the path with a small mark on it.

Everyone stood silently for what seemed an eternity. Vladimir and Anna paid their respects, laying the bouquet where their daughter lost her life. Tatiana stood by to catch any questions there might be. There were none.

Detective Meyer and Gendarme Henckels stepped back, returning to the police car where they waited. After a few minutes, the others arrived. Anna was clutching a handkerchief as she held hands with her husband. There was a further moment whilst they looked back at the spot, eventually getting into the car.

Meyer drove off in silence.

When Jason Evans got back to the flat, he put the DVD on, flicking through it on fast forward until he got to the bit that featured Nadia.

She was indeed a stunner, every man's dream. Olga had said she was from the Ukraine, yet in the video she spoke German. At the beginning of the movie he noticed something odd about her manner. She didn't like the camera, looking as though she was pressured into making it. Sure she was over eighteen, but something told him she wasn't appearing in it willingly even if she seemed to be cooperating. He had to think about that.

Jason watched fascinated, wondering how much she was paid. He was curious who the guy was with her. It wasn't Muller, and who was the person filming the movie? Flicking it back and forth, at one point he saw the outline of the camera operator in the shadow of the light. Further on the cameraman got his head partially in shot.

"That's Muller!" said Jason aloud, confirming his thoughts as to who the cameraperson was.

He could see the movie was filmed in a modern and continental looking flat. It could have been made anywhere in Europe. However, the flat didn't look like Luxembourg, of that he was certain. On the label it said Frankfurt. Jason knew it couldn't have been filmed there as one shot revealed a marina. On closer inspection, it looked like Spain or Portugal. Having been to Spain to visit his brother when he worked there, Jason realised the apartment was by the sea somewhere in Spain. The question was, where in Spain?

He turned the DVD off and made a cup of tea. Something told him he would have to talk to Olga to find out more about this movie. She might know something about it, but she might not. There was only one way to find out.

After a pleasant lunch on the terrace of a restaurant in Place Guillaume, the police officers escorted Nadia's parents to the Ukrainian Embassy. They found themselves in a large open hallway of an old traditional Luxembourg residence.

As they walked up to a reception desk, Meyer said to the receptionist in French, "*Bonjour madame.* Detective Meyer to see the Ambassador."

Replying in French, she said, "Ah yes, just a minute." She picked up the phone. "A Detective Meyer to see you." Replacing it, she added, "He'll be right with you."

After a few minutes the door opened and the Ambassador appeared. Walking over, he said, "Sorry to have kept you. I'm Viktor Kuchma, the Ukrainian Ambassador."

Meyer introduced the group and the ambassador shook everyone by the hand, saying, "Please come this way."

He led them into a large room with a high ceiling. A long old-fashioned chandelier hung in the centre, and a large desk stood in a corner in front of some French windows. There were several lounge seats.

"Please be seated," said the Ambassador.

Everyone sat down and the conversation began.

"I asked the secretary to bring in some coffees and some water. Will that suit you?"

"Thank you," said Meyer.

"Perhaps I should say a few words to Nadia's parents in Russian?"

"No problem, sir," replied Meyer.

Turning to the Ponomariovs, the Ambassador said, "I am extremely sorry to have heard the news about your daughter's death. A suicide is terrible and I give you my condolences."

"Thank you," they replied.

"This sort of thing is far too familiar in Luxembourg these days. Unfortunately, there's little the authorities can do to stop it, but this is the first incident I've heard of involving a Ukrainian."

"Are the other Ukrainian girls safe here?" asked Vladimir.

"That's a good question. As you know there are quite a few working in the cabaret bars. Most work semi-legally as I'm sure you're aware. No one asks too many questions. The girls are watched over for their own protection as much as anything."

"I see," said Vladimir.

The secretary came in and served the coffee. The conversation lightened up whilst everyone drank it.

A while later the Ambassador said, "Returning to the matter in question, I do have some papers I'll need you to sign so the body can be released." He went over to the desk and returned with them. "There's nothing to worry about. Please have a look through these. If you're happy with everything I'll just need your signatures. Thank you."

He passed the documents to Vladimir and together he and Anna read them.

After a few minutes, they signed the document and handed it back to the Ambassador who said, "Well, that's all the officialdom out of the way."

"Could you let us have the documents by Friday evening as the cargo flight leaves at nine thirty," Meyer said.

"No problem. You'll have everything by tomorrow morning."

"Thank you. Well, it's time for us to leave."

"Good. Thank you for coming to see me this afternoon."

Looking at the Ponomariovs, the Ambassador said, "I hope you enjoy the rest of your time here in Luxembourg, sad though it must be."

"Thank you," they replied.

Everyone got up and Meyer led the way. At the door he paused and said, "Ambassador, *Merci.*"

"My pleasure."

They shook hands and the group departed, walking outside to the police car. Once everyone was seated, Meyer drove off towards the nightclub.

By now, it was too late for Jason Evans to go to Trier for the day so he spent the later part of the afternoon sightseeing around town.

He went to the tourist information office in the Place d'Armes, where he asked if they had any walks around Luxembourg City. They did, so after looking at the choices he found himself on a city tour, which took him round some of the historic parts of Luxembourg City. He quite enjoyed the trip.

Meyer rang the bell of the Eastern Delight nightclub. After a few moments, Boris Tarovsky opened the door and said, "Good afternoon, do come in."

The Ponomariovs and the police officers stepped inside where they discovered a closed bar. It was dark, so Boris turned a light on. As he did so, a girl appeared. He said, "Can I introduce you to Nadia's best friend—Olga Yeltsin."

"Hello," she said in Russian.

"Hello Olga, how are you?" said Meyer.

"Oh, I'm fine thanks."

After he had introduced everyone he said to Boris, "We've just been to the Ukrainian Embassy to see the Ambassador. Unfortunately that delayed us slightly."

"No problem," replied Boris.

"Good. Well, if it's all right with you, maybe Olga could show Nadia's parents round her old apartment."

Boris nodded his approval

Turning to Olga, Meyer said, "Before I forget, did Nadia send you a postcard of her holiday to Spain?"

Olga looked at him and said, "Yes she did. Would you like to see it?"

"Yes please."

"I'll bring it down to you when we come back."

"Thanks. We'll wait outside as I'm sure you don't need us!" he said, winking at her.

Olga knew he had a point there. She smiled and led the way and Nadia's parents followed.

That left Boris the manager of Eastern Delight in the company of the police. He asked Meyer, "Have you found anything more yet?"

"We're working on a few leads," Meyer replied coyly.

"Well, if you need anything else, you know where I am," grinned Boris.

"I do indeed. Look, we'll be in the car. Thanks for your co-operation. We've got another rendezvous with Nadia's parents at four so if they take too long, can you chase them for me?"

"No problem," added Boris.

Meyer led the way and the three of them waited in the police car where they relaxed, chatted and had a couple of cigarettes.

As Nadia's parents departed the nightclub, Boris presented Anna Ponomariov with some flowers. "The girls wanted to give you these," he said.

"Oh, thank you," said Anna with tears in her eyes.

Nadia's parents and Olga walked outside, over to the police car where Olga leaned down to speak to Meyer, exposing the top of her breasts in the process. "I brought this for you," she said when Meyer wound down the window. She handed him the postcard.

"Ah, thank you Olga. I'll let you have it back."

Nadia's parents got in and after saying goodbye to Olga, the party set off for Limpertsberg.

The police car pulled up outside Klaus von Muller's flat in Limpertsberg. Gendarme Henckels noticed Muller watching from his balcony. Everyone got out of the car and walked up to the flat entrance. As Detective Meyer rang the bell, he noticed the label on the post-box read Klaus von Muller and Nadia Ponomariov. The door buzzer went and he led the way.

Muller was standing in his doorway to welcome them.

"Good afternoon, I'm Klaus von Muller. Please come in."

He led them into the lounge where he invited them to sit down.

"Tea, coffee, vodka, anyone?"

Tatiana translated.

"Coffee please," said Vladimir.

"Yes, I'll have a coffee," added Anna.

Tammy and Tatiana opted for a tea.

Meyer said, "I'd have a vodka but as I'm on duty better make it a coffee, thanks."

The others laughed.

"I won't be a second," said Muller going into the kitchen to prepare everything. The others sat silently looking around the room. He returned after a few minutes with a tray of drinks, passing them around before going back to the kitchen to bring out a plate of German biscuits. When he sat down Meyer started the conversation.

"Thank you for the coffee Herr Muller. It tastes and smells delicious."

"Thank you," Muller replied. "Have you had a busy day with Nadia's parents?"

"Yes, fairly. This morning we took Vladimir and Anna to the Adolphe Bridge to lay a wreath. After a spot of lunch and a brisk walk around the centre, we went to the Eastern Delight. A place I understand you know well," the Detective said dryly. Muller smiled, and he continued, changing the subject. "Is it okay for Nadia's parents to look around, see her room, her belongings, Herr Muller…?"

"No problem. Please come with me."

Vladimir, Anna and Tatiana got up and Muller gave them a tour of the flat.

In the bedroom, resting on the bed, was a suitcase and a pile of Nadia's belongings. Her parents went over to look. On seeing a teddy bear, Anna picked it up and hugged it. Muller and Tatiana left them discreetly to be alone for a moment in private.

Anna said to her husband, "Nadia loved that bear. I got it when she was two and she kept it all these years."

After a few minutes together, they returned to the lounge. Her handkerchief mopped the tears from her eyes. Muller went back into the bedroom and collected the luggage. Placing it by the door, he said, "Here are Nadia's things. If you like I can take them down to your car."

Meyer stood up and joined Muller. "We'll take these down to the car. We won't be long." With that, he assisted Muller with the girl's luggage.

Once everything was loaded in the car, they returned to the flat. On their way up in the lift, Meyer said in a more serious tone, "Herr Muller, I will need to speak to you shortly as I have some more questions to ask you. I'll leave it for now due to current circumstances."

Muller got the idea.

They walked back into the room where Meyer said to the sitting group, "Well, it's a lovely day outside so might I suggest we make the most of it?"

That was a subtle hint to go. Everyone got the gist and stood up ready to leave.

Vladimir went over to Muller and said, "Thank you for the coffee and for looking after Nadia."

"My pleasure. I'm sorry it turned out like this," he replied.

"It's a lovely flat, Herr Muller," said Anna as she took a last look round.

Meyer held the lift door open for everyone, saying to Muller, "Till the next time."

As the lift door closed, Muller replied, "The next time. *Auf Wiedersehen.*"

Outside as the group returned to the police car Anna looked up and waved at Muller as he watched from a window. Meyer shuddered as she did so. With everyone in the car, he drove off.

The police car pulled up at the ABC Hotel in Kirchberg. A commissionaire dashed out to open the car doors. Meyer stepped out and said, "Madame et Monsieur Ponomariov. This is where we say goodbye. Thank you for being so helpful today and I hope it's not been too much for you both."

"You've been very understanding—haven't they, dear" Vladimir replied.

Anna said, "Yes, and thank you, Tatiana, for all your translating. You've been a real gem these last two days."

"We'll see you on Thursday morning about nine in reception," Meyer said.

"Very well, and thank you again," Vladimir replied.

Both he and Anna departed and the officers got back in the police car.

Before driving off Meyer took out the postcard Olga had given him and looked at it. There were some people on a beach with Torrevieja plastered across the top of it.

"Ever been to Torrevieja?" he asked.

"No," said Tatiana and Tammy together.

As he started the engine and drove off, he added, "Why would Muller have a flat in Torrevieja?"

Gendarme Henckels replied, "Why not? You go to your relative's flats in Italy. Many of my friends go to Spain on holiday. It's a cheap place to go."

"Yes, I know that, but you're missing the point, Tammy. What I'm trying to say is, why does Muller have a flat in Torrevieja rather than, say, Malaga?"

"That's easy. Malaga's full of British. The Germans and Belgium's have their own resorts and as far as I know Torrevieja is one of them."

"That's fair enough," Meyer said. After a moment he said while driving, "Tell you what, let's interview Muller now in case he's up to anything and see what he's got to say."

"Good idea, Ernie."

The journey continued back into the city

CHAPTER 10

▼

Having returned to Police Grand-Ducale headquarters to drop Tatiana Cooper off, Detective Meyer and Gendarme Henckels drove back to Muller's apartment, parked outside and at the flat entrance rang the bell.

"Ja?" was the reply.

"Police."

"Yes, moment."

The buzzer went and the officers went in, taking the lift to Muller's flat. He was waiting in his open doorway as they walked out of the lift.

"Good afternoon Herr Muller," said Meyer.

"Good afternoon," replied Muller.

"There's a few things we'd like to ask you at the station."

"Well, this is a pleasant surprise. I was expecting something but I must admit this is earlier than I thought."

"Shall we go?"

"I'll get my jacket."

Muller was a little subdued in the circumstances but was resigned to going, as he was the chief suspect—assuming there was more to the suicide than met the eye.

At Police Grand-Ducale headquarters, Klaus von Muller found himself in one of the interview rooms. Seated at a table he knew half the reasons why the interview was conducted there—the psychological breakdown of barriers, change of venue, intimidation by questioning rather than a cosy chat in his flat.

Detective Meyer stood at the opposite end of the table from where he sat. Gendarme Henckels sat at the side with her tape recorder, taking notes.

Meyer assumed a peremptory tone. "Herr Muller, could you explain why Nadia was beaten?"

"What do you mean by that?" replied Muller.

"The lab report confirmed in the days before she killed herself she was beaten. Did you beat her?"

"If you're asking me questions like that I feel my lawyer should be present. Did she tell you I beat her?" Muller looked hard at Meyer, then continued: "No, she didn't. Why should I do that?"

"According to the text messages we've retrieved from one of her friends, the evidence clearly shows that you beat her. What I need to know is, why?"

"You'll have to better than that, Detective Meyer. You know I should have my lawyer here."

The Detective was getting annoyed. His mind was raging.

"All right, Muller, let me ask you another question. What do you know about the dragon on her back?"

"I told you. She had it put on just over a week ago."

"And what is its significance?"

"I don't think it has a significance. They're all the rage with the young girls."

But they don't have an inscription tattooed in them like hers, now do they? What can you tell us about that?"

"Can you remind me what you're talking about?"

Meyer was getting annoyed. Referring to his notes, he went on. "Don't play games with me, Muller. I'm talking about the inscription UB44138JS."

"I've no idea. Perhaps it's the number of the tattoo registration."

"Come on Muller. You can do better than that."

"All right, perhaps it's her mother's birthday. Look, I don't know, and if I did I certainly wouldn't tell you."

The Detective wasn't getting anywhere.

"Okay Muller, we'll play it your way. Tell me. What makes a man who works for the German Embassy have three flats in three countries?"

"Why not?"

"Why do you have a flat in Germany?"

"I'm German, in case you hadn't noticed."

"Why Frankfurt?"

"Why Luxembourg? Your question is irrelevant."

"I'm asking the questions, Muller. Now, why Frankfurt?"

"My aunt used to live there and when she died I took it over. It's appreciated over the years so it's better to keep it rather that sell it. After all, if I lose my job in Luxembourg at least I'll have a roof over my head rather than pay the exorbitant rents the landlords charge here."

"Tell me about your flat in Spain. How long have you had it?"

"What's it to you?"

"Quite a lot actually. What do you do there?"

"Funnily enough, I go there on holiday, like many other people do. The weather's better in Spain than here."

"If it's such a wonderful place, why would your girlfriend dislike her holiday, Muller? What made her hate the place?"

"She didn't hate it."

"You had a row down there. Why?"

"We're back on the lawyer stuff again," Muller warned.

"No we're not," Meyer replied grimly. "Answer the question."

"Have you never had a row with your wife or girlfriend? It does happen, you know."

"At the end of her holiday in Spain, why did Nadia hate you, Muller? What did you do to her?"

Muller smiled and made no comment.

"What made her go and get a tattoo on her back?"

"The same as any other girl who gets it done."

"Cobblers! There was a reason for it and I want to know why."

"She didn't say," Muller said with a smile.

"She had it done to get her own back at you, Muller. It was her revenge, wasn't it? She had it planned, didn't she? Killing herself, as there was no way out. It was a dead end. Whatever she found out meant there was no escape. She was trapped."

Meyer paused to let his words sink in, then continued, "She couldn't go back to the cabaret as they had her passport, and she couldn't leave you because there was nowhere else to go. And she wasn't going to go and see the police, was she? They'd have sent her home and given her complications with the mafia, eh Muller? So tell me, what's the big secret that led her to kill herself?"

"Detective Meyer, I've no idea half the things you're going on about. It's ludicrous what you're saying."

"Steady, Muller. You know I'm right."

Muller stared back at him with a tight expression on his face. "I don't have to answer any of your questions without my lawyer and you know it."

"All right, you win today, Muller. We'll leave it there for now. But I haven't finished yet, not by any means. You're free to go now."

Muller got up and as he left the room, he turned and said, "Do I get a lift home?"

"Muller! Don't push it."

Muller departed, walking quickly from the building.

In the interview room Meyer poured himself a glass of water, drank it quickly and said, "Come on Tammy, let's go to my office."

Upstairs he unwound with a coffee Gendarme Henckels had brought into the room.

"I'll get the bastard," he said.

"He's done nothing wrong."

"He's caused the girl to jump. That's what he did. The question of why, I don't know, but he definitely beat her as the texts and conversations prove—but I can't do anything about it."

"There's always the alternative way, Ernie."

"Yes, that's true. We can give him some harassment on the LPCCP. That should annoy him for a while. Yes, we'll do that."

"Look, you've got tomorrow off. Give yourself a break, Ernie."

Drinking his coffee, he said, "Yes, you're right, Tammy. I'll try and relax on my day off tomorrow, eh?"

"We'll get more intelligence in from Andre at the Villa Louvigny and that'll help us."

"You're quite right, Tammy. Listen, let's go and eat before I go off the idea."

The two ate in the canteen before going their separate ways.

The Evans brothers decided to eat out, dining in Place d'Armes. Later they adjourned to The Underground for a beer where, at the bar, Shaun said, "This is where I met Carmen. It's pretty dead at the moment, but at the weekend it's packed."

Later he said, "Let's drink up and I'll take you to another good bar in town."

Finishing their beer, they departed, walking up the hill back across Place d'Armes towards the bus station into Eighteen's café bar that was packed.

Inside Jason said, "This place has got a bit of life to it!"

"Oh yeah, it's always lively here," replied Shaun.

After several beers, they decided to walk down Boulevard Royal. Crossing the bridge they continuing down Avenue de la Liberté towards The Red Rose.

En route Jason said, "I need to talk to Olga. Do you mind if we go in Eastern Delight?"

"I was wondering when you'd ask me," said Shaun, grinning. "Have you brought your wallet? You'll need it!"

Near the entrance Shaun said, "Don't get more than a piccolo, or else it gets expensive. Remember, you're not working!"

"What's a piccolo?"

"It's a small bottle of champagne—two glasses, actually."

The doorman of the Eastern Delight nightclub greeted the Evans brothers as they went in. Jason looked around, noticing a bar to the left of where he stood. To the right was a stage with seats in front of it with more at the back of the room. They went over to the bar sitting next to a host of beautifully dressed girls.

"Two beers please," said Jason to the barman, surveying the scenery around.

"That's sixteen euros."

"How *much*?" said a staggered Jason. He paid the barman, saying to Shaun, "Christ, that's a hell of a lot for a beer!"

"Yeah, I know, but you wanted to come and it ain't cheap here."

"How much is a piccolo?"

"Seventy euros."

"That's a rip off!"

"You get at least ten minutes for that."

"What do you mean?"

"The girl will talk to you."

"Is that it?"

"That's it. Remember, they're hostesses, not prostitutes. These clubs are supposedly strictly controlled. This isn't Bangkok!"

"Oh right!" said Jason, intrigued.

"These girls only want your money, and the more champagne you buy them the more they get in commission. It's like a sales job, if you like! You've got to try it. Most blokes try it once, after which it all makes sense. Mind you, I heard what goes on upstairs is strictly between you and the girl. Get the idea?"

At that moment, two girls came over.

Looking at Shaun, one said, "Hello, my name's Alina and I come from Ukraine. Where do you come from?"

"England," he replied.

The other girl looked into Jason's eyes.

"*Bonsoir, je m'appelle Svetlana. Je suis Russe.*"

"*Bonsoir, je m'appelle Jason, je suis anglais.*"

Realising he spoke English, Svetlana said, "I come from Moscow."

The girls talked to the lads for ten minutes, after which they both asked, "Would you like to buy me some champagne?"

"Err, no, not tonight. I'm just having a drink with my brother," said a flustered Shaun.

Jason smiled and said to Svetlana, "Maybe later."

The girls smiled and departed. Shaun realised Jason was there for one reason. That reason was Olga. Seconds later the show got underway. The two lads could just see the stage from where they were sitting. During the show, they drank their beer and talked with another two girls who came round but neither bought a drink for them. Jason noticed it was the same routine. The next show started. Jason nudged his brother. "That's Olga!" he said.

As they admired her dancing, Shaun replied, "She's quite fit!"

They continued watching. During her performance, she paused for a second looking at Jason before finishing her act. Ten minutes later, she was changed and back in the bar where she walked over.

"Hello," she said in her strong Russian accent.

"Hi," he replied, delighted.

"Oh, this is Shaun, my brother," he said. "You spoke to him briefly the other day."

"Hello, you must be Olga?"

"I am Olga."

"It's good to finally meet you. So, you were Nadia's friend?"

"Yes, I was. We worked together."

Jason interjected. "I've found something out since I saw you."

He looked around, careful not to let the other girls overhear him. Before he could continue Olga said, "Would you like to buy me some champagne?"

"Err, yeah, okay."

"A bottle?"

"A small bottle," he said, remembering his brother's advice.

"A piccolo."

"Yeah," he said, smiling.

She signalled to the barman. "Shall we sit in the corner?"

They went to the other side of the room, leaving Shaun at the bar. The champagne arrived and Jason paid seventy euros to the waiter.

Olga said, "We can talk here. If I drink this slowly, I can make it last half an hour. If I don't like the guy I stay ten minutes."

Jason thought she was remarkably frank.

"Normally I don't say that to anyone as we're not meant to tell you. Anyway, what have you discovered?"

"Not a lot, but I did find out his surname," replied Jason.

"Which is?"

"von Muller"

"That's it! How did you do that?"

"I went to his flat yesterday using the address you gave me. When I got there, his full name was on the post box. Returning to the flat, I looked on the internet and found his phone number. When I rang it he answered."

"So what did you do?"

"I hung up."

"Why?"

"I only rang to see if he was there, and as he was I went back after lunch. The funny thing was, when I returned a police car went past me and dropped him off. I was further back in the street so I took his picture using the zoom on my camera."

"Have you got it with you?"

"Funny you should say that, but yes, I have. I've also brought the ones I took on the bridge on Friday."

Getting them out, Jason asked, "Is that Nadia?"

She nodded. "Yes."

"That's good."

"What about this one? Could this be Klaus von Muller?"

Olga looked closely. The photo wasn't good, but it was good enough for her to say with excitement, "Yes, it is! How did you get that?"

"Don't ask! Actually, it was luck more than anything."

"That's the guy she was living with."

Jason felt delighted. "There's something else I want to ask you."

"What's that?"

"Well, I went to the video shop today and whilst there I discovered the adult section."

Olga laughed, saying, "Oh yes!"

"Yeah! Anyway, guess what I found?"

Olga shrugged her shoulders, adding, "No, what?"

"Well, I discovered Nadia or someone like her made a porn movie. Did you know she made one?"

"Oh yes, she told me. Most of us have made one at some point." She laughed as she said it, adding, "They make them in Moscow or Budapest. We need the money and at the time it's good money, which you get in dollars. We're talking three years money for one film, so it's worth it. We don't see it in Russia so why not? The films all go to America, Holland or wherever?" She shrugged her shoulders.

"Oh," said a surprised Jason. "But how does Spain fit into all this?"

"Well, if a girl's lucky, and the good looking ones are, they are taken on holiday to a good resort. Sometimes this is where the films are made."

"Oh I see," said a fascinated Jason.

"Like, I told you she met this German guy who took her out of the bar. Well, he took her on holiday to Spain for a week. Apparently he's got a flat there."

"Has he now!"

"Yes."

"Where?"

"Ah, that's a good question. I can't remember. It was by the sea. She did tell me but I forget."

"That's a pity. There was a marina shown in the movie so I'll have to ask someone else if they recognise the place."

During the conversation, the waiter returned. "Excuse me sir, would you like another drink?"

Having not finished his conversation with Olga Jason ordered another beer. Her drink remained largely untouched, as she didn't intend to squeeze him like the other punters. Jason was her friend and she too wanted some answers.

"Have you got any information?" Jason asked her.

Olga replied. "Actually, I have. Yesterday afternoon I got a call from the police. The woman told me they wanted to show Nadia's parents around my flat. Imagine! Soon after my boss came up and told me the same thing. I nearly freaked out."

Jason looked at her.

She continued. "Well, I didn't. I don't normally get up till two. Today nearly killed me as I had to get up early to tidy the flat! Anyway, this afternoon just after three they arrived, five of them, including a translator called Tatiana, a Russian like me. Of course, she wasn't needed as we speak Russian. I took them up to the apartment where I showed them around and had a quick chat."

"Did you find anything out?"

Olga updated Jason on what she knew of the Ponomariov's visit.

"That is interesting. Thanks for that," said Jason.

"Oh, and they go home on Thursday."

"What are they doing tomorrow?"

"They have a free day. Actually, I'm meeting them in town for a coffee. Why don't you come along?"

Jason winced.

"Did I say something wrong?" asked Olga.

"No, but I intended to go to Trier tomorrow as I didn't get there today. What time and where are you meeting them?"

"We arranged to meet at the bandstand in Place d'Armes at four thirty."

"Right. Where shall I meet you?"

"How about outside here at four fifteen, only don't be late as I don't want to miss them. Look, if you are, meet us in Place d'Armes. That might be better."

"It sounds a safer bet," said Jason.

"So, what happens next?"

"I don't know, do you?"

"No, but if anything comes up, call me." Olga looked at Jason and said seriously, "Listen, when you do, keep it brief. Phones have ears, especially international calls."

"Oh!"

"When you come from Russia, you know these things!"

Jason was surprised by this but got the gist of her comment.

Olga added, "After tomorrow we can meet at the Place de Paris like we did before,"

"Good idea."

"I'd better go, otherwise you'll have to buy me another drink!"

"Well, see you tomorrow."

Olga knocked back her champagne and left him. Jason returned to the bar where Shaun sat and they departed.

CHAPTER 11

▼

Jason Evans was determined to get to Trier, having not made it the day before. He drove over in the Corsa, parked next to the station and walked down to Port Nigra, a Roman arch his brother had mentioned.

He spent a while wandering around the city. Feeling hungry, he found a bar in Glockenstrasse. He sat outside and relaxed over lunch and a German beer. Later, he toured along the Moselle valley on the Luxembourg side, returning to Luxembourg City in time for his rendezvous with Olga and Nadia's parents.

Nevertheless, he was late. He knew it and cursed the fact, having not allowed enough time for delays. Parking his car had taken considerably longer than he envisaged and he was now ten minutes late. Rushing towards Place d'Armes, he heard the band playing. He hoped Olga would be there and looked for her. The square was awash with people. Scouring the tables, he saw her sitting at a table with two other people under some trees near the bandstand.

He walked over and on seeing him she waved, standing up to greet him.

"Sorry I'm late," he said. "I couldn't find anywhere to park the car. It's a nightmare in this city."

"That's okay." Turning to her guests, Olga added, "Jason, I'd like you to meet Vladimir and Anna Ponomariov." Speaking in Russian, she said, "This is my friend Jason Evans."

They stood up and shook Jason's hand.

"How do you do," said Jason, not knowing any Russian.

He sat down next to Olga.

"How was Trier?" she asked him.

"Oh fine. It's so different to Luxembourg."

The waiter arrived and Jason ordered a beer. The others already had their drinks.

"Olga," said Jason. "Can you translate for me so I can talk to Nadia's parents?"

"Of course," she replied. "I guessed you'd ask me! By the way, I mentioned it was you and your brother who saw Nadia jump. I also told them the main points."

Jason looked a little shocked. "Did you mention the film?"

"No, of course I didn't," she said.

"Thank God for that. They're probably upset enough without realising she's a porn star!"

Looking at Nadia's parents and speaking slowly for Olga's benefit, Jason told them how he and his friends had got involved, ending up at the police station being interviewed by Detective Meyer, adding, "I understand he is looking after you?"

"Yes, that's right, he is," said Vladimir. "We are naturally very upset about all of this as we would have preferred Nadia to look after us. Nevertheless, we are coping with the situation. Yesterday we laid some flowers under the bridge and went to Olga's flat. We also went to the embassy and saw Klaus von Muller."

"So I heard. Was he okay?"

"He was fine but I wouldn't trust him," said Vladimir.

The waiter arrived with Jason's beer.

Vladimir continued. "I think he's the cause of my daughter's death and I want to know what he's up to. If he is, I'll kill the bastard."

Anna put a hand on his arm. "Now, now, Vladimir. Calm down, it could have been anyone. We don't know yet. Let the police investigate. It will all take time."

"Olga said you are also investigating," continued Vladimir.

"Yes, she may have mentioned, I'm on holiday, staying at my brother's flat. This whole thing has taken over my life! I'd like to get to the bottom of this. When I find out, I'll let you know via Olga. So far, what I've discovered is all luck and obviously the police are working on the case."

"We appreciate any help you can give us. We want to know why she killed herself."

The band struck up with a lively tune and everyone watched. Jason drank his beer but thought it best to leave. He was glad to have met her parents, feeling that in the circumstance it was an unexpected bonus. Finishing it, he said, "Olga, I'm going to leave now as I've got a few things to do. I'll catch up with you when I know some more."

"Yes, okay Jason. Thanks for coming down. I know Nadia's parents are pleased to meet you."

Looking at Vladimir and Anna, he said, "In such circumstances, it is still a pleasure meeting you. I'll be in touch some time in the future. Just give your address to Olga. She will do the rest."

Anna said, "Thank you for coming to see us this afternoon. We really appreciate it."

They shook hands and Jason left them to watch the band playing.

On Wednesday night, the two lads met up with Carmen who came round to the flat. They were due to depart for a restaurant on the Place de Paris when Jason said, "Carmen, can you help me with something?"

"Yes, sure," she said, somewhat surprised.

Jason explained about the DVD. "I can understand if you say no, as I know most girls don't watch porn movies. Anyway, the bit in question is not actually porn, it's sea front, and that's the bit you might be able to help me with?"

"It's okay Jason," she smiled. "I've seen these movies before!"

He got the idea. The DVD was at the point where it showed the view of the marina. Playing the tape, he said, "Do you recognise the place?"

At first, Carmen shook her head, saying, "I come from Barcelona, and I've not been to every beach resort—but it could be Torrevieja or Torrelamata." She peered at it more closely. "Wait. I think its Torrevieja. I recognise the marina."

"Torrevieja—where's that?"

"Just south of Alicante on the Costa Blanca."

Jason hadn't been there. He knew Spain but only the places his brother had taken him when he had been there visiting. Showing Carmen the pictures, he said, "Look, that's Nadia on the right of this photo, and here's one of Muller."

As Carmen looked at them, Shaun interjected: "Are we eating tonight, people?"

"Sorry," said Jason. "Thanks, Carmen, for your help."

"No problem," she replied.

With that they departed, enjoying a meal outside one of the restaurants on the Place de Paris.

Later, at Shaun's flat after Carmen had taken a taxi home, the two lads did some late night talking.

"What are you going to do?" said Shaun.

"I don't know," replied Jason. "Do you have any suggestions?"

"As you're not working, why not continue your holiday and go to Spain? But, before you rush off, why don't you find out more about Muller? Mind you, I'm still not convinced you need to get involved."

Jason intervened, "I know, I know, but…let me think about it."

As they sat there, he thought it through. "We'll look in the telephone directory, like I did before. Maybe he's in the Torrevieja directory."

"He might be—it's worth a try," said Shaun a little sceptically.

With Shaun looking on, Jason logged onto the internet.

"This beats yellow pages. There can't be too many Muller's in Torrevieja," he said.

"Or anywhere," replied his brother.

After a bit of hunting Jason found what he was looking for.

"*There* it is—Muller, Klaus von. Brilliant!"

Shaun said, "He won't be there now, will he? Didn't you say Nadia's parents saw him yesterday?"

"Yes, but you never know. He could have nipped back. What's that old English saying, 'Nothing ventured, nothing gained.'"

"More like a wasted call."

Jason dialled the number on his mobile. Much to his disbelief, his call was answered—by a girl.

"*Si?*"

Taken aback, he said, "Oh, do you speak English?"

In a Spanish accent the girl replied, "Yes, a little."

"Is Klaus von Muller there?"

"No, he's at his flat in Frankfurt. Do you want to leave a message?"

Jason was unprepared, so simply said, "Oh, no it's all right, I'll catch him another time, thanks anyway," and hung up.

Looking at Shaun, he said, "That's a result. Not only does he have a flat in Luxembourg and Spain. He's got another in Germany!"

"Has he really?"

"Yeah!"

"What is this guy? A millionaire or what!"

"I'll check it out tomorrow," said Jason, closing the internet.

CHAPTER 12

▼

At Police Grand-Ducale headquarters, Detective Meyer and Gendarme Henckels were at their desks at eight, knowing they would have a backlog to sort after their day off. Both were anxious to examine the latest intelligence from Andre and the team at the Villa Louvigny.

Checking the one flagged up as URGENT, he said, "You're not going to believe this, Tammy, but Muller's in Frankfurt."

"Frankfurt!"

"According to Andre, the Panda recorded him leaving his flat just after three yesterday afternoon. The LPCCP wiretap picked up a call at eleven ten to a man called Volkert. They traced the call to Munich. Muller's meeting him on Friday morning at his flat in Frankfurt at nine-thirty."

"Perhaps you're right, Ernie. Maybe he's up to something."

Meyer was engrossed looking at his screen.

"Andre's sent us a lot through. They've managed to get Muller's messages and numbers. I'll forward you a copy."

After studying the messages Gendarme Henckels said, "This one's an unusual one to his father. 'The yellow light is at the end of the tunnel.' Now, is that cryptic, or what?"

"Here's another," Meyer said. "'The rain in Spain is mainly on the plain. But in Luxembourg the sun is ready to shine'."

"What about this one? 'I am working on your task'. What task?" added Gendarme Henckels.

"There's a lot of messages to this Frankfurt number saying, 'Meet me at whatever time' to this Volkert. Who is he?"

"And these are going to his flat in Spain. His contact there is a girl called Martha. That could be his ex girlfriend, the one Nadia didn't like."

They spent a while cross-examining the numbers and messages, comparing them with Olga's, during which Gendarme Henckels said, "Here's one that's interesting."

"Go on."

"One of the numbers Olga Yeltsin phoned was to the Englishman Shaun Evans. We missed it the other day."

"So, she's in touch with the Englishmen, eh!"

Gendarme Henckels looked at the time and said, "Ernie, we'd better leave. We've got to be at the hotel by nine."

"You're right. Let's go."

Jason Evans was woken by his brother who eventually departed for work. Now fully awake, he got up, made himself a cup of tea and, as he sat in the lounge sipping it, wondered what he was going to do.

Right now he was on holiday, had seen a suicide and been dragged into all the pleasantries that go with it; nevertheless, he was intrigued, having been caught in the after effects.

Did he want to follow it through or should he give up now like his brother had suggested. He was unsure but felt compelled to take it further. The trouble was, he was a very determined person.

Years ago, his boss had told him to look at life as a challenge and not to waste it as one only had one life! He remembered the phrase and had since looked at each day as a challenge.

Jason had time on his hands. He could delay his return to England—another week wouldn't hurt. Anyway, he quite fancied a trip to Spain. First, he would go to Frankfurt, which he had never visited. He'd have a look round and check the address out on the back of the DVD porn movie.

Just before nine, Meyer and his team pulled up outside the ABC Hotel in Kirchberg. As they went into the reception area they saw Vladimir and Anna Ponomariov sitting on some seats surrounded by luggage.

Going over to them, Meyer said, "Good morning. Have you been waiting long?"

Tatiana continued to translate everything.

Vladimir replied, "About five minutes. We thought it best to be early."

"It's a lovely hotel," said Anna, looking around her.

"Is this Nadia's luggage as well?" Detective Meyer asked.

"Yes," replied Vladimir.

"I've arranged for it to be collected and delivered direct to you in Kiev."

"Thank you," said Vladimir.

"I'm afraid its time to leave," Meyer said softly. "Your flight leaves at eleven-ten and we need to get you to the airport on time. Are you ready to depart?"

"We are."

"If you can wait here a few moments I'll return shortly."

Going over to the reception desk, he spoke to a receptionist. Everyone waited and on his return he said, "We're just waiting for some porters."

They came over. One took Nadia's luggage away; the other collected her parents' luggage. The group walked outside to the waiting police car. The porter loaded up the boot and once everyone was in, they departed for the airport.

At Shaun's flat, Jason Evans decided to log onto the internet. He hunted for the Deutsche Telecoms directory enquiries site. After several clicks, he discovered there were many Mullers. Eventually he found what he was looking for—the web page showing Muller's address in Frankfurt.

'Great,' he thought, wondering which was the best way to get there.

Searching the internet, he located a map of Germany and a basic map of Frankfurt, printing both out. On the web site he was on, he'd have to pay for a more detailed map. Consequently, he decided to get one once there.

Unplugging his charged mobile, he rang his brother. "I've decided to stay another week, if it's okay?"

"Yeah, its fine," replied Shaun.

"I'm off to Frankfurt."

"Frankfurt! When?"

"This morning."

"What happened to Spain?"

"One thing at a time. Anyway, Frankfurt's nearer for starters! It'll be fun."

He rang his neighbour and parents in the UK to advise he was staying another week, then grabbed his bag and stuffed a few bits in. When he felt ready he left the flat, went down to the car, dumped the bag in the boot, slammed it shut, got in the car and drove up the street.

At the departures area of Findel, Luxembourg's airport, Tatiana Cooper, Gendarme Henckels and Detective Meyer waited while Vladimir and Anna Ponomariov checked in their luggage. Returning to where the officers stood, Vladimir said, "Well this is it, time to go. Thanks very much for all your help."

"I hope it's been all right for you," said Meyer.

"Yes, your hospitality has been marvellous," Anna added. "The hotel was super and our visits I shall always remember."

"It's been our first trip to the west and, considering the circumstances, it has been a sad one," said Vladimir, adding, "But we're so happy to have seen and relived Nadia's last moments. For that we thank you."

Meyer nodded.

"I must say a special thank you to you Tatiana. You've been a real treasure," beamed Anna in-between a tear.

Vladimir wiped one from his eye. Anna blew her nose several times. They shook hands and kissed everyone before making their way through passport control.

As Meyer watched them disappear he said to the girls, "They're a lovely couple. It's a pity their visit was in these circumstances. Anyway, shall we make tracks?"

The three officers walked out of the terminal back to the police car.

At Police Grand-Ducale headquarters, Meyer dropped Tatiana and Gendarme Henckels off before parking in the underground car park. He made his way to his office where Gendarme Henckels was studying her emails. Next to her were two coffees.

"Well done, Tammy, you read my mind again," he said, hanging up his jacket. He collapsed into his chair and sipped his coffee. "That's that little exercise over."

"Don't forget we're going to visit the tattoo shops this morning."

"I hadn't forgotten, but first I'll check my emails." He started to look at them but changed his mind. "Okay, I'll look at these later. Are there many Tattooists in Luxembourg?"

"There's not many in Luxembourg City but quite a few tattoo shops outside, including Esch-sur-Alzette, Clervaux and Dudelange."

"How many in Luxembourg City?"

"Two."

"Okay, let's try there first."

"Fine."

Looking at Gendarme Henckels, he said, "Didn't you say you had one?"

"Yes, on my back. Look."

She pulled up her blouse at the back, held down her skirt, stood up and turned round so she could show him.

He looked at the dragon, and her g-string.

"Well, what do you think?"

Not knowing what to say, Meyer said, "I can see the similarity but it's still different."

"Yes," replied Gendarme Henckels, tucking her blouse back in and returning to her seat.

"Where did you get yours done?"

"In Esch-sur-Alzette. A friend of mine has got a shop there."

"We can always pay a visit if we don't get any joy in the city."

As Meyer shut down his computer he grabbed his jacket, mobile and cigarettes. "By the way, did it hurt when you had it done?"

"Of course, but the level of pain depends on which bit you're having done."

Meyer decided it was an appropriate moment to leave.

After setting off, Jason Evans decided to stop at a petrol station just outside Luxembourg City. Remembering a garage he had passed at the weekend, he located it, filled the tank up and went in the shop next to the forecourt. He looked around and found several road maps of Germany. He selected one, picked up a sandwich and a bottle of coke and took everything to the cash desk.

Outside on the forecourt he started the car and drove off. Finding a place to stop, he pulled over and studied the map he had just bought, wondering which was the quickest route. Leaving Luxembourg, he followed signs on the motorway for Trier. Once in Germany he continued on the autobahns, following signs for Frankfurt, and eating his lunch en route.

Detective Meyer parked the police car outside a small quaint looking art shop in the rue du Nord in the old town of Luxembourg City. Next door was a tattoo shop called 'Body Tattoo and Piercing' that had different tattoo designs down one side of the window.

After looking at the paintings in the art shop window, the police officers made their way into the tattoo shop. The doorbell buzzed as they entered.

Meyer glanced round, wondering why some people liked putting holes in themselves. Self-mutilation, he called it. He couldn't see the attraction of tattoos but knew they were popular with the youngsters, especially girls, another necessity in the female 'must haves', or was he getting old? Even his daughter had one like Gendarme Henckels. He knew attitudes had changed. Years ago, only sailors or gay men had tattoos. These days anyone had them.

A tall Luxembourgish man covered in tattoos and body piercing emerged from the back room. On seeing the police officers, he said, "*Moïen*, can I help you?"

Detective Meyer said, "Good morning, we're enquiring about tattoos."

"We do body piercing if you're interested," replied the tattooist.

"No, we're just looking at tattoos, thanks."

"What sort of tattoo did you have in mind?"

"One of a dragon," continued Gendarme Henckels.

"We have many designs including some with dragons. Perhaps I could show you some?"

"Yes, thanks."

The tattooist went over to a drawer and pulled out several small brochures that he brought over to the counter. Flicking through a few, he said, "This is the sort of thing we do."

The officers flicked through the brochures. As they did so, the tattooist said, "I can quote you the price once you've selected the one you want. But it depends also on how large you want it and where you want it."

Laughing, Gendarme Henckels said, "Oh, it's not for us!"

"Well, providing they're over seventeen, we can tattoo them."

"No, it's not like that. Actually, we're undertaking an investigation into a suicide and the person who died had an unusual tattoo on them."

"Oh, I see," said the surprised tattooist. "What sort of design are you looking for?"

"As we said, we're looking for dragon designs," she said. "You know, the type you put on your lower back."

The tattooist picked up one brochure and flicked through it until he got to some pages with dragon designs on. "Is that the sort of thing you're looking for?"

"That's it," said Gendarme Henckels.

Detective Meyer looked at the different designs.

"Do these tattoos have a meaning to them?" he said.

"They can do, but most are mass produced."

"Do you have any more?" he said.

"No, unfortunately that's all we have. Had you one in mind?"

Meyer decided to show the tattooist the design they had. Producing the photo of the dragon he said, "This is what we are looking for."

The tattooist studied it closely. "Well, it's similar to what we do but I must say I've not seen this particular one before."

"Could this design have a meaning to it?" Meyer asked.

Still looking at the photograph the tattooist said, "It could be a triad or clan symbol. They're particularly popular in Hong Kong and China."

"Right," said Meyer. "Does this one mean anything to you?"

"I'm afraid not."

"Well, thanks for the information." Meyer turned to his partner. "Okay Tammy, let's go."

"If it's any help, you can take the brochure," said the tattooist.

"Thanks," added Meyer.

Picking it up, both said '*Äddi*,' as they left the shop, the door buzzing as it opened and closed.

Outside in the rue du Nord, Gendarme Henckels said, "I take it we'll try the other tattooist in the Grund?"

"Yes," said Meyer.

They got in the police car and drove off.

Detective Meyer parked the police car in a car park near a stone bridge in the Grund. As he and Gendarme Henckels crossed it on foot, they looked out at the Alzette River that reflected the old town on the surface. They walked along a narrow cobbled road round to the left, passing through one of Luxembourg's oldest quarters. At a junction, they took a left and walked down a narrow street looking for the second tattoo shop.

As they passed a narrow side alley Gendarme Henckels said, "There it is."

They walked up to the shop called '21st Century Design.' Its windows were darkened with Chinese lanterns and candles burning in the window. As they went in, an old bell on the door rang as it swung open.

"This looks more promising," said Meyer.

The room was dark and musty from burning incense. It had a Far Eastern feel to it. Chinese ribbons hung from the ceiling at the back of the shop. On one wall were pictures of different body piercings. Another had tattoos plastered over it that Detective Meyer went over to and looked at.

An old Chinese looking man appeared from behind an oriental designed curtain. "*Bonjour Madame et Monsieur*, can I help you?" He spoke French with a Chinese accent.

Replying in French, Meyer said, "*Bonjour monsieur*. I'm Detective Meyer. We're looking at tattoo designs."

"Ah so, we have many. What part of the body is it for?"

"The back," said Meyer.

"We have many for back. Here, let me slow you."

The old man shuffled away into a corner and ruffled through a pile of papers.

"See here. Only the best."

"We're looking for one with a dragon on."

"Dragon. Vely good, have many."

The old man turned some pages of his book.

"See here. Many dragons, big and small. What you want?"

The police officers looked at the designs.

"Do you have any special dragon designs?" asked Meyer.

"Special. What you mean special?"

"Like this." Meyer took the photo out from his jacket.

The old man drew his breath. "Hah so. Where you get this? This vely special. Old Chinese dragon."

"Yes, but how special?" Meyer leaned over the counter, realising he had hit the nail on the head. He continued, "Does this have a meaning?"

The old man drew away and said nothing, coming back to the counter saying, "Where you get this?"

"This *Monsieur*…

"Cheung," said the old man.

This, *Monsieur* Cheung, we got from someone who's now dead. We'd like to know its meaning. Do you recognise it?"

The old man looked worryingly at it. Eventually he nodded. "Yes, I know this design. It vely unusual. Where you get this?"

"From a girl called Nadia Ponomariov. Do you know her?"

The old man shook his head. "No, me not know her."

"She's Ukrainian," said Meyer, not believing him.

The old man shuffled his feet. After a moment he said, "Wait. Girl come here maybe two weeks ago. Want tattoo. She pay money, I give her tattoo."

"Did she have blonde hair?" asked Meyer.

"Yes, girl have blonde hair. Vely beautiful."

"Why did she have this particular tattoo?"

"Me not know," replied the old man.

"Did she choose it from one of your designs?"

"Ah yes—and no. Not sure."

"Well, either she did or she didn't."

The old man paused. "She bring one with her. I adapt."

"Adapt? What do you mean?"

"She want more."

"More?"

"Yes, she want number added. I think vely strange."

Detective Meyer produced his second photo that showed *UB44138JS*.

"Yes, I put this on her. She insist."

"Did she say why she wanted it?"

"No, secret, she say."

"This design is special, isn't it *Monsieur* Cheung. What does it signify?"

The old man again drew his breath. "Me not know. Old Chinese dragon. That is all."

Detective Meyer didn't believe him. Turning to Gendarme Henckels he said, "Have you got any questions?"

"Did the girl leave you a copy of the tattoo?"

"No, girl take away. Me not have."

"Thank you," she said, turning to Meyer. "Okay, I'm ready when you are."

He looked at the old man and said, "Thank you for the information. We may need to come back, but in the meantime, *Au Revoir*."

"Thank you vely much," said the old man, putting his arms into a Chinese prayer gesture.

As they made their way out the old shop doorbell rang. Meyer closed the door behind him. He said to Gendarme Henckels as they walked down the narrow passage, "I didn't believe a word he said."

She replied, "Funny, nor did I. He's hiding something."

"That Chinese guy knows full well who that symbol belongs to. He was terrified when we showed it to him. You could see it in his eyes. We might just pay him another visit…"

They continued back along the old cobbled street to the police car where, shortly after, they drove up one side of the Pétrusse valley towards Police Grand-Ducale headquarters.

Detective Meyer was sitting at his desk reading his emails. Gendarme Henckels had her laptop on his desk checking hers when the phone went.

Answering it he said, "Meyer."

"Ernie, it's Andre."

"Oh, hello Andre. What can I do for you?"

"Ernie, we've got intelligence in that the Englishman is planning on staying in Luxembourg for another week's holiday. Not only that, but as I speak he's on his way to Frankfurt."

"Frankfurt?"

Andre explained and concluded, "Well, I thought you'd like to know."

"Good man, Andre. Yes, I am extremely interested in this information."

"If I hear any more I'll call you."

"Yes."

"See you"

"*Äddi.*"

Meyer wrote down some notes.

"What's Andre got for us?"

"You won't believe this, Tammy, but you know Muller's at his flat in Frankfurt; well, it seems he's shortly going to have company. The Englishman's gone too."

"The Englishman?"

"Yes, the one who's on holiday here. We interviewed him on Friday after the girl jumped. Andre says his unit's watching him as well. This morning he spoke to his brother telling him he was going to Frankfurt. He also rang his neighbour and parents in England to say he was staying in Luxembourg another week. From what I can deduce, he's on a similar mission as ourselves and wants to find out why the girl killed herself. With any luck he'll help us from another angle."

"Why's he going to Frankfurt?"

"That's what I'd like to know."

"Perhaps he's just on a day trip, Ernie."

"Perhaps, but I have hunch he's not."

He paused for a second. "I think a little trip to Germany for us won't go amiss, eh Tammy?"

She looked at him.

He continued, "I'll inform my contact in Frankfurt of the situation and arrange for him to meet us this evening where we can update each other. He should be able to help us find out more about Muller. I'm not quite sure where all this leads us, but if we stay overnight in Frankfurt we can check out Muller's meeting tomorrow morning. It'll probably mean an early start."

"What you mean, Ernie, is that I'll need my overnight bag."

"You've got it, and I'll need mine," he said, laughing. "Oh, and Andre's got the Balaclava boys paying Muller's flat in Limpertsberg a visit tonight."

"That'll be nice for him."

"It should be nice for us. Let's see their results." Looking at his watch he said, "Perhaps if we break off now and rendezvous back here at four we can be in Frankfurt by seven."

CHAPTER 13

▼

Frankfurt, Germany

It took over three and a half hours for Jason Evans to drive to Frankfurt. It was further than he thought and the traffic had been bad. When he got close to the city he followed the 'centre' signs and once there found himself a car park. That was an experience, parking, getting a ticket, yet really, it was something like being in the UK but in another language!

Once out of the car park he strolled around, soon realising Frankfurt was a large city. Finding his bearings, Jason discovered it was a short walk to the tourist information office. Having located it, he went inside, going over to the information desk.

"*Guten tag*," he said, practicing his limited German to the girl who served him.

"How can I help you?" she said in English with a German accent, having heard his English accent.

"Oh, you speak English?" he said in a surprised voice.

"Yes I do, and French."

"I'm looking for a map that will show me these streets," he said to her, showing her the two addresses.

The girl looked at the names. "Just a minute," she said and went out of the room. After a couple of minutes she came back with two maps. Laying them on the desk, she said, "One of the addresses is in the centre of the city. It's near the central station about ten minutes from here if you are walking—see, just there." She pointed at the map. "The other is out of town in a suburb on the southwest of the city, near the autobahn." Swapping the maps over and pointing to a place on the second one she said, "As you can see it's a long road, but is quite easy to find."

"Thanks very much," Jason said, pleased.

She pointed at the city centre map. "This one is free, but the other is five euros."

"That's okay." Jason paid her the money.

The tourist information girl gave him some brochures about Frankfurt and a free plastic bag with everything in.

"*Dankeschőn*," he said to her.

"*Bitteschőn*," she replied.

"*Auf Wiedersehen.*"

Jason walked outside and, finding a bench to sit on, took the maps out to study. It was now late afternoon so he decided to have a look around, see a bit of the place, the shops, and the attractions. The city seemed attractive—it was old and new, but the sixties architecture looked concrete and ugly.

Later whilst sightseeing, he came across a small hotel and went in to enquire if they had a cheap room for the night. They had and after viewing it, he took it, paying upfront. Checking the car parking arrangements with the receptionist he explained where his car was. The receptionist drew on his map a route for him to swap car parks. Jason thanked her. "I'll be back later," he said. "*Auf Wiedersehen.*"

After moving his car, he returned to the hotel, put his bag in his room and set off again on foot to locate the address that was near the central train station. Crossing various junctions and not really having a clue where it was leading him, he eventually located the street in a grubby run down area that formed part of the red light district.

"Dodgy!" he thought.

Jason found the number of the building and took some photos to show his brother. After a quick look round, he decided to return to the hotel.

Detective Meyer and Gendarme Henckels pulled up outside Frankfurt Central Police Station in a black VW Golf. They were casually dressed even though on duty. Leaving their Luxembourg police ID badge on the dashboard, they went into the reception of the police station. Going up to the front desk, Detective Meyer said in German, "*Guten Abend*, Detective Meyer and Gendarme Henckels from Luxembourg to see Wolfgang Steinacher."

"Moment," said the receptionist.

She picked up the phone and after a short conversation said, "He'll be right with you. Please take a seat."

They walked over to where a set of chairs were situated and waited. After a couple of minutes a door swung open and Wolfgang Steinacher walked up to them, saying in German with an American twang to it, "Ernie, how are you? Long time no see."

They shook hands.

"Hello Wolfgang. I'm fine, thanks. Let me introduce my colleague Gendarme Tammy Henckels."

As Wolfgang shook her hand he said, "Ernie told me he had a handsome assistant. I believe he's right. How are you, Tammy?"

"Fine thanks."

"Well, enough of the introductions. May I suggest we adjourn to one of my favourite bars? We can discuss everything over a drink."

"That's an excellent idea Wolfgang. I'll let you lead the way."

As they walked towards the main door Wolfgang said, "Before I forget, I've booked you both into the DW Hiltone. Is that okay?"

"Fine," they replied.

The three of them left the building and drifted into the streets of Frankfurt.

In downtown central Frankfurt it was a hot sunny evening. Many people were relaxing on the outdoor beer terraces, including Detective Meyer, Gendarme Henckels and Wolfgang Steinacher. They were outside a large bar called the Bavarian Beer Keller.

Sipping a large German beer Wolfgang said, "I got your emails, Ernie. Sounds an interesting case you've been assigned. I've been looking into your requests but first tell me the situation from your end."

Detective Meyer and Gendarme Henckels updated him on the story so far. Wolfgang said, "Like you say, Ernie, there's more to it than meets the eye, and from the information I've discovered today I'd say Muller is definitely up to no good. Let me explain." He took a sip of his beer. "Your man Klaus von Muller lives in Luxembourg and works at the German Embassy. He's resident there so comes under your jurisdiction. Nevertheless, his main base is actually in Frankfurt. He uses the embassy as a cover for his 'leisure activities'. That's where it starts to get interesting."

Detective Meyer's eyebrows shot up with interest.

"Muller's current sideline that I gather you're unaware of is making porn films. He has a company here in Frankfurt that makes and sells them into the porn market. That's the reason he's based here. He spends his spare time making these films, jetting off to his other flat in Torrevieja in Spain. It's all above board and as he's not doing anything illegal we can't do much about it. He's also got diplomatic immunity should he get himself into any trouble, so he's got his arse well covered. His Spanish operation is looked after by an ex-girlfriend called Martha. He goes down there every so often, generally taking a new girlfriend with him to impress them. When they get there he normally tells the girl he would like her to star in a movie. In this instance, we're talking porn movie, not Hollywood!"

"How do you know this, Wolfgang?" asked Gendarme Henckels.

"We sent an undercover girl in. She did everything except the movie, going sick at the last moment."

"I see."

"Anyway, he offers the girl large amounts of money to star in the action and once she agrees he gets various friends to co-star alongside her. He never goes front of camera but films the action. It's interesting what you say about this girl hating him. From the file I read this is the first instance I've heard of where the girl apparently has had a bad experience. Normally these girls love it. They're up for it as it's a free holiday for the sake of a screw. Sorry Tammy, but you get the idea."

"No problem," she replied.

"I've got something that'll assist you, Ernie."

"Oh, what's that?"

"It's Muller's latest movie. It's the one that features Nadia. There's actually another five girls on it but she seems to get promoted the most and I guess that's because she's the prettiest girl."

"I take it you've seen the movie?" smiled Meyer.

"Actually no!" He returned Meyer's smile. "I only saw the promotional covers on the DVD. Ernie, listen! I went out this afternoon and bought it especially for you and I don't do that everyday, I can tell you! Still, if it's in the course of duty…but I knew the place to get the new releases, knowing it might help. I'll give it to you later."

The waiter walked past and Meyer signalled to him.

"Another beer, Wolfgang?"

"Why not! It's all on expenses so what the hell."

"Tammy, another beer?"

"Just a small one this time Ernie, thanks."

Wolfgang continued. "The guy Muller's meeting tomorrow morning is his business partner. He's a German by the name of Volkert Graf. He lives in Munich. Here's a photograph of him. You may find it useful." He passed the photo to Meyer. "We're not sure how they met but he's been working for Muller for the last ten years or so. When we previously watched them, we noticed they didn't always communicate in German. Muller, I think, speaks basic Luxembourgish and Russian. We're not currently keeping tabs on either of them but now you've brought this to our attention I'll put them back on the DPCCP and see what unfolds."

"Yeah, that would be great," said Detective Meyer.

Wolfgang continued. "Muller, as you know, is actually East German. He was born in East Berlin. Grew up there. When he left school he worked on the railways, moving into various office jobs. When the wall came down, he was one of the first to make the most of the situation and head west. He didn't go far, managing to get himself a job with the newly unified German foreign office in Berlin. He worked there for the first few years before getting a transfer to Morocco. After a few years there, he got a transfer to Luxembourg, which is where he now is, of course."

"So how do the porn films come into it?" asked Gendarme Henckels.

"The embassy is Muller's day job. His outside interests or hobby are the films. It's more of a business actually. His operations are small, almost part-time in relation to what we usually deal with. At some point in his life, I guess, he discovered an easy way to make money was by making porn films. We think he started long before the wall came down. When it did, he used his knowledge of the Eastern block countries he gained on the railways to put to good use. He regularly used to travel by train to the border towns of Poland, down to Leipzig and across to Prague and Budapest to pick up girls who used to jump at the chance of three hundred Deutschmarks cash for a couple of hours of sex. He made thousands of Deutschmarks from these films, selling them to the porn barons. After a while, he started to invest his earnings in cash purchases outside Germany. When he got the posting in Morocco, he invested in property. The Moroccan secret police picked up on him carrying cash into the country. One time he was stopped and when they opened his suitcase, there it was, fifty thousand Deutschmarks."

Detective Meyer's eyebrows rose.

Wolfgang continued, "He hadn't done anything illegal so they couldn't touch him, but they did give a warning in their own way. That's probably one reason why he got the posting to Luxembourg. I don't think he fancied a spell in one of their prisons. Anyway, whilst working in Rabat for the embassy, he continued making porn films, only this time using cheap Moroccan tarts. His other interest was in property, which the Moroccan police never quite got to the bottom of. As far as we know, Muller owns several Riads and umpteen flats in and around Marrakech. Just how many we don't know. He set up various companies. Possibly runs them from his Spanish flat. Though he's kept a low profile in Morocco recently. His property deals happened about five years ago, climaxing just before the change over to the Euro. Soon after, he ceased buying property in Morocco and started investing in Spain. We know quite a few Germans who undertook similar such operations as we worked with the French and Swiss police in an undercover operation to try to stop the flood of Deutschmarks out of the country into Switzerland."

"What happened to the money?" asked Gendarme Henckels.

"Once across the border the cash was deposited in Swiss bank accounts. A lot of black money was transferred out by telegraphic transfer to The Cayman Islands, Bermuda and other offshore havens. We know of umpteen operations that we can't touch—yet. However, a lot of the black market Deutschmarks ended up in Morocco. It was deposited cash in hand into property through the purchase of flats and Riads. The network of cash runners used either the ferries or cheap flights from Spain to get it in there. Muller was a cash operator to Morocco and used his flat in Spain as cover. We think he's part of the network."

"You mean there's more?" suggested Gendarme Henckels.

"Oh yes. He's only a small cog in the works. Where the wheel starts to turn is still a mystery to us. You may recall yourself, Ernie, there were several similar operations in Luxembourg?"

"Yes, and one of them left a bad taste in my mouth. I messed up on one during my divorce and it almost got me kicked out of the force. As you know I've been doing surveillance for a while now and this suicide has reopened the door for me."

"Well, I'm pleased for you, Ernie. You deserve it."

Wolfgang took a gulp of his beer before resuming.

"The other places many operators put their dodgy money in was Spain. They purchased everything, from flats to villas, all along the Costa Blanca and Costa Brava. In fact, it helped fuel the property boom along the Costa's. Huge amounts became untraceable. That's another reason Muller could be in Spain but again we can't prove that. There's been a huge money laundering operation going on for years now. The final destination of it we're still not sure."

"I thought you said it was property?" said Gendarme Henckels.

"For the moment it is. However, our Spanish connections have noticed one or two of the properties being sold recently. The sales make it clean money. Most have appreciated in value, making even more for whoever controls the operation. The proceeds are again filtered through the banks, most returning offshore. There's an elaborate network out there in operation making our investigations difficult. We simply don't have the resources to trace it all."

"I know the feeling," said Detective Meyer.

"Do you know where the other money's coming from?" asked Gendarme Henckels.

"We think the Far East. Again, there's several big operators out there but it could be the drug barons in Afghanistan. Where else do you get large amounts of black market money?"

"Is that where the dragon comes in?" asked Gendarme Henckels.

"Yes, there's a strong possibility."

"What do you know about this symbol, Wolfgang?" asked Meyer, showing him the photograph.

"I think it's the symbol of one of the many Chinese secret societies or triad organisations."

"But you don't know which one?" asked Gendarme Henckels.

"No, that's been the problem. We've been trying to find that out for a while now."

"Have you seen this particular symbol before?" she added.

"I haven't as it's not my domain of work, but I'll get my colleagues to check it in case they've got something. I tell you, this girl was smart to put it on her back. She knew exactly what she was doing. Even the numbers and letters were a clever idea of hers."

"We think the meaning of the letters and numbers signifies a date and possibly a bank account number," said Gendarme Henckels. "What do you think?"

"I agree with you. In Ernie's email, he said UBS in Switzerland. It's a strong possibility as Muller has travelled to Switzerland in the past going via France to get there."

"How do you know that?" said Gendarme Henckels.

"He got stopped once when going through Germany, so switched routes and started going through France. We think we only picked up on him at the tail end of his trips to Switzerland, as soon after he stopped his visits. As for the date, well, that's a wartime date and that interests me a lot."

"Oh, whys that?" said Detective Meyer.

"Because it's not so much Klaus von Muller it applies to, even though it involves him now."

"Who does it apply to?"

"I have a hunch here, Ernie. I think it applies to his father."

"His *father*?" said Tammy, astonished. "What's his father got to do with it?"

"He was a Nazi."

"So?"

"During the war he was in the SS. We know this from his Stasi records that we recovered after the unification. We think he knows the meaning of this inscription."

"Why do you say that?"

"They showed us his SS wartime postings and the date on the inscription could tie in with them."

"So where was he posted?"

"Luxembourg."

"Luxembourg!"

"Yes, I thought that might surprise you."

"It does."

"He worked at a place called The SS Villa. Does it still exist?"

"Oh, the building exists, but it has a different name these days." Meyer smiled. "They even have a sign outside saying it was used by the Gestapo."

"Well, Muller senior started his SS career in Luxembourg, living there for a couple of years. Married a local girl I discovered, but you know all that."

Detective Meyer nodded vaguely.

"He got posted to Paris for a year, but came back every month to see his wife who remained in Luxembourg. The tide turned for the Nazi's and with the allies closing in on Paris, he used his Gestapo contacts in Luxembourg to get him a rapid transfer back. However, that didn't last long as he was posted to Berlin to help defend it from the Russians. He got caught by them and was sent off for ten years hard labour, spending the rest of his working life living in the eastern block."

"What's that got to do with this inscription?"

Checking his IPOD, Wolfgang said, "Look at it. It says *UB44138JS*. The dates are 13th August 1944. Agreed?"

"Yes."

"Well, from what I can establish from his Stasi file that's the brief period he was back in Luxembourg. He was there for about a month. What he did during that time we don't know."

Gendarme Henckels butted in. "Am I missing something here?"

"No, just let me finish, Tammy."

"Sorry."

"The point I'm trying to make is, judging by the date, Muller senior must have gone down to Switzerland in August 44 either to open an account or to deposit something, possibly both."

"Yes, we thought of that, but as yet, haven't taken it any further," said Meyer.

"The Swiss authorities opened many Nazi bank accounts a couple of years ago," said Gendarme Henckels. "So the chances are they opened this account."

"They did, but that's what you'll have to discover. Is there a link between what's on the girl's back and a Swiss bank account?"

"So why is Klaus von Muller involved with this, after all these years?"

"That's easy, Ernie. His father is an old man now. He lives in a nursing home in Berlin. He's been confined to a wheelchair since a hit and run accident back in the late eighties. Our file tells us at the time he lost interest in everything. He seems to have recovered over the years but is still in his wheelchair."

"And?"

"He was an SS officer, Ernie."

"So?"

"He's one of the last still alive. Look, this number tells me he's got something of value hidden away. I'm guessing his accident prevented him travelling."

"So what's this got to do with his son?"

Wolfgang gave Detective Meyer a look of exasperation.

"Look Ernie. An SS officer made a vow to the Reich to serve and obey. That's a vow made for life. The fact that the Reich doesn't exist anymore is irrelevant. There's many old Nazi's still out there, okay? Not so many these days but the point is they kept many secrets and still have their own network of contacts. Muller senior is now very old. My guess is he still holds a few secrets and has realised that he had to pass them on to someone before he dies, or they'll be lost. This date and number I think relates to an operation Muller senior ran. It's got to be worth something for him to have passed it onto his son even though that goes against the oath of the SS. If that's the case, which I think it is, you're onto something good, Ernie. The question is, what?" Wolfgang paused and took a few swigs of beer. "I thought you might find that interesting."

"Very," replied Meyer.

"These cross border meetings we have—we should do them more often, Ernie. I know it's easier these days to simply use all this new technology to check people out, but I find a session like this so much more rewarding. Don't you?"

"Yes, very," Meyer nodded.

"The thing is, what's your next move?" Wolfgang leaned back in his chair.

"Well, we intend to investigate the meeting tomorrow morning at Muller's flat."

At that moment Gendarme Henckels said, "Will you excuse me a minute? I'll be right back."

She got up and made her way to the ladies.

Meyer continued: "From what you've told us I think it's a much larger operation we're involved with than we realised."

"Possibly Ernie. Look, sometimes one has to look at these things stage by stage. See what happens."

"True. But I don't really have an answer yet, it's too early."

"Well, if the girl's suicide is connected with the inscription, I'd say a few more days wont matter after almost sixty years!" Wolfgang laughed.

Meyer continued: "What we do know is Muller beat up the girl, but as there was no complaint from her we can't touch him."

"Tomorrow may give you some leads. Every little helps, as you know, Ernie. Your Englishman may give you some answers."

"He may. However, I find his actions weird. He seems to be spending a lot of effort on this."

"Only as much effort as you are, Ernie," he said laughing. "Let's face it, you've got some competition and I don't think you like it."

"Oh come on, Wolfgang."

"Look, the guy's doing you a favour. By the way, you'd better have this, Ernie." He passed over a plastic bag. "It's the DVD, before you ask." Wolfgang put his hand in his pocket and said, "This also might be useful. It's a tracking devise. You can use it on Volkert's car. You might need it, the way things are going."

"Thanks," replied Meyer.

Wolfgang took something from his jacket. "This could also come in handy."

He passed the small package to Detective Meyer who said, "What is it?"

"Half of it's a bug that if you insert under the passenger seat will transmit conversations for a radius of ten kilometres. The other half you'll need to listen to the conversations on. However, the problem will be getting it fitted, so the tracking device may be your best bet."

"Great!"

"Your request for a set of German number plates is sorted. I've arranged for them to be delivered to your hotel tonight so you can use them in your undercover operation tomorrow."

"Thanks Wolfgang."

"If you need anything else, shout and I'll see what I can sort out for you."

"*Wunderbar!*"

Gendarme Henckels rejoined them on the terrace. "I don't know about you two, but I'm hungry," she said.

"Yes, I think we could do with something inside us."

"Good. Well, there's a nice little restaurant up the street I'd like to take you to."

"Sounds interesting," said Meyer.

"Tammy?"

"Yes, fine."

Wolfgang waved to the waiter and settled the tab. The three of them got up and strolled down the street towards the restaurant.

CHAPTER 14

▼

After taking a shower, changing and relaxing in his hotel room for a short while, Jason Evans decided to hit the town. Finding a couple of bars, he drank several local German beers before deciding on some food. Walking down the road, he found a Vietnamese restaurant where he ate.

To give his stomach time to digest the meal he walked round Frankfurt for a while looking at the nightlife. Deciding on the lowest form first, he walked towards the station into the red light district, looking round it before returning to the central shopping area. He opted for a small club where he sat at the bar drinking a couple of beers, talking to some German girls who spoke some English.

Feeling tired he didn't stay long and returned to his hotel where in his room, he lay on the bed and channel flicked before crashing out.

After spending an enjoyable evening at Wolfgang's favourite restaurant, Detective Meyer and Gendarme Henckels had walked back with him to Frankfurt Central Police Station where, standing outside, Wolfgang said, "If you can wait here a few moments I'll fetch the portable DVD player for you, Ernie." He nipped into his office and after a few minutes returned with it. "There you go. Enjoy the movie!" he said, smiling.

"Thanks for that Wolfgang." Meyer grinned. "Well, we'd better go now as we've an early start. It's been good to see you again. Thanks for all your help."

"My pleasure," replied Wolfgang, shaking hands with both of them.

Gendarme Henckels added, "Yes, we've really enjoyed our evening."

"Don't leave it so long next time, Ernie, and keep in touch Tammy, eh!"

They all said, "*Auf Wiedersehen*," shook hands and departed.

Detective Meyer and Gendarme Henckels jumped in a taxi that took them to their hotel.

On arrival at the DW Hiltone Hotel Detective Meyer and Gendarme Henckels checked in at the reception desk, picked up their keys and retired for the night. Gendarme Henckels was exhausted and in her room went straight to bed. Meyer in his room took a shower, then hooked up the DVD player to the TV and watched the porn movie with Nadia in. He found it intriguing.

'So this is Muller's flat in Torrevieja.'

He thought it looked nice and could understand why Muller's girlfriends enjoyed their holidays if all they had to do was lie back and think of Spain. However, he could see why Nadia hated Muller as from the start it clearly looked like she was coerced into making it. He instantly recognised Graf when he showed up in the movie. Nadia had given him and the cameraman, who Detective Meyer knew was Muller, some very negative comments. He guessed the beginning had had to be re-shot several times because of her unhelpful attitude. The sex he thought was rough but nothing unusual.

The DVD he didn't rate in his top ten but it allowed him to see Nadia, so to speak, hear her voice and gave him some ideas about her. Above all, it enabled him to put a further piece in the jigsaw to help solve the case.

Luxembourg

In the early hours of Friday morning in Luxembourg, the BBB's or Black Balaclava Boys arrived at the Glacis car park at the start of their mission. Earlier at the Villa Louvigny Andre Biever had given his undercover squad their instructions.

Leaving their old Citroen with false number plates, they walked across the Glacis. They were dressed from head to toe in black, including their balaclavas and gloves. On the corner of the street, they split up. The first man waited whilst the second took the long way round the block to get to Muller's flat.

Checking his watch, the first man walked up the street. It was deserted, not a moving car in sight. He checked for any late night stragglers. It was midweek; the nearby disco was closed that night. With many people away due to the holidays meant it was quiet, making perfect conditions for a visit.

On reaching the flat, the first man took out his special key and silently unlocked the door. As he opened it, his colleague arrived and the two of them slid in, making their way towards the lift. Momentarily they listened for movement in the flats. There was none. Everyone was either asleep or were away.

Creeping up the stairs they arrived outside Muller's flat, letting themselves in. Once inside, in silence, they glanced around. Each had a job to carry out. The first man went to Muller's video, undid the back using his tools and inserted a transmitting device before sealing the unit. Next, he took some sellotape and put a small strip next to the handle of the glass door of the video unit, a calling card. He went into Muller's bedroom and on each of the small bedside tables put four strips of sellotape on the lower glass shelf, another calling card, adding a bug in the bedside radio. Moving to the bathroom, he saw an opened tube of toothpaste and, using a toothbrush on the sink, carefully put two dabs on the radiator. He marked the mirror with an 'S' which, to the naked eye, remained invisible. In a flash, he moved the toilet roll holder by forty-five degrees to the left and tore the paper at the bottom of the previously untorn roll. Returning to the lounge, he planted a bug in the artificial flowers.

During this the second man accessed Muller's computer and downloaded the hard drive, the process taking no more than five minutes.

Each gave the thumbs up sign to indicate they had completed their tasks before they silently exited the flat.

Frankfurt, Germany

In Frankfurt, Germany, Jason Evans had risen early in order not to miss the continental breakfast. At nine twenty-five he checked out of the hotel and went round to the car, dumping his overnight bag in the boot. After paying the attendant at the underground car park, he drove out into the Frankfurt traffic, following the map he bought and various road signs. After more than a couple of wrong turns, he eventually found the road where Muller lived.

Detective Meyer and Gendarme Henckels waited in their black dark screened Volkswagen Golf. They were parked at the far end of a large outdoor car park. It formed part of the modern high-rise apartment block where Klaus von Muller lived in one of the outer suburbs of Frankfurt.

Just after nine-thirty, a German registered black BMW pulled into the car park and parked near the entrance. A tallish man of about thirty-five got out of the car and picked up a case from the boot of the vehicle.

"That's our man," said Gendarme Henckels.

"It looks like it is," replied Meyer, photographing him.

The man walked over from the car to an entrance door of the flats. Opening it, he went in.

In the Golf, the officers watched.

"Where's the Englishman?" asked Gendarme Henckels.

"Oh, don't worry, he'll be here," Meyer said. "If he isn't I'll be surprised."

After a while he said, "Wait here for a moment, will you."

Nipping out of the car he made his way to the black BMW, walking round to its rear. After a short while he returned to the Golf where Gendarme Henckels said, "What were you doing?"

"I was putting a tracking devise underneath his rear bumper. We'll be able to track him using the global satellite system wherever he goes. Its the devise Wolfgang gave me last night."

"I don't remember that."

"Ah, that's when you were in the ladies. By the way, what did you think of last night?"

"Good—it introduced us to the real world of Klaus von Muller! You were right to pursue this guy."

"So far I think we've touched the tip of the iceberg. Something tells me there's a lot more underneath."

As Gendarme Henckels poured herself a cup of coffee from a flask, she said, "Do you want a cup?"

"No, I'm fine," replied Meyer who was smoking a cigarette.

He relaxed and after a while said, "This is the joy of surveillance. We sit here getting paid for doing nothing!"

In his kitchen Klaus von Muller prepared a peculator of coffee for himself and Volkert Graf. When it was made they sat drinking it in his lounge.

Speaking in German, Muller said, "I'm glad you could make it this morning, Volkert. Was the traffic on the motorway as bad as ever?"

"At the time of the morning when I set off, Klaus, it was fine," replied Graf.

"Well, I've lots to tell you, but I've left it till now as I never trust the phone. Listen, I got the letter—thanks. I've made a mental note of it but we may have to put it on hold as we've got a big problem."

"Oh, what's that?"

"I'm sorry to tell you that last Friday night Nadia committed suicide. It was while I was here for the weekend."

"Shit, that's terrible!"

"It is, because the stupid bitch has opened a can of worms."

"I told you she wasn't to be trusted!"

"She was trouble right from the start. I was stupid taking her out of the cabaret."

"You only wanted to screw her, Klaus."

"Yes, I know, and we both enjoyed it, right? Nevertheless, with hindsight I should never have taken her to Spain and kicked her out after the first week. Now she's dead and the police are investigating."

"But *you* didn't kill her…"

"No, of course I didn't. She killed herself." He took a sip of coffee before continuing. "You know, these last few days have been a nightmare. I'd not been back an hour on Monday when I got two dodgy phone calls. An hour later the cops turned up to tell me. Naturally, I was upset. They took me down to the morgue. I tell you it was an eerie experience seeing her stare at me. There was a kind of smile on her face. It read, 'I'm going to get you.' What made it worse was that the police showed me a photograph of the tattoo she had had done, the one of the dragon on her back. She had it put on deliberately after she discovered our operations and that's one reason I beat her up. It was clearly her way of getting back at me."

"I'd say the other was taking her life."

"Yes, I got the feeling she felt trapped once she found out what she knew. Stupid bitch."

Graf listened.

"It gets worse Volkert. The police not only interviewed me but her best friend where she worked. They even flew her parents over from Kiev."

"Did they really! That was decent of them."

"Well, they had to so they could take the body back, which incidentally leaves tonight. However, they were clearly after some background information on Nadia. On Tuesday afternoon, the police brought her parents round to the flat to collect her belongings. It was surreal. I had to be polite as hell. I tell you the police are investigating this big time and you can bet your bottom dollar it won't be the last I see of them."

"You've only got yourself to blame, Klaus. Your problem is you've too many fingers in too many pies. Cut a few out."

"That's what I intend to do, but this time it could be too late."

"Yeah, but don't worry about it too much. Technically you've not done anything wrong so they can't arrest you."

Muller grimaced. "No, but it's all our other stuff they'll check on and you know what that means."

"I do indeed!"

"The police are bound to find out about our Spanish operation, but like you said, it's not illegal. As you know, Nadia went ballistic after we shot the video. She sussed what we were doing here in Frankfurt and flew at me so I beat her to shut the bitch up. In Luxembourg, I discovered she'd gone through my paperwork and found out what I'm doing there. I beat her up again big time so she got the message to keep her mouth firmly shut. There's too much to lose, Volkert."

"The police are bound to check it out."

"Not if we play it right. I don't want our nice little earner being blown."

"You're not just talking about Frankfurt, are you?"

"No, that's why we're meeting today. I think we should shut down our operation here for the moment. If we go into the office this morning, we can clear it out and move everything down to your lockup in Munich. Luckily, the distribution of the films is not our problem. We can get fresh meat in the future, but meantime we'll have to cool it. Hopefully this'll all die down—then we can start again."

"But surely you'll have to watch your back?"

"Yes, that's partly why we're here now. Any communication by electronic means is out, Volkert, and watch who you sit next to in the pub. Chances are they'll put a couple of informers drinking lemonade or water next to us."

"Klaus, if they're investigating you means they'll check out the flat in Spain. The evidence is on the DVDs. What about Martha?"

"Oh, she'll be okay. I sent her a letter with instructions last night."

"Look, Klaus. You're panicking. We've done nothing illegal so they can't touch us."

"But they can harass us and mark my words, they're very good at that. The police have their methods, which they'll use if necessary. More coffee?"

"Ah ha." As Muller poured them both another cup Graf continued, "Well, I'd better watch my back, Klaus. At least you've got diplomatic immunity if the shit hits the fan."

"Yes, it comes in handy. Nevertheless, there's another consideration in my life to sort."

"What's that?"

"My father's little operation."

"Oh, what's happening on that?"

"He expected everything done by now and it isn't. I've got to speed things up. If I don't get it sorted in the next two weeks he said he'll find his own solution."

"Why two weeks?"

"He's fed up with my excuses. Look, can you come over on Sunday—then I can show you what I've prepared?"

"It'd better be worth it, Klaus. I'm a busy man."

"Look, Volkert. Call it a social visit. You know it makes sense."

"I do."

"If my father could walk and was younger everything would be easy, but as you know the communists and history did him no favours. He's a stubborn bugger, one of the few remaining. You know he wrote to me last week saying he might have to get help from certain friends, and I tell you, even you don't want to get involved with those!"

"Christ, Klaus. Don't get into more shit. If the Dragon finds out about that…"

"It's a separate issue."

"Klaus, I'll have to go back on Sunday night as I'm meeting one of the Dragon's contacts on Monday night. I get the feeling there's something in the pipeline again. I know it's been blocked recently but I have an uneasy feeling. I can fly up on Tuesday if that's any good for you?"

Muller didn't look too happy.

"All right," he said. "But I want to honour the promise I made to my father and I don't like to let him down."

"You won't. Look, I'll book the flight. What time's the plane?"

"From memory there's two a day, one in the morning and one in the evening from Munich."

"Well, I can't do the morning so I'll try and get the evening flight. I'll let you know."

"Just remember the phone is sure to be bugged," said Muller.

They drank another coffee. Both were deep in thought before Graf said, "Look Klaus. Let's go downtown and take it from there."

"Okay, that's good with me."

They got up and made their way down to the BMW.

Locating the car park entrance of Klaus von Muller's flat, Jason Evans drove in, parking halfway down the outer row. Walking round the vicinity, he took a couple of pictures of the flats in the process. As he did so, Detective Meyer and Gendarme Henckels watched him from inside their black VW Golf.

"There, I told you he'd turn up, Tammy!" he said gleefully.

"What's he up to?" she said. "We've sat here now for more than an hour without anything happening."

"Patience, Tammy! Have faith. I'm sure the Englishman will lead us to something."

Jason went to a nearby doorway, opened it and went inside—but discovered that beyond the entrance hallway was residents' access only.

There was a wall of post boxes on the left hand side. One of them bore Muller's name. Nearby was a bell board with residents' names on. Again, his name was on it.

At that moment, an old woman came out of the building. In English Jason said to her, "Excuse me, do you speak English?"

Shaking her head, she brushed him aside and went on her way. Feeling he wasn't getting anywhere he went back to the Corsa, sitting inside it with the radio on. Wondering what to do next, he suddenly saw two men carrying cases come out of the door that went to the flats above. They were walking across the car park towards him.

"Amazing!" said Jason to himself, realising the girl in Spain had been right. "It's Muller and the guy on the DVD."

Muller and Graf stopped at a black BMW that was parked nearby, putting the cases in the boot. Getting in, Graff reversed into the aisle and they drove off.

Jason had a hunch and decided to follow at a distance. Following both of them using their global satellite tracker signal was Detective Meyer and Gendarme Henckels.

After a short distance, Jason realised Muller and his friend were driving into the city. Continuing the pursuit, he guessed where they were going.

Jason followed the BMW into the red light district in Frankfurt. Driving past Muller's office Graf searched for a car parking space. In the adjacent street, he found one. Passing Graf's car Jason also located a spot in the same street to park. Using his rear view mirror he watched as the two men walked up the street towards him. He looked at his map as they passed the Corsa on the other side of the road.

Detective Meyer and Gendarme Henckels drove past them both, turning right at a corner and right again before parking in a newly vacated space twenty meters beyond Muller's office.

It was dustbin day and the bins still had to be emptied. Jason noticed a dustcart collecting rubbish nearby. As the two men walked down the street, he saw Muller take something from his pocket and put it in a wheelie bin that stood amongst a line of others still to be emptied, before turning the corner.

Getting out of the car, Jason crossed the road and walked up the street to where the bin was. He stopped, lifted its lid and looked at the rubbish inside. After a moment, he found what he was looking for.

What he discovered was an envelope addressed to Herr Muller, which he quickly put in his pocket. He followed the two men, turned the corner and walked at a quick pace to keep up, keeping his distance. At the next crossroads the men turned right, going down the street for another two hundred metres.

"Here they come," said Gendarme Henckels as she looked in her rear view mirror. Shortly after she said, "And here comes the Englishman."

"Wolfgang did us proud," said Detective Meyer as he watched. "I never would have thought we'd end up here."

Having got half way down the street, Jason saw Muller and Graf go in the building and, feeling he couldn't do much more, turned round and retraced his steps to the Corsa where he took the envelope out of his pocket. It was addressed to Muller at his German flat. The postmark on the envelope was Munich.

Inside he discovered a letter with a Munich address. Looking at it closely, he saw someone called Volkert had signed it. Reading its contents, Jason tried to understand the letter; but not speaking German didn't help. He wasn't sure whether it was all in German. Most of the words looked German, but then some of them didn't. Now he was puzzled. Maybe it was Czech or Polish as the borders were relatively close. He hadn't a clue but decided to study it later.

Feeling hungry, he got out of the car, walked down the street and located a sandwich bar. He bought a drink and sandwich and ate them in the car.

Afterwards he decided it was a good time to drive round and see a few sites in Frankfurt before returning to Luxembourg.

For the police officers it involved an hour and twenty minutes wait in the VW Golf.

"This is a really bad area," said Gendarme Henckels.

"I'm told it's worse at night, full of pimps, prostitutes and drug addicts. Just the sort of place for a porn business."

"Yes, Muller kept that quiet, didn't he? By the way Ernie, how was the movie?"

He laughed. "It was interesting, but on a serious note it assisted me with the case. I got some information from it and learnt a thing or two about Nadia. Do you want to watch it?"

"Not unless I need to, thank you Ernie," she replied quickly.

"I thought you might say that. That's why I didn't mention it till you asked."

Just at that moment, Muller and Graf appeared from the building.

Watching in their rear view mirrors Gendarme Henckels said, "There they are, Ernie."

Graf walked up the street while Muller stood by a vacant parking spot.

"What are they doing?" asked Gendarme Henckels.

"By the look of it I'd say Graf's getting his car," replied Meyer.

Two minutes later Graf parked the BMW in the parking spot, returning with Muller into the building. A short time later, they returned carrying cases and various bags, dumping them in the car before returning to the office

With a smile on his face, Meyer said wryly, "It looks as though they're clearing out their office."

"You mean they're panicking."

"I think you're right there."

Five minutes later the two men returned with more boxes. A further trip followed, after which the police officers saw Graf lock the door of the building and the boot of the car.

"I think that's the lot Tammy."

"What now?"

"We follow them."

As the men got in the car and drove off, Detective Meyer turned on the tracking device and for several minutes monitored it.

"They're going back to his flat. Let's go."

He started the engine and drove off.

When the police officers arrived at the car park of Klaus von Muller's flat, they saw the black BMW parked in the same spot as before. They parked in their previous spot and waited.

"What do you think he's done with the gear in the boot, Ernie?"

"My guess is its still there as they were emptying the office in the red light district to relocate somewhere else."

"Where?"

"How do I know? I doubt Muller will want it here, so my hunch is Munich."

"Munich?"

"Well, that's where Graf lives, right?"

"Yes."

"I doubt he'll put the gear in his flat, so the chances are he's got an office there. We don't know a lot about this guy. Is he still working for Muller? We'll have to find out."

At that moment, the two men reappeared, walking from the entrance of the flats towards the BMW. The police officers watched them. The two men were engrossed in conversation. Finally, they shook hands and Graf got in the car, reversed into the aisle and drove off. Muller waved as he departed before returning to his flat.

Looking at Detective Meyer, Gendarme Henckels said, "What now, Ernie?"

He paused, lighting a cigarette.

"How about a little tracking using my new toy?"

He turned it on and they watched the display board.

"Actually, if I'm right we'll see the BMW head south to Munich."

"We haven't got time to go to Munich, Ernie. Don't forget we've got to be back in Luxembourg tonight in time for the flight to Kiev."

"I realise that, Tammy."

Finishing his cigarette, he added, "We can't follow him now so let's have some lunch before we return to Luxembourg."

"Good idea."

CHAPTER 15

▼

Luxembourg

After a long drive back to Luxembourg Jason Evans arrived at his brother's flat, feeling tired. He relaxed under a hot shower that made him feel fresher and more awake. After dressing, he borrowed his brother's washing machine, popped some laundry in and turned on the TV.

Detective Meyer and Gendarme Henckels arrived back in the Grand Duchy calling in at a petrol station in Wasserbillig to fill up with cheap petrol and cigarettes.

Returning to Police Grand-Ducale headquarters in Luxembourg City, they unloaded their overnight bags from the car, went inside and took a coffee before changing into uniform.

Later in his office, Meyer was checking his emails when Gendarme Henckels knocked and entered. As she went to check hers, he said, "You might want to leave most of those for now as we've got to see Inspector Bruns at seven."

Checking the time, she replied, "We've a few minutes."

They sat in silence, reading their screens after which Meyer said, "Okay, we'd better go, Tammy."

They departed for the Inspector's office.

Shaun Evans returned home, greeted his brother and after they briefly updated each other, said, "I've arranged a meal with the girls on the basis you'd be back."

"Great!" said Jason.

"I'm meeting them at The Red Rose at seven thirty."

"Well, you'd better get a move on," said Jason jokingly as he watched TV.

Shaun jumped in the shower, changed and in a short time was ready. Looking at the clock he said, "Let's go."

They left the flat and walked up the street towards the pub.

Detective Meyer knocked at Inspector Bruns' door. He looked up and said, "Ah, Detective Meyer, Gendarme Henckels, come in. Take a seat, please."

They sat down.

Looking inquisitive he said, "How was Frankfurt? Did you solve the case?"

They laughed and updated the Inspector at the end of which Meyer said, "We're still checking our emails. I know Andre's team has sent us more information."

"Well, don't worry about that now," the Inspector replied. "Whilst you were away I got him to fill me in."

"I see," said Meyer.

"He's got the lab team working on the download from Muller's computer that the undercover squad recovered this morning. The results should be known some time tomorrow. This is turning into an interesting case for both of you. I get the impression you're making progress, but there's a few points I'd like to run through with you." Bruns paused. "I think it was an excellent idea going to Frankfurt. Your contact Wolfgang proved extremely useful. Now we know about Muller and, maybe more importantly, his father."

"His father?" said Meyer.

"You said Wolfgang had a hunch about him. Well, so do I. What did he do in August 1944, Ernie? Did he go to Switzerland? Recheck Klaus von Muller's text messages to see if you've missed anything. You'll better check with Europol and Interpol to see what they've got on dragon symbols. Find out what organisations use the symbol."

Inspector Bruns paused for a second whilst he blew his nose.

"Muller's definitely got more than one string to his bow. I mean, making porn films, dodgy property deals in Morocco and possible money laundering, is, I must say, unusual. However, all these might not be a connection and nothing to do with our case. What we've got to find out I think is what the date and symbol on the girl's back signifies. Are they related or not? I'm guessing they are separate issues. The link is Muller junior. At the end of the day, though, we mustn't loose track of the fact we're investigating a suicide."

"Yes sir."

"Well, I'd better let you get off—I know you've got to be at the airport shortly. Keep me updated on developments."

"We will."

"Good. Enjoy your day off—I'll see you on Monday."

Detective Meyer and Gendarme Henckels got up and made their way down the corridor where Meyer said, "We'd better get a move on, Tammy, or we'll miss the flight!"

The Evans brothers found a table to sit at on the patio outside The Red Rose. Again, it was busy and still very warm. Sipping his pint, Jason said, "It's hard to believe a week's gone by since I first came here."

Minutes later, Carmen and Maria arrived, greeted the brothers and sat down. Shaun bought them a drink. They let the girls do the talking and eventually the subject of what Jason had been doing came up. He updated them.

"You're turning into another Inspector Clouseau, aren't you?" Carmen smiled, looking at Jason.

He laughed. "Actually there is something you can help me with." He showed them the letter he found. "What do you make of that?" As they read it, he added, "It's not all in German, is it?"

Maria shook her head. "No, it's not. If you look, some words are in German and others are in Luxembourgish, which I speak. Most, though, I don't understand. The words are similar to Luxembourgish—see, look at that word there—and here."

"I don't know!" Jason looked at Carmen. "Do you know, Carmen?"

"No, I don't speak Luxembourgish," she replied.

Maria continued: "It's definitely a Germanic language. The languages I speak are mainly Latin based, which is why it's easy for me to learn French and Spanish. I've grown up with the other two languages but struggle with both. If you wait a minute, I'll ask my friend who's at the bar—and whilst I'm at it I'll get the next round. Same again?"

Everyone nodded and Jason said, "That's very kind of you."

Maria went inside to the bar and ordered.

"You're at the table outside?" said the barmaid.

"Yes," replied Maria.

"I'll bring the drinks out to you."

"Thank you." Maria paid for the round.

She took the letter over to a guy at the end of the bar who was a Luxembourger.

"*Moïen*," she said to him.

They embraced each other before he continued in Luxembourgish. "Hello Maria, how are you?"

"I'm fine Carl. Say, could you help me with something?"

"Yes, what's that?"

She showed him the letter.

"Is this yours?" he asked.

Not quite knowing what to say she said, "Oh no, it's a long story. Actually, it's a friend's. Does it mean anything to you?"

He looked down his nose at the letter. "Hum, let me see…It's definitely not all in Luxembourgish. Let me ask Luc." Carl leaned over and prodded him. "Luc, this girl needs help. Does this mean anything to you?"

Luc looked at the letter, putting on his glasses to read it properly. Eventually he replied, "You're right, it's not Luxembourgish. It's Jenisch."

Surprised, Maria said, "Jenisch! I've heard of that. It's an old language, isn't it?"

"Yes it is," Luc replied. "It's still spoken, mainly in Pfaffenthal."

"Do you speak Jenisch?" she said to him.

"No, I don't, but try one of the locals in Pfaffenthal."

"Good idea. Thanks very much, both of you," she said, rushing outside to rejoin the group.

"Well?" said Shaun.

"It's Jenisch."

"Jenisch! What's that?" said Jason. "You mean Danish?"

"No, Jenisch—it's an old local language or dialect spoken by some people in Pfaffenthal. I've heard about Jenisch before but have never seen it. We were never taught it. When I was at school, I learnt Luxembourgish. This was in the period when Luxembourgish was being taught on a more formal basis."

"What do you mean?" asked Shaun.

"Well, if you are over thirty you'll find that anyone over this age speaks Luxembourgish but doesn't write it very well. For centuries it was mainly spoken. French and German were taught as written languages. However, something changed in the mid-eighties. I think it was 1984."

"You mean big brother stepped in!" joked Shaun.

"Not quite big brother, but the next best thing. Actually, it was the Luxembourg government. It was something to do with a European directive which forced the government to act."

She paused. The group sat there fascinated.

"Please continue," said Jason, spellbound.

"Well, before 1984 or around that time each town had its own dialect or language. The government of the time forced everyone to learn the language so that everyone in the country spoke it."

"You mean it brought the country together," interjected Shaun.

"That's right."

"Anyway, the local dialects began to fade away as everyone learnt Luxembourgish. Now only the old people speak these dialects. But, if you look around you'll see that anyone under twenty speaks and writes Luxembourgish fluently."

"Well, *you* speak it," said Jason.

"Yes, I do. However, I sometimes have difficulty writing it. I am, how do you say, one of those people in-between. I'm twenty-four and was taught it at school, but it was different to how they now teach it."

"What do you mean?" asked a puzzled Jason.

She continued with the others listening, riveted.

"These days anyone under twenty speaks and writes Luxembourgish. It's what the government wants. I'm second generation Portuguese, so grew up with my native language and Luxembourgish. I also learnt German, French, English and a bit of Spanish."

"What do you mean, second generation?"

"My parents moved here from their village in Portugal; soon after, I was born here—in Luxembourg."

"I wish I could speak as many languages as you," said Jason.

"Yes, it's good in Luxembourg as you need it for a job and to socialise. In ten years' time the country will really benefit."

"So where does Jenisch fit into all this?" asked Jason.

"It doesn't. In today's Luxembourg, most people don't know about it. I heard about it years ago but had forgotten until Luc mentioned it. You have to remember, I come from a Portuguese family, so my native language takes priority."

"Yeah, sure," said Jason.

"So where are we going tonight?" said Carmen, changing the subject rather abruptly.

"Well, I know a nice little bar in Pfaffenthal if you're interested," said Shaun. "We can check out this Jenisch, Jason!"

"Sounds good to me," he replied.

The others nodded in agreement.

"Just one question," said Jason. "Where's Pfaffenthal?"

"It's under the red bridge in the valley," said Carmen.

"I have a friend who lives there," added Maria.

"Well, I don't know about you guys, but I'm starving," said Shaun.

"I'm Jason, nice to meet you!"

"You don't give up, do you," said his brother.

Shaun pulled out his mobile phone and called for a taxi. Within minutes, it arrived. Downing their drinks, they went over and jumped in.

Sitting in the front seat Shaun said to the Portuguese driver, "*Pfaffenthal s'il vous plaît.*" As the taxi departed he said to the others, "I can't remember the name of the pub, but I know where it is, so don't worry!"

At Findel Airport in Luxembourg Detective Meyer and Gendarme Henckels found themselves in a hanger of the cargo area of Ardennes International Cargo. They were led round to where the coffin of Nadia Ponomariov was resting.

Standing next to it the cargo supervisor said to Detective Meyer, "We've prepared everything like you requested. The paperwork is sorted so if it's all right with you we'll load the body on board."

"Yes, that's fine," Meyer replied.

The man signalled to a couple of colleagues who were waiting nearby. One went away and came back with a few more workers and the coffin containing the body of Nadia Ponomariov was loaded on board the cargo plane.

Detective Meyer and Gendarme Henckels stood watching, the noise of the planes surrounding them.

With the coffin safely loaded, Meyer said, "Poor girl. What a waste of a life." Turning to the cargo supervisor, he added, "Thanks a lot for your help."

"Our job," he replied, walking off.

Meyer nudged Gendarme Henckels. "Shall we go?"

"Yes, let's," she replied.

As they departed the aircraft hanger he added, "In a way I'm glad we've got tomorrow off. It's been a hell of a week."

"I know what you mean."

They walked through the swing doors of the hanger and made for their police car. For them it was clocking off time.

As they drove out of the airport Meyer asked, "Are you doing anything tonight, Tammy?"

"Sleeping!" she replied.

"Me too, but first I'm going to relax with some friends over a few beers."

When the taxi arrived in Pfaffenthal Shaun Evans said to the driver, "Here, thanks."

He paid the fare and everyone got out of the taxi, finding themselves near a stone bridge.

"It's over the river," said Shaun.

"Nice area," replied Jason.

"It's quiet," added Carmen.

The group walked across the bridge and Shaun led them to where the pub was situated.

"Here we are," he said.

"Copacabana," said Jason, looking at the sign above them.

"It's a South American bar," Maria said. "I've been here before."

As Jason opened the bar door the sound of salsa music hit them. For a moment, it could have been Copacabana beach. They went in, discovering a long bar on the right where Shaun said, "There's more bars inside on different levels. It's an amazing place, as you'll see."

"Great music," Jason beamed. "Why didn't you tell me about this last week?"

"Well, you can't do everything in a week, can you?" Shaun laughed.

"That's fair enough."

They went over to the bar where the barmaid greeted them.

"It's my round, what would you like?" asked Carmen.

After they selected their drinks, Maria said, "Come Jason, follow me!"

He did, following her past the restaurant area in the hacienda of the bar. They went up some stairs where Jason found himself in another bar.

Flirting a little with Jason, she said, "Do you like cigars? This is the place to get them. Look."

In the corner was a cupboard with a glass door. Inside were many varieties.

"Unfortunately, I don't smoke!" he said to her.

"Castro would love this place," she added, laughing.

They had a quick embrace before Shaun and Carmen caught them whilst carrying the drinks. Continuing up the stairs Maria led them to a roof terrace where there was yet another bar.

Maria said, "Well, what do you think?"

"Yeah, its great," said Jason. looking around.

Carmen said, "It's my first time up here."

Maria added, "This is the Ipanema bar, only open in the summer. The smaller mid-level one is Flamingo and the basement Leblon. If you've ever been to Brazil you'll know these are actually beaches in Rio de Janeiro."

"Maybe we should go there, Maria?" Jason grinned.

She smiled.

The group decided to eat on the terrace.

Looking into Carmen's eyes, Shaun said, "This is wonderful."

The waitress came up the stairs and Jason asked her for the menu. Looking at it, he said, "It's very South American."

After taking their time, they decided to order a *rodizio*, a Brazilian carvery, the restaurant speciality. To go with the meal Shaun ordered several bottles of Brazilian Red. Everyone helped themselves at the salad bar and throughout the evening umpteen different meats arrived on skewers.

"It tastes delicious," said Shaun.

"*Bon Appetite!*" added Carmen.

They tucked in and the meal was a success.

Later, Maria excused herself going downstairs to powder her nose. When she came back, she said, "Did you know there's a salsa night here later?"

"No," everyone in the group said together.

"It starts at eleven."

Jason looked at his watch. It was virtually eleven. "Well, there's no point in leaving, we may as well check it out," he said to the others.

Carmen said, "I do salsa lessons."

"Do you? Shaun didn't tell me that," replied Jason.

Gazing into Shaun's eyes, she added, "That's because he's still got a lot to learn about me."

"Do you do salsa, Maria?" asked Jason.

"Yes, I go to a variety of places."

"In Luxembourg?"

"Yes, of course!" she laughed.

Carmen added, "I like to try different styles."

"Are you any good?" Jason asked Carmen.

"I'm okay. Actually, I'm Intermediate Two."

"Which is?" asked Shaun.

"Quite good," she said smiling. "I'll show you later, if you like."

In moments like these, Shaun just loved Carmen's Spanish accent. He found it so sensual.

Jason excused himself saying, "I'll be back shortly. I'm going to ask if anyone speaks Jenisch—is that okay?"

The others nodded, happy where they were. The setting was wonderful and they weren't ready to go inside just yet.

He went downstairs, passing a cellar stairway where he could hear salsa music. Reaching the bar he said in French to the barmaid, "Excuse me, do you speak English or French?"

"Both actually," she smiled.

Jason said in English, "Can you help me? I'm trying to find someone who speaks Jenisch. Do you know anyone?"

The barmaid laughed.

Jason added, "Did I say something wrong?"

"No, it's just that Jenisch is spoken by the older generation who live here in Pfaffenthal. You see that guy over there? He speaks it."

Jason looked over. In the corner was an old man who looked as if he had no teeth.

The barmaid added, "Do you speak Luxembourgish?"

"Err, no, just French and English."

"You'll need someone to help you as he only speaks Jenisch and Luxembourgish."

"Oh, right!" replied Jason.

The old man looked half-drunk, but he was happy.

The barmaid spoke to a guy at the bar, "Serge, can you help this man? He needs someone who can understand French and Luxembourgish."

He nodded, saying, "For what?"

Jason introduced himself and Serge likewise. He turned out to be a French Luxembourger. Jason briefly explained what he wanted before they went over to the table where the old man sat.

"Hello, I'm Jason Evans," he said, introducing himself.

The old man nodded and responded, Jason not understanding a word. He asked Serge, "Can you ask him if he could translate something for me, please?"

Serge translated into Luxembourgish and the old man pointed at his glass. Jason got the drift and ordered him a beer, at the same time ordering himself and Serge a beer. The old man smiled, thanking him. Looking at the letter, he spoke to Serge in a tongue Jason didn't understand.

"The old man's too drunk to help you now. Come back tomorrow at noon and he'll help you," said Serge.

"Oh right, thanks very much."

Thinking about it for a moment Jason added, "What about a translator? I don't speak Luxembourgish."

Serge replied, "Don't worry; the old man will bring his son along. You'll be fine."

Jason was delighted. He found it all a fascinating experience. Finally, he thought, he was getting somewhere. Returning to the others he past the cellar where the salsa beat was drifting up the stairs to the roof terrace. It was busy—the music of the night was happening.

"Any luck?" said Shaun.

Jason updated them.

"Well done, Inspector Clouseau!" said Carmen. They all laughed.

Shaun called the waitress for the bill after which Maria said, "Shall we go?"

"Yes, let's," said Carmen.

"To the salsa!" they said together, laughing.

The group of friends went down the stairs to the cellar bar where more drinks were bought. The music was loud and full of rhythm. Soon the girls were on the dance floor, whisked off their feet by various men. The Evans brothers could only watch as the girls showed them what it was all about! A touch of jealousy crept into Shaun's mind.

"I'm starting salsa lessons," he joked.

"I can see why," yelled Jason.

Standing there, they felt like lemons. The men on the dance floor seemed able to move the girls in any direction they wanted. The salsa music played, it was packed and the sweat rolled off everyone. Above all, it was fun, romantic, and the rhythms of the salsa beat played until closing time. For the group it had been a fantastic night.

CHAPTER 16

▼

In Shaun's flat, Jason Evans woke up late.

"What's the time?" He looked at his watch and muttered, "Oh gaud, its eleven thirty!" He yelled at his brother: "Shaun, Shaun, wake up, its eleven-thirty!"

A murmur came from the other room. "Yeah, yeah, okay, okay."

Once awake, Shaun decided to get his own back. With his brother in the shower, he banged on the door and said, "Jason, its eleven-thirty, diet coke break!"

"Very funny!" was the reply. "Can you make me a coffee?"

"Please!"

Shaun made it. Knowing Jason had to get to Pfaffenthal by midday, he pulled on some clothes. Jason dressed and they quickly drank their coffee.

Grabbing his car keys, Shaun said, "Come on, I'm giving you a lift."

"Well done, Shaun. That's what brothers are for."

"Yeah, it's a good job I extended the car hire for another week, isn't it!"

Jason looked at him. He had forgotten all about it going back. "Shit!"

"Come on, let's go."

They left the flat and Shaun drove towards Pfaffenthal.

"Did we come this way last night?" Jason asked him.

"No, this is a more scenic route, but it's just as quick."

The Evans brothers arrived near Copacabana in Pfaffenthal where Shaun dropped Jason off.

"Got the letter?" he said to Jason.

"Oh shit," said Jason, panicking. Feeling his back pocket, he took out the letter to check. Putting it back, he grinned and said, "Bastard! Anyway, thanks a lot bruv! See you later."

Shaun drove off.

Jason went in the door of Copacabana to find the bar area empty.

'Great, all that rush for nothing!' he thought.

Sitting at the bar, he waited. Eventually a barmaid appeared. He knew from the previous night she came from Brazil.

Speaking to her he said, "Hi, remember me?"

Replying in her bubbly voice she said, "Oh hi, how could I forget?"

"Well, I've come back to meet the old man I met last night."

"Yeah, I remember you mentioning it."

"But he's not here, is he?" Jason looked around.

"Oh don't worry, what time did he say he'd meet you?"

"Midday."

"Well, he'll be here, just hang on a while."

Jason waited half an hour, drinking a couple of coffees at the bar. He looked at his watch several times, wondering whether he'd done the right thing.

At twelve thirty, the door swung open and the old man walked in. Behind him was another man whom Jason thought must be his son. They strolled up to the bar where Jason was sitting.

"*Moïen*," he said greeting them.

"*Moïen*," they replied.

Jason had learnt some Luxembourgish. *Moïen* was one of the few words he knew as he had noticed everyone greet one another with it all the time.

In French, he said to the younger man, "I'm Jason Evans."

The man replied, "I'm Jean-Claude Kremer and this is my father René. It's nice to meet you."

Jason offered them a drink and while ordering got himself another coffee before they sat down at one of the tables. He continued, "I'm on holiday here staying with my brother. I'm looking for someone who speaks Jenisch and who could help me translate a letter I found. Last night I met your father who told me to come down here today, so here I am."

He produced the letter, and some lined paper he had brought with him in his other pocket and a pen. Speaking in French, he summarised what had happened so far.

The two men sat there listening. Every so often Jason stopped to allow time for Jean-Claude to translate the French into Luxembourgish and presumably into a bit of Jenisch. It all sounded the same to Jason.

After he had finished the summary, he showed them the letter. The old man had brought his glasses with him. The lenses were strong and thick with black rims.

As the two men read the letter, Jason sat there dreaming for a moment. He watched the old mans' mouth, fascinated; it reminding him of his grandfather who had to wear false teeth. That was a long time ago and he was only a kid when that had happened.

Jason drifted back to the present and noticed the old man and his son were engrossed in a deep conversation. It was all Double Dutch to him. He thought they were talking backwards. Maybe it was an early form of Klingon!

Jean-Claude asked, "Do you want us to write it in French on your paper, or do you want to write it down in English as my written English is not so good?"

Jason replied, "That's a good question! I hadn't really thought about it." Thinking for a second or two he said, "Maybe it would be better if you write it down in French on every other line. I can translate it into English afterwards."

Time ticked by. The big old-fashioned clock on the wall ticked loudly in the silent bar. Its chimes went off every quarter of an hour. Several drinks were consumed. Jason went for the soft drinks, letting the two men get on with the translating so time would not be wasted. At times, their conversation became heated. He understood little of what was being discussed. A few people came into the bar but overall it remained quiet. That suited Jason who had a bit of a hangover. He fancied a couple of hour's kip.

Eventually Jean-Claude said, "*Voila*, it's finished."

He passed the paper over to Jason who read it. The two men looked quite excited with the result and watched him look at their work.

Stopping some way down, Jason said, "What does this say?"

Jean-Claude looked at some words and amended the sentence. Jason re-read it slowly, rewriting a few words in the space on the paper, making sure he could read every word that was written down. When he was finished he said, "Thank you very much for translating it for me. I am very grateful."

"No problem!"

Jason picked up the pen and started translating the French into English during which he got more help from Jean-Claude with a couple of the French words.

When he was satisfied with the result, he looked up and said, "The thing I don't get is what the letter means. Some of it looks as though it's in some type of code and parts of it are in some form of slang."

Jean-Claude explained. "Jenisch is more a spoken language than written, always has been. It's actually more of a dialect than a language. It was used by prisoners for centuries in the jails that used to be down here in the valley. Of course, when the prisoners were released back into the community they could speak this language well. After all, you didn't get books in prison cells centuries ago, so the only method was verbal." He sipped his drink and continued. "Oh, and you're right, part of it is a slang language. There are not many words, which is half it's secret, because you can intersperse it with other words in other languages, thus throwing people off the scent if you want to lose them. This letter does that brilliantly. Anyway, the prisoners taught their families the language and so it spread and became the local language, especially down here in Pfaffenthal as it was near the old prison. You have to remember, Luxembourg was invaded by many different countries over the centuries. The fortifications as you may know became known as the Gibraltar of the north. The guards in the prisons were for example French, Austrian or Prussian, so Jenisch was a bonus for the prisoners. A hundred years ago, many market traders in the area used the language. Traces of it are still used in the trade today. Fifty years ago, many people used to speak Jenisch in Pfaffenthal. When I was a child, it was taught in the local school. It was *the* language taught, *not* Luxembourgish. We grew up speaking it." He paused to blow his nose. "As kids, we used to have fights with the boys who lived in the city at the top of the hill who spoke Luxembourgish. There was rivalry between the city and valley, always has been. When the changes happened in the eighties the next generation wasn't taught the local dialects. As the older generation grew older and died, less and less people could speak the dialects. There are very few places where you'll find it written down. I know of one such book in the National Library. Have a look—it may help you."

Jason sat there fascinated.

Jean-Claude continued, "By the look of your letter, these men know how to write and speak Jenisch. They have used it to their advantage as the prisoners did for centuries to outwit their prison guards. This is a modern-day version of that. However, this time they are communicating in code, using it and making it extremely difficult for anyone to crack it. Read the letter again when you get home. You can see there are places mentioned, dates and banks. Perhaps it will make more sense when you study it."

Jason nodded. "The thing I don't get is that it's written in Munich, sent to Frankfurt and disposed of there."

"Well, I don't know about the Frankfurt part, but I can guess the Munich connection," replied Jean-Claude. "You see, Jenisch is or was also spoken there." Sipping his beer, he continued, "Many centuries ago, what you might call travellers crossed from Munich and settled in Trier and Luxembourg. That's how I think the language started here and was spoken in the prisons—when the soldiers locked these travellers up."

"You mean gypsies?"

"Yes—well, sort of."

"Very interesting!"

Jean-Claude added, "Just to confuse the reader the letter is in three languages. It is written in Jenisch, but when there isn't a word in Jenisch, it's written in Luxembourgish. To confuse the reader further, where there isn't a word in Luxembourgish the rest is in German."

"And now you've converted it all into French!"

"Yes, and you've converted it to English," he said, laughing. "So along the way we may have lost the full meaning, but there's enough to understand what the letter is saying, if you understand me?"

"Yes, I get the idea," said Jason.

"Of course, we have only translated it for you. It is not for us to comment on the contents, but I will say this. Be careful, this letter is written in a secret language that few people speak. If I understand it correctly, what you have here is more than you imagine. How do you say, you may have uncovered the tip of an iceberg."

A shiver went down Jason's spine.

"You mean there's more to this than meets the eye."

"Yes, there's a lot more, so be careful. These people are by the sound of it involved in something big, and from what you've already told me about the girl committing suicide, I'd say she knew something she shouldn't have. It's none of my business, but that's what I think."

"Oh," said Jason, a little shaken.

"If you need any more help, you know where to find us. This is a safe and quiet part of the city; no one comes down here and my father is a regular in this pub."

The old man was sitting listening to the conversation but not understanding it. He was thinking things through. Something was nagging him at the back of his mind. He decided to talk to his son. Speaking in Luxembourgish, he interrupted them. "Tell the Englishman the surname of this man rings a bell. I can't place it at the moment but if I do tell him I'll let him know."

Jean-Claude translated the conversation.

Jason said, "Okay, it sounds interesting!"

The barmaid came over to their table. "I'm sorry to trouble you but the bar is now closed. In fact, it closed a while ago but there's no real rush down here."

"Oh, I'm sorry, I didn't know." Jason looked at the clock. He paid the tab and left her a nice tip.

"*Merci*," she replied blushing.

The three men got up. Looking at Jean-Claude, Jason said to him, "What's your address and telephone number, please?"

Jean-Claude wrote down his details on a bar mat.

"There you are. If you need anything else or want anymore translating, please let us know and we'll only be too pleased to help you."

Jason was grateful. Before the meeting, he hadn't given Jenisch much thought. Something told him he was witnessing a unique experience. It made him feel good. On another bar mat, he wrote down his brother's and his telephone number, adding his brother's flat address, which he gave to Jean-Claude.

"It's cheaper if you ring my brother's mobile as mine is an English number," he said, wondering how he could repay their kindness. He added, "Can I take you both to dinner?"

"No, no, it's okay. We are happy to have helped you. You got the drinks, it's enough." Jean-Claude patted Jason on the shoulder.

They made their way to the door, saying goodbye to the barmaid. Outside he shook hands with both men and they went their separate ways. Jason climbed the steep hill, which would take him into the city; the two men went over the bridge that crossed the river.

Right now Jason was happy. He had got a result.

Klaus von Muller arrived back in Luxembourg just after six-thirty on Saturday evening. He parked in the flats' underground car park and took the lift up to his flat. As the door closed, he saw a small dragon symbol stuck on it. Curious, he looked closely, noticing it was different to the one he knew—but it was a dragon symbol nonetheless. He ignored it, went into the flat, dumped his bags next to the settee, sat down and rested, thinking, 'Thank God that journey's over.'

Muller went into the kitchen and poured himself a fruit juice before returning to the lounge where he put the TV on. Watching the box, he noticed a strip of sellotape on the glass door of the video cabinet.

'Strange,' he thought, 'I don't remember that before.'

Pulling it off, he threw it in the bin, returning to watch the sport.

In Shaun's flat, Jason Evans woke up after a few hours' kip. He felt like sleeping for the next twelve hours but forced himself out of bed and into the bathroom. Whilst in the shower he heard the door slam. Coming out of the shower, he grabbed a towel.

As he dried himself, he yelled through the door: "Is that you, Shaun?"

"Of course it's me, who'd you think it was? Father Christmas!"

Exiting the bathroom wearing just boxer shorts, Jason crossed the lounge to the bedroom where he dressed. As he did so, he said to his brother, "Where've you been?"

"I went round to Carmen's and we went shopping at Le Robinson shopping centre in Strassen."

"Where's that?"

"On the west side of Luxembourg City. We bumped into Maria there. Apparently she's got something to show you!"

"Really!" said a surprised Jason. "So what's the plan?"

"We're meeting the girls at Carmen's flat at eight. I'm driving! We're going to a restaurant in Bonnevoie, that's south Luxembourg City, before you ask. I've got time for a quick shower."

Twenty minutes later the lads were ready. Leaving the flat, they went down to the car and headed for Carmen's.

Outside Carmen's Chávez Fernández's flat, Jason jumped out of the car and rang the bell.

"*Bonjour* Carmen, its Jason,"

"We're coming, wait there," she replied.

Thirty seconds later the two girls appeared. Jason embraced them.

Maria said to Jason, "Well, what do you think? Do you like it?"

She did a twirl. Maria was wearing a red dress perfect for the hot weather.

"Yeah! Not bad," Jason replied, genuinely surprised.

The three piled into the car and Shaun drove off, aiming for Bonnevoie.

Klaus von Muller had been in his flat in Limpertsberg with the television on for just over an hour when it went on the blink.

"Bloody cable company," he said aloud.

He had had problems following a neighbour calling them out. Ever since the TVs in the flats hadn't been the same.

Klaus felt the real problem lay elsewhere. He felt a computer pro-gramme was deliberately doing the disruption, as the timings were uncannily regular. He couldn't be sure of that, but it occurred once a day an hour after the TV was turned on.

He thought it odd, the state monitoring his television viewing habits. Mind you, nothing surprised him, as he knew the state con-trolled everything.

Later, when he visited the bathroom, he washed his hands. See-ing the dabs of toothpaste on the radiator, he said to himself, 'Funny, I don't remember those before.'

Getting a cloth, he wiped it clean before returning to the living room where he chilled out for the rest of the evening, drinking a few bottles of German beer.

In downtown Bonnevoie it was a typical Saturday night. The Evans brothers, Carmen and Maria arrived at one of Luxembourg's trendiest restaurants, Le Grand Cowboy. Walking round the central bar, they found a table in an upper area of the restaurant.

As Carmen ordered a round of drinks, Maria said, "I've never known it so hot in Luxembourg."

"Just like Spain," added Carmen.

"It's better than England," added Jason.

"But it's difficult to sleep in this weather, don't you think?" said Shaun.

"Cor! You're a fine one to talk, what with your snoring!" jested Jason.

"I dig him in the ribs when it gets too bad," added Carmen, laughing.

"Are you ready to order?" asked Shaun, giving Jason a steely look!

Everyone nodded so Shaun signalled to a passing waitress who came over and took the order.

"How did you get on today?" Carmen asked Jason.

He updated them.

"I'm really intrigued," Maria said. "At first, I thought it would all be finished in a few days, but you've found some fascinating information during the last week. What are you going to do next?"

"Ah, that's a good question. Actually, I'm not sure, but I'm open to suggestion." Pausing, Jason said, "I've a question for you, Maria."

"Yes?" she replied.

"Where's the National Library?"

"Oh, it's next to Notre Dame Cathedral. You took a photo of it from the bridge."

The meal eventually arrived and they enjoyed it. At the end Shaun said, "Why don't we go down to J. R. Flannigan's?"

"That sound's like an Irish bar," added Jason.

"It is,"

"I quite like it there," said Carmen.

"Fine," added Maria.

They paid for the meal and left the restaurant.

Whilst enjoying his night in after his journey back from Frankfurt, Klaus von Muller decided to take a shower before he went to bed.

As he undressed, he noticed the toilet roll holder at an angle.

'Did I leave it like that?' he thought.

He couldn't be sure.

Nor could he be sure about the torn strips in the paper, which to his tidy mind just looked odd.

Muller liked to enjoy a long hot steamy shower so he could relax in volumes of steam. Once he had stood under it for what seemed like hours he finally turned the water off and stepped out of the shower.

As he did so he saw what looked like a large 'S' in the mirror.

'That's odd too,' he thought.

He knew the cleaning lady was due in on one of the days he had been in Frankfurt, but why the 'S'? Was she playing around when cleaning? He wiped it with his hand and continued to dry himself before opening the window to let the steam drift out of the window. Returning to the bedroom, he dressed and sat in the lounge with another beer. The TV was back to normal and he relaxed.

Shaun Evans drove into the Pétrusse valley passing through The Grund, along the old cobbled streets that the tyres on his car didn't like, past the old houses that were being renovated. In Clausen, he parked the car in a space at the top of the hill and the group walked down to J. R. Flannigan's. Going in they discovered a band playing rhythm and blues. Jason ordered a round. As he did so, Shaun met an Irish work colleague.

"Hello Liam, how's it going?"

"Yeah, I'm fine, thanks," he replied, drinking his pint of Guinness.

"This is my girlfriend Carmen; next to her is Maria and that guy at the bar is my brother."

"Good to meet you. This is my mate Mick who's over from Dublin for the weekend."

"Hello," said Mick, smiling at everyone.

Jason brought the round over to a table the girls had managed to commandeer.

"So, where are you taking your friend this weekend?" Shaun asked Liam.

"Actually, we're off tunnelling tomorrow afternoon."

"Tunnelling?" said Shaun.

"Yeah, we're going down some secret tunnels, aren't we, Mick?"

"You're in charge."

"Secret tunnels! That sounds great!" said Jason. "Tell me more!"

"They're not really secret," said Liam, drinking half his Guinness. "Well, I don't think they are, as we're going with a friend of mine who's in a tunnel club. The Luxembourg Fortress Club is its real name but he calls it The Secret Tunnels Club. I like that name. It sounds like an adventure, eh!"

"Can anyone go?" asked Shaun.

"Well, I don't know. I'll have to ask him."

"Maybe you could find out and let me know?"

"No problem. I'll call you tomorrow lunchtime if I get a result."

"What about tonight? Is anything happening?"

"Well, after this we're going to The Scottish Piper, and then The Lift Shaft before it closes—they've got an Austin Powers night."

"Have they?"

"Why don't you come down, it'll be grand!"

"That sounds a great idea."

"Anyway we're off over the road now. See you later."

Liam and his friend Mick departed.

Shaun said, "I don't know if you heard, but there's an Austin Powers night at The Lift Shaft. Is anyone interested?"

"Groovy baby!" replied Jason.

"I love Austin Powers," smiled Maria. "Did you see the movies? They were really good."

"I didn't like the second one," said Carmen.

"Oh, I didn't see that," added Jason.

Maria said, "The best one was the last one—wasn't Tom Cruise in it?"

The group finished their drinks and left the pub, walking up the street to the car. Shaun drove off in the direction of Hollerich.

Deciding to have an early night, Klaus von Muller retired to bed to do a spot of reading. As he lay there, he picked up his book from the bedside table. In doing so, he noticed three strands of sellotape on the shelf of the glass table. Moving another book, he saw a fourth. Checking the other bedside table, he saw another four strips of sellotape.

'That's odd,' he thought. 'Were they there before? And if so, why weren't they removed by the cleaner?'

Immersing himself in his book he ploughed though it before deciding he could read no more and called it a night.

In Hollerich, Shaun Evans drove up and down the Rue de Hollerich, raging, "I can never find anywhere to park!"

"*There's* a space!" shouted Carmen.

He parked the car and the four of them walked towards The Lift Shaft. As they opened the door psychedelic sixties music hit them in the face.

"Is this groovy or what!" Shaun said to his brother.

At the bar, the barmen were wearing Austin Powers wigs.

"They're even wearing the teeth, look!" added Jason.

Maria said, "Carmen, look at the dress the barmaid's wearing. My mother used to wear clothes like that!"

They realised most of the people in the bar were dressed in sixties style clothes. The TV showed an Austin Powers movie and the art deco of the bar was very sixties. Even the signs were in the psychedelic style of the era.

"This is groovy man," Jason joked to his brother.

"Yeah, I thought you might like this place."

The four of them soon got into the party mode. The DJ was fun, the drink flowed and the place was packed.

Later, Shaun bumped into Liam.

"Oh, you made it," Liam said to him.

"We made it before you did, you cheeky sod!" joked Shaun.

The DJ got the party swinging and everyone danced where they stood. A good time was had by one and all.

Some time later Shaun yelled into his brother's ear: "There's an extension on tonight, which means closing time isn't till three in the morning. That's good, eh?"

"Groovy man!"

The party continued with more people arriving. The beat of the psychedelic swinging sixties music pumped into the night.

CHAPTER 17

▼

Sunday might be a lie in for most, but for Detective Meyer and Gendarme Henckels it was just another working day. At Police Grand-Ducale headquarters, he yawned over a cup of coffee. "I'm not used to getting up this early, Tammy. I didn't normally go to bed until now when I was on late night surveillance. By the way, did you enjoy your day off?"

"Yes thanks; actually I ended up playing basketball last night against the police team from Esch. Our Gare Police team won the match 86–44.

"Well done, Tammy!" smiled Meyer. Turning on his pc, he clicked on his mailbox. "These emails seem to accumulate when you're away," he said, glancing at them. After looking at a couple he said, "It seems Andre's been a busy little bee. Whilst we enjoyed our day off his teams have come up with more intelligence. He's got the result of the undercover squad's visit."

"And?" said Gendarme Henckels, looking at him.

Meyer paused for a moment while he read it.

"Well, the long and the short of it is they didn't find much."

"Did they find anything?"

"Oh yes, it wasn't a wasted visit. Andre's lab team spent over twenty-four hours analysing Muller's hard drive. The thing is, he's a crafty bugger."

"Why do you say that?"

"Well, according to the results, Muller doesn't forward date many items on his pc, which as you know is what we look for so we can load the dates on the LPCCP. They think he's got another lap top, as there's not many letters on the hard drive. However, there was a few they found that might assist us…just a minute whilst I look."

Detective Meyer read what Andre had sent him.

"He sent one to Martha in Spain this week advising her of Nadia's suicide and that we're investigating it. He warns her to be on guard and be wary of whom she talks to. Muller says they're likely to send an undercover squad out to sweet-talk her. He mentions the Luxembourg police are investigating. It appears he's put his Spanish film making on hold for the moment."

"You mean he's panicking and temporarily stopped making porn films?" said Gendarme Henckels, smiling.

"Yes!" Meyer laughed.

"Anything else?"

"Yes, there's a letter to his father in Berlin. Let's see…"

He read it and summed it up…"It tells him he's working on the project and will speed up its conclusion…He apologises for the delay and notes his father's deadline but can't see what all the fuss is about. Muller realises his concern but doesn't want his father's friends involved. He mentions that he will be going on another tunnels trip a week on Sunday, which Tammy, according to my maths, is…today."

"A tunnels trip?"

"Yes, that sounds interesting, don't you think?"

"Yes."

"He ends with, 'Volkert will be assisting me to find the light at the end of the tunnel.'"

"He's used that phrase before, Ernie. Do you remember when we looked at those text messages Andre sent over?"

"You've got a point there, Tammy."

"Ernie, are we investigating the wrong thing here? I mean, should we be looking at tunnel systems rather than dragon symbols?"

"Go on."

"Well, on more than one occasion he's talked about tunnels, right?"

"Right."

"So which tunnels?"

"There are so many tunnels, Tammy. Specify your point."

"Luxembourg has many under the city."

"So does Berlin, London and Moscow."

"You know what I mean, Ernie. Look, if Muller's going on a tunnels trip today the chances are it's here in Luxembourg."

"It could be in Verdun, Fort Fermont or wherever."

"Yes, of course it could. But if we re-look at the list of telephone numbers he's called recently and chase a few of them, maybe that'll give us a clue?"

"That's a good idea. Look, if you could do that, see what you come up with and I'll finish analysing Andre's bits."

Gendarme Henckels started her exercise whilst Meyer read a few more emails, his mind pondering over something. Several minutes went by before he spoke again.

"Tammy, do you remember what Wolfgang said about his father being a Nazi?"

"Yes,"

"We're looking for the connection between the inscription date of the 13th August 1944 and Muller senior's month in Luxembourg in August 1944. Maybe the tunnels could be our answer?"

"Go on."

"Well, here's my hunch. Muller senior got out of Paris and came back to Luxembourg before being recalled to Berlin. The thing is, he was here in the August, which is the date on the inscription."

"Yes."

"Well, up to now we thought the date was connected to a Swiss bank account. Suppose it wasn't. What are the alternatives? Look. The Nazis were on the run. They were retreating fast, taking everything they could with them. Muller senior was an SS officer. The chances are he was up to no good. Why are there no records of his actions?"

"Should there be?"

"The Nazis were fanatical about writing everything down, a bit like us now. We know the date means something and if Muller is writing to his father about speeding the job up, presumably it's because he's being pressurised by his father, who's threatening to send his friends round if he doesn't get it done. Think about it, Tammy. How old is Muller senior? He must be well into his eighties. It's obvious his friends must be a bunch of old Nazi's. The underground movement's been operating worldwide since the end of the war, and what with the internet, their membership I read is increasing. They're actually pretty dangerous and I'm guessing that's one reason why Muller junior doesn't want them involved. The other could be because it's financial. His father would only have told him if it benefited the family. You can take a secret to your grave, but a financial gain can be passed on. Muller senior doesn't want his son to miss out on what he's hidden. I think we could have it here, Tammy. You're talking about tunnels. What if Muller senior hid something in the tunnels?"

"That would explain the cryptic text messages that both Klaus and Nadia sent," added Gendarme Henckels.

"Yes, it would. The light at the end of the tunnel can only signify one thing."

"Go on."

Detective Meyer continued. "Something is hidden there."

"Come to think about it, wasn't there another text message that said, 'The yellow light is at the end of the tunnel'?"

"Yes, you're right, there was. What do you think it means?"

"Perhaps he's hidden some gold there!" Gendarme Henckels laughed.

Meyer looked at her in admiration.

"Actually, I think you've hit the nail on the head. Forget the dragon, it's part of what we need to investigate, but I think Klaus von Muller's main worry at the moment is recovering something for his father that could possibly be gold. Whatever it is, is hidden at the end of a tunnel."

"Nazi gold."

"Possibly, who knows?"

Meyer continued: "If you think about it, it all makes sense. Muller senior has never been back to Luxembourg since the end of the war due to the Berlin wall and his ill health. Therefore, he can't recover whatever he's been hiding. Time's ticking by for Muller senior so he's got Klaus to do his dirty work for him. The old man's getting impatient. He wants to see whatever's hidden before he dies. That's it!"

"Well done Ernie," said Tammy. "And all we've got to do is prove it."

"Indeed!"

"I must say, Wolfgang's Stasi information was brilliant. I thought the German government destroyed their records when the wall came down. Well, from what we saw they destroyed the paper records and transferred them onto computers!"

They both laughed at that.

Meyer continued. "I'd say this tunnels trip today will give us our biggest clue. It'll definitely be worth checking out."

They returned to their tasks. Gendarme Henckels checked the phone lists they had, tested a few numbers on her screen and made a few calls. Meyer read his screen, updated his files and reviewed the situation to date.

Klaus von Muller woke up to the joys of another day in Luxembourg. He had allowed himself to have a lie in, as it was a Sunday. He washed, dressed and made himself breakfast before reading the previous day's newspaper he had bought in Frankfurt.

Muller wanted to get one or two chores completed before his friend Volkert arrived at midday. Abandoning his newspaper, he went into the kitchen and put on a load of washing. Spilling some soap powder on the floor, he got himself a cloth and wiped it clean. As he did so, it hit him.

'Wait a minute. All these strange things I've noticed. There's a hidden meaning to them.'

Walking through the rooms in his flat, he had a closer look, checking the places he had cleaned. Muller had been puzzled about the previous night's occurrences, wondering if he was going senile.

'Of course,' he thought. 'Someone's been in and left me a calling card.'

He couldn't prove it as he'd wiped away the evidence. Who was going to believe him when he told them about these strange occurrences? No one!

Muller walked over to the front door, opened it, went over to the lift and pressed the lift button. When it arrived he checked the inside door.

'That's funny,' he thought.

The dragon symbol on the lift door had gone. In its place was a small Portuguese flag. He thought it very odd. Returning inside Muller went back to his paper before starting his next chore.

Having nipped out to get two coffees, Meyer returned to his office where Gendarme Henckels was eager to talk to him.

"What up's?" he said.

"I've checked Muller's phone list. It appears he's been ringing several numbers every few weeks. At first, I tried a few with no joy. However, when I rang one I spoke to someone called Monsieur Barthel. Does that name ring a bell with you?"

"No," replied Meyer sipping his coffee.

"Well, I asked him about a tunnels trip and guess what he said?"

"Surprise me."

"He's said there's one this afternoon at Fort Thüngen."

"Did he really! You were right, Tammy. Not only are the tunnels in Luxembourg, but they're right on our doorstep. What else did he say?"

"He mentioned anyone can go. When I asked him for more details, he said they would be some leaflets this afternoon. However, when I asked him about future trips he mentioned the Luxembourg Fortress Club would be going to Verdun in October."

"The Luxembourg Fortress Club?"

"Yes, I discovered this is the name of the club that runs special tours round the Luxembourg fortress and tunnel systems around the city." Sipping her coffee she added, "I'm not talking about the tourist tunnels but the ones that are not normally open to the public."

"Yes, I know of them but have never been down any. Don't tell me, Klaus von Muller is a member?"

"Funny you should say that, but yes, he is. I found that out when I mentioned his name to Monsieur Barthel."

"Bingo! So, Muller's using them to discover the different tunnel systems around the city."

"Surely his father must have told him which tunnel the gold—or whatever—is in?"

"Yes, but from what I gather the club doesn't run regular trips to the same forts. They vary their tour programme."

"No wonder Muller is ringing this man. He wants to know when the next tour is going down the tunnel he needs so he can search for whatever is there. He must be frustrated if he can only visit it occasionally. Maybe his father doesn't appreciate that."

Detective Meyer felt a tingle of anticipation.

"By the way, what time is this tour?"

"It starts at three."

"Great. I think a trip up there this afternoon will be worthwhile.

After a coffee beak Detective Meyer and Gendarme Henckels returned feeling somewhat buoyed up. As they walked into the room he said, "We'll need to plan this, Tammy. We can't go in uniform—that'll give the game away. Have you got any suggestions?"

She sat down and thought for a moment.

"Well, if we're going undercover we'll need to split up, otherwise Muller will not only recognise us but get highly suspicious at the same time."

"Yes, that seems fair enough," said Meyer.

Gendarme Henckels continued. "Why don't you ask Andre along? After all, he's doing us a few favours with all this."

"Yes, why not? I tell you what. Why don't you two go together? You'd make a lovely couple!"

"Thank you Ernie, that's very kind of you!"

Meyer added, "But if he can't go, get someone else—I like the couple idea."

"So what will you do?"

"I don't know."

"Why don't you take one of the dogs from the police dog unit? They always appreciate a walk. If anyone says anything you're simply taking your dog for a Sunday afternoon walk."

"That sounds an excellent idea. Can you ring them and sort it out whilst I update the case notes?"

"No problem."

Gendarme Henckels checked her laptop for the phone number of the dog unit. Ringing it, she waited for someone to answer.

"Police Dog Unit Milly speaking. How may I help you?"

"*Moïen*—oh, hello Milly, its Gendarme Henckels at headquarters. How are you?"

They exchanged greetings.

Gendarme Henckels continued, "Actually, Detective Meyer and I need a dog this afternoon for an undercover operation. Can we borrow one of yours?"

"No problem."

"Great."

"Which dog do you want? Do you have any preferences?"

"No,"

"Okay, then I suggest Bessie the German Shepherd—or would you prefer Bruno the Rottweiler?"

"I don't mind which one. Wait a minute, I'll ask Ernie."

Looking over at Detective Meyer she said, "You can have Bessie the German Shepherd or Bruno the Rottweiler."

"We'll have Bruno," he replied.

"Milly, did you hear that, he wants Bruno."

"No problem."

"Great, we'll be round sometime between two and three. Thanks, *äddi*."

"*Äddi*."

As Gendarme Henckels put the receiver down, Meyer said, "We can meet Andre, have some lunch then go from there. How does that sound?"

"It sounds fine."

Gendarme Henckels picked up the phone and dialled a number.

"*Moïen.* Is that Andre? Hi, it's Gendarme Henckels. Listen Andre, what are you doing this afternoon?"

"I'm working."

"Well, how do you fancy an undercover assignment? We need someone to help us this afternoon up at Fort Thüngen."

She updated Andre on recent events, at the end of which he said, "Tammy, I'd be delighted to assist. I'm not that busy and it'll make a change. Are we going disguised?"

Gendarme Henckels giggled. "I never thought of that. What do you suggest?"

"Well, if we are, I can bring my cowboy hat. It's in my car along with my jacket. You can be my cowgirl, yahoo!"

Gendarme Henckels paused for a moment before saying with a laugh, "You're mad, Andre, and it sounds fine. Can you get over to our building? We'll meet in reception, say at one."

"No problem. My, you certainly know how to brighten a chap's day Tammy. Great. See you later, *äddi.*"

Putting the phone down Gendarme Henckels said, "I don't know whether you got all that, but Andre's coming. We're meeting him at one. Oh, and we're going as a cowboy couple!"

Meyer burst out laughing. "Great, I'll look forward to it."

CHAPTER 18

▼

At Shaun's flat, the phone rang on his mobile. Jason Evans was the first awake and as it was nearest to him he answered it.

"Hello? No, it's Jason—Shaun's still asleep,"

"*Was* asleep," said a voice from the other room.

"Oh, he's awake now, hang on."

Jason walked into his brother's bedroom and passed him the phone. He went into the kitchen, put the kettle on and began to make a cup of tea. Whilst on the phone Shaun got up, went into the lounge, grabbed a pen and wrote some information his friend on the phone gave him.

"Okay, see you at two, *adios*." Looking up, he said, "I'll have one if you're making a cuppa."

"Yeah, I thought you might," replied his brother.

Shaun switched on the TV and while channel flicking said, "What a load of rubbish. There are some grotty channels. I mean, you can't even get Eastenders."

Jason brought the tea in. As he placed the mugs on the table he said, "I take it your mate spoke to his mate?"

"Yeah, he did."

"What did he say?"

"Apparently there's a special tour this afternoon at a place called Fort Thüngen. We're to meet Liam outside La Cité bar at two.

We'll have to wear some warm clothing and bring a torch. I've actually got one in case there's a blackout. Funnily enough, I only put some new batteries in it the week before you arrived, though I've never actually used it. Do you think the girls are really interested?"

"They seemed to be."

"Okay, I'll ring Carmen."

He dialled her number.

"Carmen, its Shaun. How are you? Listen, Jason and I are going down the tunnels Liam mentioned last night. Are you still interested? Great! Yeah, wear some warm clothes; yeah, I know its summer but he said it's cold down there. Okay, see you outside La Cité bar at two. Oh, have you got a torch? Can you borrow one? Right, yeah, see you later."

Looking at Jason he said, "Do you want to ring Maria?"

Shaun tossed him his mobile and Jason rang her.

"Hi Maria, its Jason. Are you okay? Still feeling groovy? Oh, take an aspirin. Anyway, we're going down these secret tunnels. Are you coming? Brilliant. We don't have much time as we're meeting outside La Cité bar at two. Oh, bring a torch. Have you got one? You have? Good, well bring it with you and wear some warm clothing. See you shortly."

The door buzzer went and Klaus von Muller answered it.

"It's Volkert."

Muller let him in and opened the flat door before returning to the kitchen. Shortly after, Volkert Graf walked in.

"Hello Klaus. Sorry I'm a bit late. I got stuck in traffic on the autobahn in Germany. I mean, on a Sunday morning you'd think there wouldn't be much traffic, but I've encountered various car accidents, not to mention Sunday drivers. Those mobile home wagons should be banned!"

"Well, don't worry, Volkert. The main thing is you're here. We've plenty of time. Would you like a coffee?"

"Thanks."

"This flat's not as pleasant as my Frankfurt one."

"Oh, I don't know. It looks fine to me," replied Volkert looking around.

"By the way," said Klaus in a more serious mood. "I've had a visit," handing him his coffee.

"What do you mean, you've had a visit?"

"Well, I can't prove it, but I think someone's been in the flat."

As Muller updated Graf on the strange experiences he'd encountered since getting back from Frankfurt they walked into the lounge and sat down.

After listening to him Graf replied, "You're imagining things, Klaus."

"If I'm imagining, have a look at this."

They walked out of the flat onto the landing where Muller called the lift. Gesturing Graf to enter, Muller followed and the door closed.

Pointing at the small Portuguese sticker on the door, Muller said, "I am not imagining stickers."

"It could have been there for ages."

Muller realised he wasn't going to convince Graf and decided to leave it. Returning to the flat, he said, "Look, whether you believe me or not, just watch your back, Volkert. These people are bastards. I've encountered it before in Morocco. I get the impression someone is deliberately trying to wind me up but I can't prove it."

"Are you keeping a note of all these instances?"

"I haven't so far, but maybe I should?"

"I would if what you say is true." Graf sipped his coffee. "I believe you, Klaus, but you've got to be able to prove it. Once you've got your evidence, take it to your lawyer for their advice."

"For what little use that'll do."

"Well, it's only a suggestion."

"Look, these people are harassing me. I'll keep you posted if anything else happens—which I guarantee you it will, as this is their punishment for Nadia's suicide whilst they investigate it further. That Detective Meyer is behind it all."

"What time are we going down these tunnels, Klaus?" said Graf, changing the subject.

"The tour starts at three, so we need to be there just before. Ah, that reminds me. I must show you something."

Muller went over to a drawer and took out an old map from a plastic folder, placing it on the coffee table in front of Graf.

"Take a look at that."

After a few moments of studying it, Graf said, "Well, it's not very helpful, is it, Klaus? Where did you get it?"

"My father drew it. Of course, he knows exactly where to go, but at the time didn't make detailed plans in case it fell into the wrong hands. If you look on the back you'll see he's put on a bit more information for me that he thought might be useful. He never bothered before, especially when the communists were in power as he didn't want them getting hold of it. My father never trusted a soul and certainly never anticipated anyone else having to do his dirty work for him. Unfortunately, as I've already discovered, finding the place, as you will shortly see, is not as easy as you might think."

"But you've found it?"

"I have now. It was a nightmare at first, as during these trips I've only got a certain amount of time. You see, access to these tunnels is limited to the Luxembourg Fortress Club, so I have to make the most of these special trips. I have to keep ringing the tour guide for details of the next tour, as unfortunately a list of dates is never forthcoming unless you ask for it. Even so, I only get a few sent through. Mind you, that's typical for Luxembourg. If you don't ask, you don't get, or you only get what you ask because you didn't ask for everything. Are you with me?"

"I think so."

"That's where you come in, Volkert. I need to show you the place so we can plan the next stage. But first a spot of lunch might be a good idea."

"Yes, that sounds excellent."

"Have you anything in mind?"

"Up to you, Klaus."

"Well, I know a nice Portuguese restaurant in Ettelbrück we can drive to before the trip. It's a bit out of town, but if we go now I can show you some real Luxembourg and we can enjoy a good meal."

"*Wunderbar!*"

The two of them got up and, taking the map with them, departed.

The sun shone through the window of Detective Meyer's office as he sat at his desk relaxing for a moment. Gendarme Henckels was checking one of Andre's intelligence lists on Klaus von Muller. As she did so, Meyer looked at his watch and said, "May I suggest you go and get changed and made up before we rendezvous at one with Andre in reception?"

"Yes, I'll do that right now."

"Good. Well, I'll also go and get changed. I don't know about you but I'm looking forward to this afternoon, it should be fun."

They got up and went down to the changing rooms. For Meyer it was easy, just a white T-shirt and jeans, his normal gear. For Gendarme Henckels it involved some makeup, wig and some clothes that she borrowed.

At the reception desk at Police Grand-Ducale headquarters, Meyer and Andre Biever waited. Gendarme Henckels eventually emerged from the lift.

"Sorry I'm late," she said. "It took a bit longer than I thought."

"Oh, is that you, Tammy!" Meyer laughed. "We didn't recognise you."

"Don't say a word!" she replied. "I think it looks terrible."

"No, not at all!" said Andre. "I wouldn't know it was you dressed like that."

She was dressed in a frumpy cowgirl dress with jacket that Meyer thought looked awful. She wore a short black wig and glasses. The applied makeup made her look ten years older.

Gendarme Henckels said, "Mind you, Andre, going with a cow-boy will be something different. But do you have to wear that hat!"

Everyone laughed.

Meyer said, "May I suggest the Vauban Mill at Mamur? We've got time to get there, enjoy a good lunch by the river, then pick Bruno up from the police dog unit before heading up to the fort."

"Fine," said Andre.

"Yes, it's good," added Gendarme Henckels.

Making their way to the car park, they located an unmarked old Volvo estate.

Meyer said, "We've got this one this afternoon. I just hope she doesn't break down."

Starting the motor, he reversed into the bay and they departed.

The Evans brothers met Liam outside La Cité bar just before two. Five minutes later Liam said to Shaun, "Did you say your girl-friends are coming?"

"They'll be here," he replied, hoping they would.

Just at that moment the two girls walked round the corner into view, embracing the small party of Jason, Shaun, Liam, his friend

Mick, their friend John and his girlfriend Judith. Everyone set off for the bus stop where after a short wait they hopped onto a bendy bus towards the Kirchberg plateau.

At the bus stop in Kirchberg, the group got off the bus and walked down the street towards Fort Thüngen. Taking a left turn, they walked through some woods, finding themselves by the side of an old looking fortress behind which was a new building.

"I take it this is Fort Thüngen?" Shaun said to Liam.

"You're right, it is," he said.

"So what's that building?" He pointed to the new construction.

"It's the new art museum."

"It looks awful!"

"Yeah, I know. There's been a lot of debate about it. Many people hate it."

As they were early, the group walked round to the rear of the fortress, split up and looked round the vicinity. What they saw was Fort Thüngen's two huge rear towers looking out over a wide lawn that gave it a bird's eye view of the city on the opposite side of the valley. On its roof stood three gilded acorns. At the fort's rear an arched stone bridge crossed a wide ditch to the entrance.

Jason went off with Maria to look at the ditch, saying, "It look's newly renovated."

"Yes, I noticed that," she nodded. "It's quite deep. Do you think it ever had water in it?"

"I don't know, maybe."

The old Volvo did a sharp left and edged its way up the steep narrow winding hill of rue des Trois Glands, passing under the railway arch. Meyer parked in the car park a bit further up on the left. While Gendarme Henckels and Andre Biever got out of the car, he went round to its rear to let out a barking Bruno.

The dog dashed over the road and cocked his leg before returning to Detective Meyer. Once a lead was attached, they set off up a wooded footpath towards the forts.

Just before ten to three Jason Evans noticed a man arrive who greeted everyone. He walked across the old arched stone bridge up to the doorway of the fort. Unlocking the door, he went in. One or two people followed him.

"Perhaps that's the organiser?" he said to Maria.

They walked round to where everyone had gathered, standing on the right. As they did, Jason glanced to his right and saw two men get out of a black BMW that had just pulled up and parked. He instantly recognised them.

Astounded, he said, "Look. Maria, you see the two men over there walking this way? Well, the one on the left is him, Klaus von Muller, and the other guy is the one I saw at Muller's flat in Frankfurt."

"Really?" replied Maria, now as intrigued as Jason was excited. She added, "What's he doing here?"

"That's what I want to know."

The two men walked over to where the group was standing.

"This is it, Volkert," said Muller. "This is Fort Thüngen. The rest follows…"

They waited at the back of the group. Jason signalled to Maria to keep 'mum' for the moment.

"We'll tell the other two at the right moment."

"Okay," she whispered.

CHAPTER 19

▼

Just after three, the man who had gone inside Fort Thüngen came out to where a large group had gathered and said in Luxembourgish, "*Moïen*, my name is Jerry Barthel. I am your guide this afternoon for the Fortress tour. We'll be visiting Fort Thüngen and three other forts, which are Fort Ober-Grünewald, Fort Nieder-Grünewald and Fort Olizy. We'll be going down some casemates so I hope you've brought a torch with you. I see you've come warmly dressed, which is good as it is cold in the tunnels. The tour will be in Luxembourgish and French."

He said the same in French. As he did so, two people slipped into the back of the tour group, namely Gendarme Henckels and Andre Biever. Both wore dark glasses and held hands. Andre was armed with a video camera.

The tour guide described in Luxembourgish a few details about the fort in front of where everyone was standing. Jason thought he looked a typical Luxembourger. Nevertheless, his mind was wandering. 'Why was Muller here of all places?' he wondered.

The tour kicked off inside the Fort in a large reception area. The guide continued his ramblings in Luxembourgish and everyone studied the maps and photos on the display board.

"Interesting, don't you think?" Jason said to his brother.

"Yes, I didn't know any of this," replied Shaun.

The two girls stood next to one of the maps away from the main group who by now were in a kitchen area of the fort.

Maria whispered in Spanish: "Carmen, there are two men in the kitchen you might want to listen in on."

"Why?" she said surprised.

"Because one of them is Klaus von Muller."

"Oh my God, is it really? What's he doing here?"

"That's what we want to know. See what you can find out, but don't say a word. Oh, and Jason said the friend with him he last saw at Muller's flat in Frankfurt."

"What does this Muller look like?"

"He's the one wearing a green sweat shirt with Mexico City on it."

The girls walked over to where the tour group was in the kitchen area of the fort. Gendarme Henckels and Andre were at the back of the room. Muller and Graf stood towards the front where the tour guide got a man to stand on a spot marked X with tape.

"Now say something," he said to him.

"What do you want me to say?"

As he spoke, his voice changed. It echoed around the room. Everyone laughed. Some tunnellers took it in turns to try out the effect.

The tour moved on with the tour leader taking the group into the round of the right tower where a bronze miniature of Fort Thüngen was on display.

Muller and his friend stood in the middle of the group along with Gendarme Henckels and Andre who filmed the model as the tour guide described its meaning. Back in the kitchen, Carmen stayed put, pulling Shaun into a romantic embrace.

"We're missing the tour," he smiled.

"Wait," she hissed as she kissed him, continuing in a whisper. "I have something important to tell you."

"Oh, what's that?" he whispered back.

"There are two men in the tour. One is wearing a green sweat-shirt with Mexico City on it,"

"And?"

"It's Klaus von Muller."

"Is it? How do you know?"

"Jason recognised him. Shush! See what he does. Don't say a word till later. Oh, and his friend Jason saw in Frankfurt."

Carmen kissed him and they rejoined the main group strolling arm in arm into the round of the right tower where she kissed him again in front of everyone.

The tour continued with the group being led down a spiral stone stairway after which everyone found themselves in a tunnel.

"Isn't it exciting!" said Maria, holding Jason's hand. "Our first secret tunnel."

"It's cold though," he replied.

They moved down it, following the passages until some time later, when the group emerged into sunlight in a large dug-out ditch.

The tour leader said, "This is the moat of the former Fort Ober-Grünewald. You can see it is gradually being rebuilt into its original form. All the forts round here were de-fortified after the Treaty of London in 1867. This whole area was raised to the ground and levelled over to give forest and gardens."

Jason was again losing interest. The tour moved on, heading round a reduit and under a former defence wall of the fort through a small tunnel bringing the tour out to an area facing the city. The tour leader stopped and started another explanation.

From the corner of his eye, Jason noticed a man walking a dog on the nearby grass verge. He was dressed in jeans and a white T-shirt. After a few moments, Jason turned to Shaun and whispered, "Don't look just yet, but the man standing on your right with his dog is the police officer who interviewed us last Friday."

"You mean Detective Meyer?"

"Yes, that's it!"

"What's he doing here?"

"Exactly! There's something funny going on. Keep your eyes and ears open."

Jason wasn't the only one to see him. Muller had also zoomed in and spotted him. As the tunnellers crossed towards a forest opening, he said to Graf, "Volkert, if I'm not mistaken the Detective dealing with Nadia's death is back there walking his dog."

"Well, he's probably out for a Sunday afternoon stroll."

"True, but don't you think that's a bit coincidental..."

They walked on behind the tour guide who led everyone along a forest trail.

Jason, who was in the middle of the group, went up to Maria and put his arm around her. As they walked along the path, he whispered into her ear, "Maria, you're not going to believe this, but we're being followed."

"Followed?"

"Yes. Look—something fishy is going on. I've just seen the Detective who interviewed us last week watching us back there. He's the guy with the Rottweiler."

"That's funny you should say that," whispered Maria. "The woman dressed like a cowgirl reminds me of someone else—but the hair is wrong," she laughed.

"Come to think of it, you're right! It's that Detective's assistant. What was her name?"

"Gendarme Henckels."

"That's it!"

"I swear she's wearing a wig."

The conversation was halted as other people in the tour closed in. Instead, they kissed and continued their walk along the forest footpath.

Later, at a clearing in the forest, the tour guide said in Luxembourgish, "We are now at the entrance of another fort. This one is Fort Nieder-Grünewald."

He said it again in French after which he unlocked the grate and made his way down to a green door at the bottom. Unlocking it, he went into the tunnel. Everyone followed.

As Muller and his friend walked down the steps, Graf paused at the grate and at the door of the tunnel to look at the locks before moving into the tunnel.

Inside, it was dark. The tour group needed their torches as compared with the previous tunnel that was partially lit, this one was blacker than a coalminer's face. Everyone stumbled along, the light of their torches bouncing off the walls and ceilings.

Jason, Maria, Carmen and Shaun had split up. Carmen was with John, Shaun with Liam and Jason with Mick. Each was trying to find out what was going on whilst not giving anything away.

In the meantime, Maria had separated herself from the gang. She was now right at the back of the tour group and was a distance behind Klaus von Muller and his friend who was wearing a black leather jacket.

As the tunnellers made their way along the passage Maria listened to what Muller was saying to his mate. She realised he wasn't just talking in Luxembourgish, but using German as well, guessing the other words could be Jenisch? She didn't understand them, but could guess their meanings, as some were similar to Luxembourgish. After Jason's visit to Pfaffenthal the day before she was sure it was Jenisch.

Maria heard Muller say, "It's this one, I'm telling you."

Graf replied, "Are you sure?"

"Yes, of course I'm sure. This is my third visit and according to the map, it's somewhere near here. The trouble is every tunnel looks the same. I've been looking for some yellow markers I previously left. Once we find those, it's easy. We look for a small piece of wood nailed into the wall that should have a paint mark around it."

"I see what you mean about getting lost. I wouldn't want to remain down here too long on my own."

"Actually I would, as I could spend more time locating and finding the treasure. My father knows its location but he's too old now and stuck in Berlin in that nursing home."

'Treasure!' thought Maria excitedly. 'What is he talking about?' keeping her distance at the same time.

Muller continued, "With your knowledge of locks, we should be able to come back another time. Best not to do anything now, if you know what I mean."

"I'm with you."

"The good thing about this club is it's allowed me time to find the location of the gold."

'Gold!' thought Maria. 'What was he talking about?' She was very excited. Her heart was pumping fast nevertheless she remained calm.

The tunnellers walked down many different tunnels, eventually surfacing onto an area next to an autoroute in Kirchberg. Gendarme Henckels and Andre realised they had been in the middle of the group.

The tour leader addressed everyone. "The main tunnel you have walked down actually led from one former fort into another. We are now in part of the former Fort Olizy. We shall see more of this fort shortly."

He allowed everyone a breathing space for a minute or two during which time Maria whispered into Jason's ear, "I've heard something fantastic which you just won't believe."

"Tell me later," he hissed back, kissing her.

The tour backtracked down the stairway. The cowboy couple made sure they were behind Muller, but some French people edged their way in-between them as they descended the steps. They ended up four people behind him. Returning along the passageway and down another at a certain point, they heard the guide stop and say, "If you go up here and continue round to your left you'll return back here."

A short time later Andre said, "We've lost him."

Gendarme Henckels said, "He can't be far. How can we loose them? They were literally in front of us."

With the majority of people back, the tour guide led the way along the passageways, allowing everyone time to explore on their own.

Muller and Graf, meanwhile, were searching for yellow markers and had been doing so for a while. Using their torches, they located two of them.

Muller said, "We haven't got much time."

Simultaneously, Maria and Jason were exploring together, holding hands when suddenly they saw Muller and Graf in one of the side tunnels.

After a couple of minutes the two men emerged into the main passageway, walking towards the entrance, past Maria and Jason who were in a lover's embrace fifty meters further up. Jason looked at his watch and after a minute walked back up the main tunnel with Maria beyond the side tunnel Muller and Graf had been in, having made sure no torchlights were in the vicinity before returning to the side tunnel. Shining their torches and not speaking, they looked.

Maria found it first, tapping Jason in the side and pointing her torch at a yellow marker. Looking around, they discovered two more on the floor. The tunnel roof at the end appeared to lower into the ground. In the dark, it was difficult to see.

Leaving the side tunnel, they slowly scanned the walls on the main passageway and discovered two more yellow markers in the walls. After not finding any more they walked swiftly back, their torches beaming on the ceiling, all around the blackness of the tunnel. Walking towards the exit, they emerged into the forest clearing where the sunlight hit them.

Climbing the steps, Jason and Maria discovered they were the last two out as everyone was waiting for them. Realising this, Maria embraced Jason, putting her arm around him and hugging him tightly. Right now, both were curious about the markers but knew they would have to remain quiet until later.

The tour continued through more woods, ending back at Fort Thüngen where the tour guide said, "This is the end of the tour. I hope you enjoyed it. The next one will be in two weeks. *Merci, Äddi et Au Revoir.*"

He handed out some leaflets and the tour group split up.

Jason knew he had to do something, so with Maria went over to the guide and, speaking in French, said, "Thanks for a good tour. May I have a couple of leaflets please?" He held out his hand.

"Yes, no problem," replied the tour guide, nodding and giving him some.

Jason and Maria rejoined their friends in the group who were waiting for them.

John, who was one of them, said, "There's a nice little café bar we can go to if you like. It's just over there."

"Why not?" replied Liam.

The others all agreed and went over to investigate.

As they did so the youngsters saw the man with the Rottweiler watching them from a distance talking to the cowboy couple who had been on the tour.

"Did you find anything?" said Detective Meyer to Gendarme Henckels and Andre.

"Not much," Andre replied. "Unfortunately at one point we got separated from Muller in the tunnels and when we got close he disappeared."

"Disappeared? How could he disappear?"

"Don't ask, but at least we've got the video to look at."

"How long did you lose him for?"

"About ten minutes. It was hard to say in the dark."

"And which tunnel system were you in when you lost him?"

"Fort Nieder-Grünewald," replied Gendarme Henckels.

"Perhaps that is the tunnel we're looking for."

Bruno barked and pulled on the lead, having seen another dog. Reining him in, Meyer said, "Okay, let's go. I could do with a drink and Bruno definitely wants one, don't you?"

The dog barked again and Andre patted him on the head before they set off back to the Volvo. As they walked through the forest, Meyer said, "The Englishmen and Muller were watching me when you were on the tour."

"Yes, they knew something was up, but I don't think they knew what exactly," said Andre.

"Did they say anything?"

"Not a word," said Gendarme Henckels. "Although the Portuguese and Spanish girls recognised me."

"How do you know that?" asked Meyer.

"Call it female intuition!" she smiled.

They continued their walk through the woods and on reaching the Volvo put Bruno in the rear section before driving off.

CHAPTER 20

▼

The group of Liam and friends arrived at the café bar where John said, "This is Junker's Cabin. Don't you think it's got that old log cabin feel to it?"

They found some seats on the terrace and waited for the waitress to take their order.

"It's so hot," said Judith.

"Yes, I'm taking off these warm layers of clothing," said Carmen.

"We'll be lugging this lot round all day," joked Maria.

They chatted amongst themselves and a short while later the drinks arrived.

"The tunnel tour was really great," said Shaun to Liam.

"Yeah, it was grand, wasn't it?"

"Did you like it, Carmen?" added Shaun.

"I liked it!" she replied firmly.

Jason and Maria remained calm, not saying a word as to what they had seen and heard in the tunnel. All four of them had seen Muller and his friend disappear immediately after the tour.

After a while John said, "Does anyone fancy a scenic walk back into town? It's too nice to go on the bus."

The others agreed and a leisurely stroll was taken down a winding, descending road into the valley towards Clausen.

When the group arrived at The British Inn in Clausen, Liam said, "Does anyone fancy a pint?"

"Actually, I'm afraid we've got to go," Shaun interjected. "Unfortunately, we're meeting friends. Thanks anyway for a great afternoon."

Liam, John and his girlfriend Judith walked into The British Inn while the others crossed the road towards an archway opposite.

Once through it, Shaun breathed a sigh of relief. "Sorry about that. Listen, I know we're not meeting anyone but realise we need to discuss what we saw. I need a drink and I'm sure you do, so let's walk back along the river where it's quiet. We can talk en route and have one in the Grund."

"Good idea," said Jason.

The four of them turned right and crossed a bridge over the Alzette River. Crossing the road, they walked down some steps where a river walkway greeted them.

"Did you see Detective Meyer back there?" said Jason

Carmen replied, "Who was he talking to? The cowboy couple were watching Muller and his friend throughout the tour."

"That cowgirl was Detective Meyer's assistant Gendarme Henckels."

"Was it really!" Carmen exclaimed.

"Yes, she was wearing a wig. I don't know about the guy but I guess he was an undercover detective."

"Why do you say that?" said Carmen.

"Because they're watching Muller following the girl's suicide," Jason said. "Come to think of it, they could easily be watching us as we're witnesses."

"But why would Muller be on a tunnel trip?" asked Carmen.

"That's easy," said Maria.

"What do you mean?" said Carmen.

"Well, I was listening to what he said."

"So was I, but I didn't hear anything unusual," added Carmen.

"Actually, I discovered something with Maria," said Jason.

"Oh, what's that?" asked Shaun.

"Well, when we were in the tunnels, Maria and I were watching Muller and his friend from a distance."

"And?"

"We passed them down one of the side tunnels. When they came out Maria and I were pretending to be kissing."

"What you mean, pretending? We *were* kissing!" smiled Maria. "And it was a good kiss!"

"Let me finish. We went back up the main tunnel to fool Muller and his sidekick before we backtracked into the one they had been in."

"Go on."

"After a bit of exploring we found a yellow marker in the wall and two more on the ground. Later we found two more."

"How do you know he put them there? Anyone could have left them."

"Let me explain," said Maria.

"Oh?" said Shaun, intrigued.

"At one point I was walking in the tunnel on my own at the back of everyone. I was behind Muller who was behind his friend."

"So?"

"Muller said he had been there before and was looking for some yellow markers he had left on previous occasions. He mentioned something about an old piece of wood with paint around it on the wall."

"Did he say anything else?" asked Jason.

"Oh yes," smiled Maria, adding sweetly, "He said his father was in a nursing home in Berlin and was too old to find it."

"Find what?" added Shaun.

"The Treasure!"

"Treasure!" the other three exclaimed together.

"What sort of treasure?" asked Jason

"Well, I wondered at first because they kept swapping languages. But I think he said he had only joined the Fortress Club so he could find it. I wasn't sure if I understood everything as they were talking in Jenisch with other words in German and Luxembourgish. It wasn't easy following them at a distance in the tunnel."

"Get to the point, Maria," added an intrigued Jason.

"Well, it looks as though Muller is looking for gold."

"Gold!" exclaimed the other three excitedly.

This prompted the group to stop in their tracks.

"Are you sure?" said Jason.

"That's what Muller said, for sure."

"Maria, I'm impressed," added an amazed Carmen.

"They also talked about coming back when no one was around."

"Really?" said Jason.

"Oh, and I forgot to say he mentioned something about his father wanting him to locate it."

"What's his father got to do with it?" asked a puzzled Carmen.

"That's easy," said Shaun who had been thinking rapidly.

"What do you mean?" asked Carmen.

"Well, how old is Muller?"

"I don't know, maybe fifty."

"Exactly! Don't you get it?"

"Get what?" she said, laughing a little.

"Look! If Muller is fifty his father must be, say, eighty odd."

"Well, they're looking for gold, right!"

"So?"

"Well, didn't you ever study history in Spain?"

"Of course we did."

"Well, think about it. What Muller's looking for must be some secret Nazi gold his father must have hidden there during the war. Bingo!"

"Bloody hell," said Jason.

"This is incredible," added Carmen.

"Exciting, don't you think!" responded Shaun.

"This calls for a drink," added Jason.

The four of them headed for Amundsen's, a Norwegian pub in the Grund.

After dropping Bruno at the dog unit Meyer drove the Volvo back to Police Grand-Ducale headquarters. In the underground car park, as the group split up, he said, "Thanks for your help this afternoon, Andre."

"My pleasure, Ernie. Actually, it was quite enjoyable. I hoped it helped."

"Oh yes, it did that. At least we know which tunnel to watch. All we've got to do is wait to see what happens next. Keep in touch if you get anything new."

"Yes."

"See you, Andre."

"Yes, *äddi*."

As Andre departed Detective Meyer said to Gendarme Henckels, "We'll catch up with everything tomorrow."

"That's fine with me."

"Good, well see you in the morning…"

As he walked off he said, "By the way Tammy, you look nice as a cowgirl!"

"Thank you Ernie! I shall look forward to my normal uniform tomorrow."

At Amundsen's bar in the Grund the Evans brothers and the girls sat on the terrace looking out at the view of Luxembourg City where they relaxed with their drinks, the Alzette River an arm's length away. Some ducks quacked nearby.

The subject of gold was intriguing everyone.

"What do you know about Nazi gold in Luxembourg, Maria?" asked Jason.

"I don't, I'm afraid. We were taught at school about the Nazi's who invaded and occupied Luxembourg during the war but that's all. I mean, one does hear stories about it but they're just stories."

"Do you know of anyone who has ever found any?"

"Like I said, if I did I would tell you. Why don't you find someone else to ask?"

"Like who, Maria?" added Jason.

"Someone who was here during the war."

"Do you know anyone?" asked Shaun.

"I'm afraid I don't know many, if any of that age," replied Maria.

"Oh, lets leave it for now," Carmen interjected. "Where are we eating tonight? I'm hungry."

"Me to," added Maria.

"Let's go to Place d'Armes," suggested Carmen.

Everyone agreed and the rest of the evening was spent eating, drinking and relaxing in the square as the sun descended.

Klaus von Muller and Volkert Graf had spent the evening in Limpertsberg devouring a couple of large steaks in a nearby restaurant to Muller's flat. On their return, Graf said, "Listen Klaus, I'd better be going—it's a long journey. If it weren't for the meeting tomorrow I'd stay. Thanks for the meal and hopefully I'll see you on Tuesday night."

"No problem."

"I'll text you tomorrow with the confirmed flight times."

"Good, it gives us plenty of time."

"Great. Well, I'll be off."

Graf got into the black BMW, wound down the window and said, "Don't worry Klaus, we'll find the bloody gold if it's the last thing we do. Another few days won't matter. Catch you later, *tschüs!*"

As he drove away Muller waved, walked up the path and pulled out the dustbins from the storage area, putting them on the path ready for the refuse men. Returning to his flat, he spent the rest of the evening relaxing in front of the TV before taking a shower and then sat down for another session with his new novel.

In Shaun Evan's flat later that night, Jason lay on the sofa bed in the lounge, his mind buzzing.

"Shaun, I've been thinking," he said.

"Really!" he replied, already in his room.

"Yes, listen, I've made a decision."

"What's that?"

"I've decided to take a month out before reviewing my position. Can I stay a bit longer?"

"Sure, but as long as it's not forever. I need some space, you know."

"Yes, I realise that, but I've been thinking about what I should do next. I'd like to continue finding out about the girl who jumped. I find the whole thing intriguing. What with this gold theory today. Do you think the two are connected?"

"They could be," added Shaun.

"Is it worth following?"

"It's up to you."

"Well, as you know, I've got a bit of time at the moment. The summer is here and right now I'm enjoying myself."

"Didn't you talk about going to Spain?"

"I did, but it's been pretty active here, don't you think?"

"Sure!"

"Not many people can say they've discovered hidden treasure."

"It was Maria actually."

"Yes, but it was a group effort, if you think about it. However, I'm still curious. Surely the authorities would know about it?"

"They probably know about most of the gold. After all, the Nazi's must have stashed a fair wad in the Luxembourg Banks."

"Don't they have banking secrecy here?"

"They do, but with time and the revelations of the war, no bank would keep Nazi gold; or would it?"

"I don't know. Anyway, this gold isn't in any bank. It's stashed away in a tunnel."

"You would have thought someone would have located it by now. After all, think about how many people were in that tunnel today. If there is any, it means that for nearly sixty years anyone who's ever gone down there must have walked right past it."

"True." Shaun was getting tired.

"I mean, you would have thought someone would have used a metal detector down there," added Jason.

"Maybe no one thought of that. Anyway Jason, let's sleep—I'm tired."

With that, they called it a night.

CHAPTER 21

▼

In Limpertsberg, Klaus von Muller had risen at his normal time of six forty-five. He had washed, dressed and made some coffee before having his usual continental breakfast.

An hour later, he was ready to leave and make his way into the office after more than a week off. Grabbing his yellow jacket now looking presentable after dry cleaning, he picked up his mobile and left his flat. As he walked out of the flat's entrance he bumped into the dustbin that was standing in front of the entrance door. Walking past it he practically tripped over a long stick that was lying on the ground before walking onto the street and seeing the three dustbins that he had put out the previous night.

Realising something funny was going on, he scanned the area. Nothing unusual was happening so he walked over to the dustbins to check they belonged to the flats. They were, and had been emptied.

This he found weird but at that moment instinct told him he had been set up.

He sensed someone was sending him a hidden message. An extra dustbin, a long stick. What with the things in his flat and now this, he felt there were too many coincidences happening for it to be normal.

Checking the area again, he noticed the Fiat Panda still sitting there.

He thought it strange—it had been there a week and not moved. He guessed he was being watched but couldn't prove it. He sensed the Panda was where he was being watched from. Again, he couldn't prove it.

As he stood in front of the car his mobile went off. Answering it, all he got was five beeps. Replacing the phone in his jacket, he walked off down the street towards his office. Two minutes later, he received another call on his mobile. Again, it was five beeps.

'Bastards,' he thought.

Muller wasn't daft. He knew instantly Meyer's mob were deliberately setting out to worry him.

He thought it made sense, the Panda sitting there recording his every move. He realised the chances were the phone was bugged as well. It could explain the problem of the cable TV playing up.

'State interference, of course! It was easy, just link into the cable line *et voila*, instant population control.'

As he walked into town he thought, 'sod 'em!'

Muller knew he'd done nothing wrong but was aware someone from the state was deliberately giving him a warning because they didn't like what he was doing.

At Police Grand-Ducale headquarters, Detective Meyer hadn't been at his desk more than ten minutes when the phone rang.

"Meyer. Ah Andre, how are you?"

Andre replied down the phone, "Oh, I'm okay thanks. And you?"

"Fine, it's the start of another week."

Looking out of his window Meyer said, "How's Luxembourg looking this morning?"

"Why don't you come over and see for yourself, Ernie. I've got a few bits that might interest you."

Meyer paused for a second. "Yes, what time?"

"Say nine o' clock."

"I'll be there as Tammy's been seconded onto other duties this morning."

"Okay, see you shortly."

Meyer left his office at Police Grand-Ducale headquarters and walked up through the city towards Andre Biever's office at the Villa Louvigny. He had given himself plenty of time to stretch his legs with the walk between the two. He walked through the municipal park at a more leisurely rate as he found it relaxing. On reaching the entrance to Villa Louvigny, he walked in past some parked cars. As he did so he looked up at the tower and thought 'It's a pity Radio Luxembourg moved out' before continuing towards the entrance.

Passing a 'Ministry of Education' sign on the wall, he went into the building over to a reception area where several security guards sat. He greeted them and said, "Good morning, Detective Meyer to see Andre Biever in the 'Special Needs' department."

A guard replied, "Good morning Detective Meyer. Could you wait a moment please?"

The guard picked up the phone, dialled a number and said, "Herr Biever, a Detective Meyer to see you." Replacing it, he said to Meyer, "This way please," escorting him to a lift.

The doors opened and they went in. The guard produced a special key and inserted it in the 15th floor button. The lift started its ascent and moments later, the doors opened and Meyer arrived at another reception area with 'Special Needs Department' plastered over one wall. He walked over to a girl at another reception desk and said, "Detective Meyer to see Andre Biever."

She smiled and said, "Good morning, Detective Meyer, we're expecting you. Please go in."

She pressed a button, a door opened and he went in.

A vast communications and special operations room awash with operators wearing headsets greeted him. Andre Biever, seeing Meyer, walked over from his desk and shook hands. "Hello Ernie. Thanks for coming over."

"Good morning Andre."

Andre walked over to his desk and looked out of the window. "As you can see, it's still a bit hazy but the view's as good as ever."

"Yes, I envy you that. All I see from my office is a block of flats!"

"Have a seat, Ernie."

He pulled up a chair next to where Andre sat.

"Coffee or tea before we start?"

"Coffee would be great."

Signalling to a girl nearby, Andre said, "Danni, could you get us two coffees please?"

Andre turned to Meyer. "Now to business."

"What have you got to show me?"

"About an hour ago the Panda reported Muller walking over the stick that we delivered last night. Here, let me show you."

Andre clicked a few buttons on his screen and replayed the scene. "As you can see, he found the extra dustbin we left him."

"Yes," replied Meyer, watching.

The coffee arrived and they sipped it.

Having viewed the clip, Andre said, "It's quite funny to watch, especially the bit when we phone him and give him the beeps. That worried him."

"Indeed?"

"When Muller arrived home on Saturday night he gradually discovered our calling cards but it took him until Sunday morning to make the connection.

We listened to him go round checking everything. It's amazing the technology one can hide in a flat, not to mention a Panda. Oh, and the small dragon sticker that we left on his lift door we replaced with a small Portuguese flag sticker during the night. Subtle, aren't we, Ernie?" He laughed.

"As always, Andre. You always know how to do a good sting operation."

"Let me show you yesterday afternoon's video. I transferred it to DVD."

He clicked on his screen.

"Have a look at this, Ernie."

The DVD showed Muller and Graf at several points during the tunnel trip.

Andre said, "If you look at this bit you'll see Graf peering at the locks at the entrance to Fort Nieder-Grünewald. Is he going to pick them? If I rewind, you can see the two Englishmen with their girlfriends at various points clearly watching and following Muller."

Andre skipped to the next track.

"If you look here you can see the Portuguese girl beaming as she comes out of the tunnel. There she is, whispering something to one of the Evans boys."

"Oh yes," murmured Meyer.

"It looks as though she's discovered something. That's the only point I can find where the couples are not acting normally. When they come out of the tunnel, they are seen as lovers. However, if you notice they're the last out and are several minutes after everyone else. Don't you find that a bit odd, Ernie?"

"Normally I wouldn't take any notice of two lovers, but in the circumstances I have to agree with you."

"You remember we said at some point we lost Muller and Graf in the tunnels? Well, it was during this period."

Meyer said, "I agree there's something funny going on. Have you pulled in any intelligence off their mobiles?"

"So far there's nothing. But it's still early."

"Can I have a copy of the DVD?"

"I thought you'd ask so I copied one already for you." Andre passed him the disk in its case.

"Thanks, and keep me posted on any other developments," Meyer said.

"Well, if you look at your emails you'll see I've sent you the latest intelligence."

"Good, it should be useful." Meyer finished his coffee.

"Oh, and whilst you're here, have a look at this. It's a video shot of Muller talking with Graf last night outside his flat."

They watched it, after which Meyer said, "I'd better get back. I'll review the new data. Thanks for the coffee."

"Thanks for coming over."

"I'll be in touch. *Äddi.*"

"*Äddi.*"

As Meyer walked out he thought, 'Good old Andre—never lets me down.'

At Shaun's flat, Jason Evans had drifted back to sleep after his brother's early departure for work. Just after ten, he got up and made himself a cup of tea. Looking out of the kitchen window, he was a little unsure as to what to do.

Finally, he turned his brother's computer on and scanned the Jenisch letter and the translation of it, just in case the originals got lost. Printing a few copies, he put them all in a safe place.

Deciding to stretch his legs, he set off for a look round the shops.

In Luxembourg City centre Jason Evans contemplated his next move. Seeing a bookshop, he went in to look at what they had on

Spain but found the choice limited. The next bookshop he was delighted with, discovering many travel books in a variety of languages. Flicking through several including Spain he realised he didn't know what he was looking for.

Whilst walking round the shop something caught his eye. It was a book called *Jenisch*. Picking it up, he looked inside, realising it must be the book the two men in Pfaffenthal had mentioned. However, they had said it was out of print and could only be found at the National Library.

Flicking through it, he noticed it said 'Reprinted 2003'. Fascinated, he decided to buy it. He went over to the sales counter and paid for it, saying to the sales lady, "I heard this was only in the National Library. Do they reprint it often?"

"No, I think the last time was ten years ago."

"Oh right. Do they print many?"

The woman shook her head. "Hardly a demand for it, eh!"

Jason thought she had a point.

"Thanks," he said and walked out of the shop.

Jason Evans decided to call in at Eighteen's café. Walking over to the bar, he sat at one of the stools, ordered himself a beer and fell into a conversation with a Luxembourger called Heinz.

During their discussion, Jason asked his new acquaintance, "Do you know anything about metal detectors?"

Heinz laughed. "Unfortunately I don't, but my colleague might." Turning to his friend he said in Luxembourgish, "Jos, what do you know about metal detectors?"

"What do you want to know about them?"

"No, it's not me. It's the Englishman here."

"I'm Jason by the way."

"Nice to meet you Jason," replied Jos in English, shaking his hand.

"The thing is, do you know where I can buy a metal detector in Luxembourg?"

Jos thought about it and said, "I'm not sure you can."

"I know in some countries they're not allowed. Does this apply here?"

"Ah, I'm not sure on that either."

Jason realised he wasn't getting very far but added, "I'm curious about their penetration depth when looking for metals."

Jos replied, "I can answer that as my friend has one in England. We used it when I visited him. They don't go very deep—about thirty centimetres."

"That's interesting," said Jason.

"Yes, but if you're thinking of using one in Luxembourg, forget it!"

"Oh, why's that?"

"Well, you need permission from the Minister of Arts and Science."

"Really!"

"Not only that, the Ministry of Justice regards it as a contravention of the law."

"I see. So what you're really saying is in Luxembourg they're not allowed."

"You've got it, and if you did find anything I think the state would automatically claim it."

"Well, thanks for the information, Jos. It's better to know these things than break any rules, eh!"

"Good luck with your hobby."

The conversation moved onto other subjects before Jason finished his beer and left.

Walking down Grand Rue in the city centre, Jason Evans passed a travel agent. After looking at the special offers in the window, he decided to go in and look round.

"Can I help you?" a woman said in Luxembourgish.

"Do you speak English?"

"Yes, I do."

Jason took a seat at the desk where the woman was sitting.

"Do you have any brochures on Torrevieja in Spain, please?"

"When would you like to travel?"

"Do you have any last minute deals?"

"Yes, I'll have a look for you."

"What about flight only? Is that possible?"

"Yes, but it depends on which airline you want to take. What sort of price are you looking at?"

"Well, not too expensive. What have you got?"

The woman scanned her computer and after a few moments came up with a few examples which she showed Jason. They discussed a few options after which he said to the sales woman, "Thanks for the information."

Having strolled round town, Jason decided to call in at a Portuguese delicatessen shop near his brother's flat. Whilst at the checkout he recognised a man further on in the queue.

"*Moïen*," Jason said to him, smiling.

The man said, "*Moïen*," grinned, and once he had paid turned towards the exit. Jason decided to make his move.

"Hi, it's Jerry Barthel, if I remember?"

"It is, and let me think—you must be the Englishman who came on the forts tour yesterday?"

The two stood there, each holding their shopping.

Jason continued, "That's right, I'm Jason Evans. My friends and I thoroughly enjoyed it and can't wait for the next one."

"Well Jason, our club does have other forts to visit. Did I not give you some information regarding our next trip?"

"You did, but I have something important to tell you which I think you may find extremely interesting. Say, do you have time for a quick drink where we can discuss it?"

"Well, I have the shopping here, and I have a few things to do this afternoon, but as it's such a nice day, why not?"

"Great!" replied a delighted Jason, adding, "When?"

"I could meet you at four. Perhaps the Place de Paris would be better, eh?"

"Fine, see you there at four."

At Police Grand-Ducale headquarters, Detective Meyer strolled into his office after a heavy lunch with his colleagues in a local restaurant. As he sat down Inspector Bruns popped his head round the door and said, "Good afternoon, Ernie."

Meyer looked up. "Inspector Bruns, sir."

"Can we meet up, say in quarter of an hour for an update?"

"Yes sir."

A few minutes later Gendarme Henckels walked in.

"Ernie, I'd better let you know I'm not feeling too good."

"Oh, take a seat, Tammy. Is it serious?"

"No, it's just a migraine, but it's getting worse. I may have to go home if these pills don't shift it."

"We've got a meeting with Inspector Bruns in ten minutes. Can you survive that?"

"I should, but if I'm quiet you know the reason."

"Oh, don't worry, leave it to me," Meyer muttered, concerned.

After checking their emails, they made their way to the Inspector's office.

The door was open as Detective Meyer and Gendarme Henckels arrived.

On seeing them Inspector Bruns said, "Come in, take a seat." Starting the conversation on a lighter note, he said, "I hear you've been out with a cowboy, Tammy. Is that true?"

They laughed and she replied, "Yes sir, it's true, though strictly business."

"Of course! But did you find anything out that will help with the enquiry?"

"Actually, we discovered a lot sir," said Meyer.

They both updated the Inspector with everything since their last meeting.

Meyer finished the update saying, "As you can see sir, we have changed tactics. For the moment we are concentrating on the tunnels and whatever is down there rather than our original thoughts concerning the dragon. This, we think, is a separate, unrelated issue that still needs investigating. Muller is—or was—involved with both, but we think because of his father's pressure he's having to concentrate on the tunnels ahead of anything else."

Inspector Bruns listened to their reports in silence. After a moment he said, "Hum, so what you're saying is, nothing's going to happen for a few days."

Meyer said, "That's right. Gendarme Henckels and I have spent some of this morning on other duties, but we'll need to prepare a plan of action."

"What do you suggest?"

"Well, it would be good to involve Andre and some of his team. I'll need to run it through with him."

"Fine, Ernie. Do what you need to do and we might have a result sooner than later, eh!" The Inspector laughed.

"Anything else, sir?" Meyer asked.

"No, that's all for now."

"Thank you, sir," they both replied, shaking hands with Inspector Bruns and departing.

As they walked back, Gendarme Henckels put her hand to her head and said to Meyer, "Ernie, I'm really sorry, but I'll have to go home. This migraine is killing me."

He looked at her. "No problem. I hope you feel better tomorrow."

She walked down the corridor and Detective Meyer returned to his office to write up his report.

CHAPTER 22

───────────▼───────────

Jason Evans sat at one of the tables outside his favourite restaurant on the Place de Paris, relaxing and sipping his coke in the afternoon sunshine. He was waiting for his rendezvous with Monsieur Barthel, having returned from his flat.

Just after four, Monsieur Barthel arrived. On seeing him, Jason waved and he walked over to where Jason sat.

"*Moïen* Monsieur Barthel. Thanks for coming,"

The two-shook hands and Monsieur Barthel sat opposite Jason.

"Oh, it's no problem. Actually, it's rather nice to get out of my flat in this weather. Now tell me, you mentioned that you have something interesting to discuss?"

"Oh yes," replied Jason. "It was fortunate I saw you earlier because I wasn't sure what to do."

At that moment the waitress arrived.

"What can I get you?" asked Jason.

"A beer will be fine."

"Two beers please."

The waitress went away to get them. Jason continued.

"Where was I? Oh yes. Yesterday, as you know, my friends and I went on your tour. We enjoyed it. The thing is, when we were down one of the tunnels Maria, my girlfriend, overheard two men talking about buried treasure. Actually, we think its Nazi gold."

Monsieur Barthel smiled. "Well, there are many stories about gold. I myself mention it in some of my tours. Maybe your girlfriend heard one of these stories."

Jason thought about it. Had Maria got it wrong? But he knew there were too many other instances.

Jason replied to the comment. "Well, she could have done. Nevertheless, in this situation I don't think so. The thing is, when we were down one of the tunnels, I think it was in the last one, we encountered something unusual."

"You mean Fort Nieder-Grünewald?"

"It could be. It was the one in the forest."

"Yes," nodded Monsieur Barthel.

The beer arrived which Jason paid for. Both he and the waitress exchanged smiles before he continued.

"As I was saying, my girlfriend was on her way up the tunnel behind this guy. She overheard him talking to his friend about some treasure that his father wanted him to find. According to Maria, and from what she could understand, the men were conversing in three languages during their conversation. The odd thing was they were speaking in German, Luxembourgish and Jenisch."

Monsieur Barthel looked up. His eyes seemed to light up.

"Jenisch. That's interesting. Are you sure?"

"Yes, I'm sure. She couldn't understand every word but it is I gather similar to Luxembourgish, is it not?"

"Well, I'm not an expert on Jenisch and not many people are these days."

"Anyway, the man said his father is in a nursing home in Berlin. She also heard them talking about some yellow markers he had placed on previous tours. Apparently, this guy only joined your club to help trace the gold."

"Do you know the name of this man?"

"I do. His name is Klaus von Muller. Do you know him?"

Monsieur Barthel thought about it. "Yes, I've heard the name. If I remember rightly, he's German."

"He is," Jason continued. "Anyway, later on the tour Maria and I were looking around the tunnels on our own when we stumbled across Muller and his friend acting suspiciously in one of the smaller tunnels. We carried on exploring but later went back to where we had seen them."

"Many people explore the tunnels on our tours."

"Yes, but let me finish! What we discovered were some yellow markers in some cracks in the wall and on the floor; you would have to look hard to see them in the light. With not many people going down the tunnels means they'd remain undetected for months."

"And what do you think these markers mean?"

"From what my friends gathered, that's where the gold is buried."

"Well, I must say I admire your thinking. But don't you think you may be taking this a little too far?" Monsieur Barthel sipped his beer.

Jason continued, "Normally I'd agree with you. But there's more. During the tour we noticed that we and Klaus von Muller were being watched by some undercover police."

"Oh, this is incredible! Your imagination is running wild. You are wasting my time." Monsieur Barthel thumped down his glass.

"No, no, I'm serious. Look, just over a week ago I arrived here on holiday. On my first night in Luxembourg, my brother, his girlfriend, her friend and I witnessed a girl commit suicide off the Adolphe Bridge. It was terrible. Afterwards we had to go down to the police station. The guy walking his Rottweiler during the tour was the guy who interviewed us."

"He could simply be out for the afternoon walking his dog."

"We think there were another two undercover detectives on the tour. Do you remember the cowboy couple yesterday? He had a video camera with him…"

Monsieur Barthel nodded.

"…and was filming everything and, on reflection, everyone; well, his partner, according to my girlfriend, was the assistant of the man with the Rottweiler. She normally has long ginger hair but yesterday she was wearing a black wig. Oh, and I know Muller through his ex-girlfriend's best friend who, believe it or not, is a stripper in the Eastern Delight nightclub!" He paused, taking in the bewildered look on his companion's face. "It's a long story but I hope you get the idea. What I am trying to say is, something funny is, or was, going on, and I wanted to tell you about it."

Monsieur Barthel looked dubious. "Well, what you've said is most interesting. You know, I've been running these tours for many years now and you've certainly amazed me. How long did you say you've been in Luxembourg?"

"About eleven days."

"Well, Jason. For someone who's only been here a short time I think you have a good imagination. You've still a lot to learn about our country. What you say is all interesting stuff, but I've heard it all before. I mean, discovering gold is hardly new, is it?"

Jason realised he wasn't convincing him. "Look, I realise it sounds incredible, but none of us is making this up. My girlfriend is Luxembourgish and both she and I saw the markers. I believe what she said."

"You could be right." Monsieur Barthel shrugged. "Anything is possible."

"I even asked someone about the use of metal detectors and they said if anyone discovered any sort of metal or treasure the state would keep it. That doesn't bother me. All I'm saying is, wouldn't it be great if we found it ahead of Klaus von Muller?"

"So what are you suggesting?"

"Well, if there was the possibility of going back down the tunnel I could show you the markers and we could take it from there. I promise you, I'm not wasting your time."

"Well, the next tour for the club isn't for another month. However, I do have a private tour there tomorrow. Would that be any good to you?"

"Would it! That would be great. What time?"

"Three o' clock, as usual, but this tour is for a French group."

"Great!"

"I would suggest you join the tour and afterwards we can look for these markers; then I can see if your story is genuine or not. How does that sound?"

"Fine!"

Monsieur Barthel stood up. "Until tomorrow."

The two shook hands.

"Yes, and thanks for your time. *Äddi.*"

Jason was delighted. He had a result. All he had to do now was prove he was right. Sipping his beer, he relaxed and went over in his mind the events of the last few days before he picked up his mobile and called a number.

"Is that Olga? Hi, it's Jason. How are you? Yes, I'm fine. Where am I? I'm in the Place de Paris having a beer. What are you doing right now? Nothing? Great! Well, do you have time for a quick drink? I've lots to tell you. Okay—see you in five minutes."

Ten minutes went by during which Jason ordered himself a coke. After wondering where Olga had got to he suddenly looked up and saw her standing in front of him.

"Sorry I'm late," she smiled as Jason got up to embrace her.

"Oh, don't worry," he replied. "I only called on chance."

"Well, you were lucky!" she laughed, sitting opposite him. "You said you had lots to tell me?"

"Yes, that's right."

The waitress arrived and said, "*S'il vous plaît?*"

"What would you like?"

"A coke please."

"Make that two cokes, *merci.*"

The waitress departed and Jason resumed the conversation. "Where was I? Oh yes; well, it's been an interesting week. I've been checking out this Klaus von Muller. He's quite an interesting character from what I've discovered so far."

"What do you mean?" Olga lit a cigarette as she relaxed in the afternoon sun.

Jason related the events of the previous days, ending with, "So there it is. Have you managed to find out anything?"

Olga smiled. "To be honest, it's been a quiet week. My life is not as exciting as yours. I'm amazed at your discoveries. You sound like an undercover detective."

"It's luck more than anything." He smiled. "You know what I mean."

The conversation changed course and a while later Olga said, "Look, I'll have to go now Jason. I've got a few things to do."

"No problem. Can I meet you again?"

"Yes, of course."

"When?"

"When you've got some news."

The two of them laughed.

Getting up to kiss Jason on the cheek, Olga said, "See you soon."

"Yeah, bye."

The two went their separate ways.

At Police Grand-Ducale headquarters the phone rang as Detective Meyer sat down. "Meyer," he said.

"It's Andre, Ernie."

"Andre, what a pleasure. What's up?"

"We've received intelligence that Graf has booked his flight. He's flying AirLux tomorrow evening."

"Great. What time's his plane?"

"He's leaving Munich at 7.00 p.m., getting into Luxembourg at 7.30 p.m. Says he'll meet Muller at his flat."

"Perfect. How long is he here for?"

"He's booked a return ticket for Thursday morning."

"Excellent."

"Can we expect a bit of action?" Andre added, laughing.

"It looks like it," Meyer replied.

"What are you going to do?"

"I'm not sure yet. Any suggestions?"

Andre paused for a moment. "Perhaps we could discuss it over a beer?"

"Yes, that sounds a good idea. When?"

"Say six-thirty at The Grand Canyon bar?"

"That will be fine. See you shortly, *äddi.*"

"*Äddi*"

Meyer smiled as he replaced the receiver. Something told him the next stage of the operation was about to start.

Meyer was late arriving for his rendezvous. As he walked up to the Grand Canyon bar he saw Andre sipping a beer on the outdoor terrace.

Andre raised his glass to show him he had seen him coming.

Meyer sat down next to him. "Sorry I'm late. I've been rushing around doing odds and sods."

"Where's Tammy?"

"She's not feeling so good; had a migraine this afternoon so went home to sleep it off."

A French waitress came out and Detective Meyer ordered a beer.

"So the action starts tomorrow night, Andre?"

"Yes, but I did say he was here for two nights, so it could be Wednesday before it really starts. He's simply flying in tomorrow."

"True."

"The Panda and the bugs we planted will tell us what's happening. As soon as I know we'll let you know. By the way, what are you going to do?"

"That's a good point. To be honest I'm not sure. I'm hoping your intelligence stakeout unit might have some ideas?"

"Yes, we can help you there."

"From what you and Tammy said we can't get access to the tunnels as it's controlled by this tunnel club."

"You're forgetting I hold the master key, Ernie."

"Of course! However, as I've never been in those tunnels I'd rather act on the surface. From what you have described it's a bit of a maze."

"Yes, I see your point. Tammy and I simply followed the crowd, but it's easy to get lost if you take a wrong turn, especially on your own."

"What do you think Muller's chances are of finding anything?"

"It's hard to say really. After all these years, is what they are looking for still there? I mean, surely the government checked those tunnels?"

"They did on numerous occasions after the Nazis left but didn't find anything, or so they advised the media. You know how it is, Ernie…"

"Oh, don't I," he replied, smiling. With his curious face on he added, "I mean, think of all the thousands of people who must have been down there since. Why has no one discovered anything before?"

"That's easy, Ernie. We just walked through the tunnels for fun; we're not excavating them! Look, no one was searching for anything except us and I can assure you, when you've seen one tunnel you've seen them all."

Meyer nodded.

Andre continued. "Whatever is hidden is not going to stare us in the face, is it? That's why Muller is having difficulty. Quite frankly it's like looking for a needle in a haystack."

The waitress came out to serve another customer. Andre called her over and ordered another two beers.

"Listen Ernie, do you want to know what I think you should do. Here's my suggestion…"

The Evans brothers decided to have a night in, chilling out with the beers Jason had bought that afternoon. The TV was on with a European football match showing. As they sat watching Shaun said, "I can't go out every night, Jason. I need to recharge my batteries."

"I know what you mean," replied Jason. "You can read my new book on Jenisch if you like?" He passed it over. Shaun glanced through it.

Jason continued, "I was in a few bookshops this morning looking at books on Spain. I didn't find anything I wanted."

At that moment Shaun's phone rang. He answered it.

"It's for you," tossing his mobile over.

"Hello?" said Jason.

"Hello Jason, it's Jean-Claude Kremer. We met on Saturday afternoon."

"Yes," replied a surprised Jason.

"Listen, you remember my father saying that something was at the back of his mind? Well, he's found the answer and wants to tell you. Can you meet him at the same bar tonight?"

"Yeah, no problem. What time?"

"Say at nine."

"Okay, see you. Bye."

He hung up and looking at Shaun said, "So much for a night in! That was the guy I met on Saturday afternoon in Pfaffenthal. His father wants to meet me tonight in the same bar. Apparently he's got something to tell me."

"Oh," said Shaun who was watching the TV and didn't fancy going anywhere.

"Don't worry, I'll get the bus and walk the rest. I checked the bus number on Saturday on my way back."

Jason Evans walked into Copacabana bar in Pfaffenthal where some salsa music was playing. A few of the locals were seated at the tables, including the old man at one of them. At the bar was Jean-Claude Kremer who, on seeing him, said, "Jason, just in time. What can I get you?"

"A beer, thanks."

"One more please?"

As the barmaid poured the beers, she said to Jason, "Well, this is a pleasant surprise. Can't keep you away, eh!"

"It's a great place," he responded.

Still standing at the bar, Jean-Claude said, "Thanks for coming down so quickly."

"My pleasure," said Jason curious as to why he was there.

The beer arrived with a cheery smile from the barmaid.

"*Merci*," said Jean-Claude, handing her a note.

They took the beers over to the table where the old man was sitting.

"*Moïen*," said Jason to him, shaking hands.

"*Moïen*."

"Actually, Jean-Claude, I've forgotten your father's name—sorry!"

"René."

"That's it."

The old man nodded and sipped his beer. Jason remained, fascinated by the man's false teeth that made his jaw move oddly.

"So your father has some information for me?" he said.

"Yes," Jean-Claude nodded.

He spoke to his father in Luxembourgish who suddenly had a light in his eye that made him seem twenty years younger.

"You remember on Saturday my father said something was nagging him?"

"Yes."

"Well, later that night he remembered what it was."

Jason was intrigued. Jean-Claude continued: "My father's an old man now, nearly eighty, lived in the area all his life, so knows everyone. Okay, these days he doesn't know all the Portuguese who now live down here, but what I am trying to say is, he remembers all of the locals who used to live here. More importantly, he remembers a girl called Ellie Pitt. She was Jenisch, was around his age and apparently was very good looking."

Jason looked at him, wondering where the conversation was going.

Jean-Claude continued: "The thing is, during the war she married a Nazi."

"And…"

"The letter we looked at on Saturday was sent to a Klaus von Muller, right?"

"Yes."

"Well, Ellie Pitt married a German called Erich von Muller."

"You mean this Muller is his son?"

"He could be. My father tells me for many years the Pitt family lived close by to his family. They were a poor Jenisch family who struggled to survive, especially pre-war. In those days Jenisch people were treated like dirt by the Luxembourgers, who despised them. Anyway, by marrying a Nazi the family became better off. The thing is, she was blonde and Hitler liked blondes for breeding purposes."

"You mean the Aryan look?"

"Yes. Actually, he was an SS officer, so the family at the time lived well. Anyway, when the allies advanced, the Germans retreated. Muller was recalled to Berlin. From what my father can remember Ellie went with him. She hurriedly left Luxembourg and was never seen again."

"Surely she must have come back after the war?"

"No. You have to remember she was Jenisch, not Luxembourgish. Therefore, to marry a Nazi, especially an SS officer, meant the family would have been treated, how do you say in English, like lepers, after the allies arrived in Luxembourg. It was better for her to be with her husband. My father as you can see is quite excited by all this. It brought back so many memories. I haven't seen him like it for years." Jean-Claude paused to sip his beer. "Yesterday afternoon he met an old friend of his to discuss your situation. Not only that, but in the afternoon they went to the local church to check the marriage records. They spoke to the local cardinal who was most helpful. Amazingly, the old wartime records were still there. Anyway, after a bit of searching, they found what he was looking for. Ellie Pitt married Erich von Muller on 4th June 1942." Jean-Claude stopped again to sip his beer before continuing. "From what they could both work out, Ellie and Erich survived the war. My father's friend remembers hearing from the family that she used to send them letters from Berlin. However, she lived on the Russian side of the city where communications were not good. The Russians punished Erich. He was sent off for ten years hard labour in a prison camp and was lucky to survive. Anyway, on his release he returned to East Berlin where he was reunited with Ellie. Nine months later his son was born. This is where it gets a little hazy. As far as they know, the son was called Klaus. My father remembers seeing a photo of him as a baby that his mother sent back to Luxembourg. It was all very hushed up, as only a few people knew what had happened to Ellie. In the late fifties the family moved out of the valley and never returned. That's all we know."

"Fascinating," said Jason, still taking it all in.

"So, Jason—have you come up with anything new?" said Jean-Claude.

"Actually I have, but first another beer?"

The old man and Jean-Claude nodded. Jason went up to the bar and ordered the next round. Returning to the table with the beer he said, "Yesterday my friends and I went down some secret tunnels at a place called Fort Thüngen. If I hadn't met one of Shaun's friends on Saturday night I wouldn't have known they existed."

He went on to update the two men of the events of the previous day after which Jean-Claude said, "Well, you and your friends have certainly got yourselves involved in quite an adventure, eh Jason! But like I said before, be careful."

They finished their beer and Jason said, "Same again?"

"No, not tonight thanks, I've work tomorrow. We'll go now. You have your information. Let us know if you discover anything."

The three of them got up. Jason shook hands and said, "Thanks a lot."

"Not at all."

They departed with Jason returning to the flat where during a few cans he updated a surprised Shaun.

Both had an early night.

CHAPTER 23

▼

There was little cloud about as Jason Evans arrived at Fort Thüngen a couple of minutes before three. A coach was parked near the rear of the fort. A group from it were waiting outside the entrance.

Just after three, Monsieur Barthel arrived, greeted the coach party and Jason before walking over the stone arched bridge to unlock the fort and go inside.

Jason realised it might be the same procedure as the previous Sunday as Monsieur Barthel came out and started the tour. He followed at the back, half listening to what was being said, contenting himself with the knowledge that the best bit would be later.

As the group entered Fort Nieder-Grünewald, Jason made sure he was the last person to descend the steps. Unbeknown to him at that moment, he was being watched.

In the bushes beyond the clearing lay two undercover agents.

Once everyone had descended, and on seeing Jason Evans, one of them phoned headquarters.

"Andre, its Graham at the fort. The tour group's arrived and descended into the tunnel."

"Thanks, Graham," said Andre, thinking that it was a good job they had tapped the tour leader's phone.

"Oh, Andre," added Graham. "There's something else you should know."

"Oh, what's that?"

"The Englishman's with the tour."

"The Englishman! What's he doing there?"

"That's what we're going to find out."

"Yes, keep me posted."

Underground in the tunnels, Jason tried to remember where he had been the day before. Retracing his steps down the passageways, he scanned the walls looking for a yellow marker, keeping his distance from the group in front whose torches faded rapidly leaving him alone, his torch beaming on the wall. Eventually, he stumbled across a yellow marker wedged in a wall. Knowing he was close, Jason carefully searched for the next one.

It was located two passageways further on. He realised the tunnel he was searching for was on his right, having seen it the previous Sunday. If he hadn't been looking he would have gone right past it.

Going down the narrow tunnel, he remembered what Maria had said about a small piece of wood in the wall with a paint mark around it. Shining his torch and using his brother's to give more light, he searched the walls.

"There it is!" he said aloud as he found the remnants of a rotten piece of wood in the wall. Around it, he noticed, the wall had been painted black and yellow over a small area.

He produced a water bottle from his pocket and placed it on the floor after which he caught up with the tour. By now some people were on their way back, so he turned around and returned to the surface via the secret entrance in the forest.

Monsieur Barthel was the last one out and once he had noted Jason was looking at him from above, locked the door and the grate before leading the party back to Fort Thüngen.

As he walked along the forest path Jason caught up with him.

Further back, Graham crept out of the clearing and followed the group.

"Did you find anything?" Monsieur Barthel asked Jason with interest.

"Yes, I found what I was looking for. I've left a water bottle in the tunnel as a marker so it's easy to find later."

Once they were back at Fort Thüngen the tour group split up. The undercover agent who was following mixed in with the group, listening for anything Jason might say. There was nothing, so he carried on walking, passing slowly through the group to the right of the rebuilt fort, admiring its beauty as he did so.

After Monsieur Barthel had gathered the group together and spoken with them, he came over to where Jason was standing and said, "I'm afraid you'll have to wait another half hour or so. I've been invited for a drink over at Junker's Cabin. Why don't you join me? We can search afterwards."

They walked over to the log cabin. As they did so, Graham phoned the second undercover agent to meet him at the rear of the fort.

The tour group including Monsieur Barthel and Jason found themselves a place on the terrace and when the waitress came out ordered a drink.

A short time later, the undercover agents sat down at a table close to where Jason and Monsieur Barthel were talking to some of the group. They ordered themselves two mineral waters and sat there relaxing, looking out on the old forts, occasionally talking to each other at odd moments in Luxembourgish. Most of the time they listened to what Monsieur Barthel and Jason Evans were discussing.

Jason spoke with a few of the tour group in French whom he discovered were from Paris. They were on a mini fortress tour of Europe, and Luxembourg was their first stop. For the two undercover agents listening, it didn't provide any leads.

When Monsieur Barthel and Jason had finished their drink, they made their excuses and left the group, walking past Fort Thüngen, back through the forest to the secret tunnel entrance.

As they did so, the undercover agents split up and followed, making their way back to their lookout point in the forest.

Monsieur Barthel opened the grate and descended the steps that led to the locked door of Fort Nieder-Grünewald, which he opened.

He said to Jason, "I'll let you lead the way!"

Meanwhile Graham was watching from his concealed position in the forest. Reporting to Andre on his phone he said, "Barthel and Evans are now back in the tunnels."

Underground, as they walked along Jason said, "Why are these passageways so low?"

"They didn't need to be high as the soldiers were shorter than those today."

"You mean they were midgets?"

"No, no," Monsieur Barthel laughed. "In those days people weren't as tall."

"What were they used for?"

"When the tunnels were built under the original fort the smaller inner ones were used as storage, the outer ones as defence, so if the enemy attacked and was above the tunnel they could be blown up. It would collapse in a way so the enemy couldn't penetrate the tunnels, and later another tunnel could always be dug."

The two men walked on, shining their torches as they did so.

Some way down the tunnel system Jason located the first yellow marker.

"There's the first one," he said.

"Oh yes," said a surprised Monsieur Barthel.

The two proceeded to the second marker after which Jason located the tunnel where he had left the bottled water.

"This one," he said as he shone his torch up the narrow tunnel.

Walking up it, he located a yellow marker in the wall. Pointing his torch on the floor he said, "See, here's two more."

"So there is!" said a still surprised Monsieur Barthel.

"Earlier I was looking for a piece of wood with paint around it." He flashed his torch around. "I couldn't find it at first but…ah, here it is," he added, triumphantly shining his torch at the remnants. "As you can see, there's not much left after all these years, but there are still traces of some black and yellow paint on the wall."

"And this is where you say the gold is?"

"Well, it's somewhere here. The question is where?"

Both of them looked around for further clues.

Jason added, "Perhaps there's a secret doorway that's been boarded up."

Monsieur Barthel shook his head. "No, it can't be that. If you look along the walls, they're solid rock. There are only two places your gold could be."

"Oh, where's that?"

"It's either buried somewhere along this passageway or the tunnel continues further along."

"You mean it doesn't end here—what we see is false?"

"Possibly. The tunnel could have been made into the shape it now is, so to the naked eye it looks as if the tunnel ends here."

"This is where a metal detector would come in handy."

"Not if it's buried too deep,"

"Oh yes, I forgot. So where could it be?"

"Well, my guess is to look at the floor."

Both of them shone their torches along the passageway.

Monsieur Barthel said, "Look carefully. You'll notice the tunnel floor at the entrance starts off as stone. Further along it becomes earth and stone and towards the end, it is earth. If you look, you'll see this is the natural line of where the rock in places ended and the earth began. Also, after the forts were demolished, the whole of the surface area round here was levelled and over time the forest grew up making this an ideal place to hide something."

"I see, so now what?" said Jason.

"Let's go back to the car. I brought some tools with me just in case."

"What do you mean?"

"Just in case you were right, Jason! So far you are. Let's go."

On the forest path Monsieur Barthel and Jason Evans walked quickly back towards Fort Thüngen. As they did so, Graham informed HQ, "Barthel and Evans are heading for the main fort, will follow."

As Monsieur Barthel walked along, he got his mobile out and made a call in Luxembourgish. "*Moïen*, Roland. How are you? Good. Yes, I'm fine thanks. Listen, what are you doing right now? Nothing? Have you got a couple of hours to spare? Good! Are you feeling fit? Do you want to help me find something interesting? No, I'll tell you more once you arrive. Where am I? I'm at Fort Thüngen. Listen, can you bring your largest torches, gas lamps, spade and a pickaxe with you, please? We'll meet you in Fort Nieder-Grünewald. I'll leave the gate unlocked for you. When you arrive, shout and you'll find us further up on your right. Great! See you in half an hour." Monsieur Barthel was excited as he talked to his friend. He finished the conversation by saying, "Roland, this is the moment we have talked of for many years. *Äddi*."

He hung up and put his mobile in his pocket.

As he did so, the undercover agent said on his mobile, "Did you get that call? Sorry, I didn't catch the conversation."

Andre replied, "Communications will relay the message to us shortly."

Jason asked nosily, "Who was that?"

"That's Roland Halsdorf, a good friend of mine. He's also in the LFC club. Like me, he's retired and got a bit of time on his hands since his wife died last year."

"Do you have a wife?" asked Jason, feeling embarrassed for having asked the question.

"Yes, Josephine and I have been married for thirty-one years." He smiled. "She lets me out every so often and as a part-time hobby I run some of the tours."

"Good idea."

"At my age it keeps me fit."

"What did you used to do?"

"I worked on the railways—used to be a train driver. Years ago, I drove steam trains. With the onset of diesel, I retrained. Actually, I still drive steam trains today."

"Today?" asked Jason, surprised.

Monsieur Barthel laughed. "Yes, I'm a member of a local steam train association and every so often we go on trips to various places. The last one was Koblenz in Germany. Have you been there?"

"Not yet,"

"It's a good day out as the journey on the train takes you through some wonderful countryside including a breathtaking journey along the Moselle River. As it passes under the bridges the steam goes everywhere. It's a delight to watch."

"I must try it," said Jason. "What's Koblenz like?"

"There are some lovely shops to look round and the walk on the promenade where the Moselle meets the Rhine is a must. If you've got time, there's a huge fort to visit. I went there years ago with my wife."

"You said something about steam trains?"

"Oh yes—well, as a member of the steam engine association I get to take my turn driving the steam train, and sometimes when we swap over I keep the fire burning."

"Really! That must be fun. I've always wanted to do that."

"Yes, it takes me back to the golden years of steam trains in Luxembourg. Those were the days."

In the forest, the undercover guy watched as Monsieur Barthel and Jason reached his car in Fort Thüngen car park. He opened the boot and pulled out a couple of spades, a barrow, two gas lamps, three white safety hats, another large torch and a pickaxe. He put all of them in the barrow.

"You came prepared!" exclaimed Jason.

Monsieur Barthel laughed. "Yes, I came prepared. Actually, Jason, if you're right, this will be a major discovery. I have to confess I'm as excited about the prospect of finding gold as you but didn't want to say anything until now."

"I see you brought some safety hats. We didn't use those yesterday,"

"Ah, but we weren't digging for gold, were we!"

"True."

"Where we're going to be digging you're likely to hit your head more than once on the roof of the tunnel. It's really low."

After Monsieur Barthel locked his car they set off towards the forest with Jason pushing the barrow.

At the forest clearing where Fort Nieder-Grünewald was situated, Jason Evans and Monsieur Barthel heard what sounded like a large twig break in the forest nearby. They both looked in the direction of the noise but neither could see anything beyond the thickness of the forest.

After a moment, Jason passed the barrow down the steps to Monsieur Barthel. Back underground, they found their way back to the location of the side tunnel where the water bottle had been left in a more prominent place.

"So what do you suggest we do first?" asked Jason.

"Well, I propose we start digging towards the end of the tunnel. Let's see if we come up with anything. I hope you're feeling fit, Jason. You're a bit younger than I am."

The gas lamp was lit and placed in front of them while the torches were placed at separate points, one at the other end of the tunnel, the other close by to where they stood. The two of them set to work, digging at a point where the roof made it difficult to dig and where the floor was earth towards the end of the tunnel.

"If you look carefully," said Monsieur Barthel, "you'll see the tunnel roof appears to slope downwards. It's a little deceiving to the human eye, as it is so black down here. Nevertheless, if you adjust your eyesight you'll see that the earth slopes upwards slightly. Not a lot, but enough to give us a clue that maybe something could be here."

At some point Jason pulled out his phone and said, "I'd better turn this off or I'll run out of battery. I forgot to charge it."

"Well, it's no good down here," replied Monsieur Barthel.

After a few shovelfuls Jason said, "The earth is hard to dig in places and easier in others. Is that normal?"

"Yes, I noticed that. I must admit it's a bit unusual."

During the first quarter of an hour, Jason updated Monsieur Barthel of the events since their previous meeting on the Place de Paris.

Outside in the forest the two undercover agents lay waiting and watching. Suddenly they saw a man walk into the clearing from the forest path and descend the steps into the tunnels of Fort Nieder-Grünewald.

Underground, Jason Evans and Monsieur Barthel heard an odd sound. It was like a wolf whistle from further round the tunnel system. Monsieur Barthel stopped his digging and shouted in Luxembourgish: "Roland, down here!"

Roland Halsdorf appeared at the end of the passageway.

"What have we here?" he asked in Luxembourgish, surprised.

He placed his tools along the passage. As he did so, Monsieur Barthel said in an excited tone, "Well, don't just stand there. Light your gas lamp and come and help us."

Roland Halsdorf lit the lamp, placing it at the end of the passageway. He picked up his pickaxe and walked back to where the two were digging.

Monsieur Barthel continued, "It's a long story, but this is Jason. He's an Englander."

"How do you do?" responded Jason, shaking Roland's hand.

"Hello Jason," said Roland, speaking and continuing his conversation in English. "Well, as you can see, I've brought the bits you suggested, Jerry. I guessed something was up by the tone in your voice."

"You'd better wear this," said Monsieur Barthel to Roland.

He gave him a white safety hat.

As they dug, Monsieur Barthel told Roland in Luxembourgish the story so far, at the end of which Roland said in English, "This is very exciting. To make a discovery after all these years would be, like you say in English, hitting the jackpot!"

Monsieur Barthel interjected, "Of course we may not find anything, but if we don't try we won't find out."

"But surely, if this Klaus von Muller was smart enough, he would have been back by now?"

"Why should he rush?" said Monsieur Barthel. "After all, it's been nearly sixty years since his father was in Luxembourg. Incidentally, Jason, you said his father was in the SS?"

"That's right. However, what regiment I don't know!"

"Ah, that's easy. Your old man friend said he checked the records in the church. It will be recorded in there, but in all the excitement he probably forgot to tell you."

"We know the SS had the plans of the tunnels. My guess is that Muller had access to them. Knowing he was on the losing side, he decided to offload some of the gold in his authority to a safe place. What better place than the tunnels?"

"Muller could have hidden it in the weeks before the allies arrived, to pick up later on a rainy day," said Jason jokingly. "Mind you, it's been a long rainy day!"

"It's a good theory."

"Yes, you'll have to find out more, Jason."

"Oh, don't worry, I intend to. After all, I've got the time."

"And the inclination, by the sound of it. I'm amazed by your research so far."

"It's luck actually, but it's interesting. If the girl hadn't committed suicide none of us would be here now."

"True. But did you find out why she killed herself?"

"No, that side's gone a bit quiet. The police are still looking into it."

The three of them continued to dig, transporting the earth into the barrow and depositing it in a nearby side tunnel.

Some minutes later Jason said, "The thing I don't get is, where did they get the gold from? Was it in a Luxembourg bank before the allies arrived?"

Monsieur Barthel replied, "Oh, I doubt that. In those days the banking sector wasn't what it is today. Most gold was usually held in Switzerland, as that was a neutral country favoured by the Nazis as a safe haven. Mind you, I'm not saying there wasn't any held here in the banks. As from where it came from…"

The digging continued with the smell of hot sweaty bodies.

"Maybe we're digging in the wrong place?" Jason laughed. "Maybe it's the wrong kind of earth we're digging!"

By now, there was a large hole forming across the narrow passageway.

"I think we'll have to go a little deeper," said Roland.

They readjusted the lighting and continued.

After about five minutes Roland said, "Wait a minute, I've got something here."

He dug round the area with his spade to identify the object but discovered it was a large rock. As he dug it out the gas lamp flickered and faded. Monsieur Barthel went over to it and, using his torch, changed the gas canister before relighting it.

After a while Jason said, "This is hard work!" By now the sweat was pouring off his forehead.

"Listen to him, Jerry. Anyone would think he hadn't done a hard day's work in his life."

"Well, he did work in a bank!"

The two men laughed.

Volkert Graf walked through customs and out into the arrivals area of Findel airport in Luxembourg. He dressed casually, carrying his overnight bag. Outside he took a taxi.

In Limpertsberg, Detective Meyer and Gendarme Henckels waited in their black VW Golf for Volkert Graf to arrive.

As he got out of the taxi Gendarme Henckels said, "There he is!"

"Yes," Meyer nodded.

Graf leaned over the seat. He paid the driver who got out and took his bag from the boot.

"*Merci* monsieur," said Graf, who walked up the path and rang Muller's bell. The door buzzed and he made his way up.

"What do you think he'll do next?" asked Gendarme Henckels.

"They'll act tonight as Muller's booked tomorrow off, starting later as it's quiet at this time of the night."

Gendarme Henckels added, "I don't see why he doesn't do his digging in the day. No one goes down there, Ernie."

"They might not, but people use the forest paths and they don't want to be seen acting suspiciously."

"Well, you can't get more suspicious than at night."

"You know what I mean, Tammy."

As the lift door opened, Graf saw Muller standing in the doorway waiting for him.

"Good evening Volkert. Thanks for coming," said Muller, shaking him firmly by the hand. "Come in."

They went into the flat where Graf dumped his bag on the floor.

"Did you have a good flight?" asked Muller.

Graf replied, "Yes, not bad, and there were no delays, which is good."

"It's going to be a long night Volkert."

"I'm sure it is. That's why I need to eat, Klaus, before we do anything."

"How about a takeaway? It's quick."

They decided on an Indian and Muller phoned the order through.

Putting the phone down, he said, "That's sorted. If we leave in ten minutes it'll be ready when we arrive."

"Good."

"Would you like a cup of coffee?"

"I fancy a beer, Klaus. Have you got one?"

"No problem."

He went into the kitchen and brought two cold beers from the fridge. Returning to the lounge, he passed one to Graf. "That should cool you down."

"Cheers."

"Cheers."

"Buy the way, how did last night go?"

Graf paused. "Don't laugh, but it was cancelled."

"Cancelled! Why?"

"I don't know. All I know is, they'll be in touch shortly."

"How do you know that?"

"Some Chinese girl personally delivered a note to me yesterday afternoon."

Graf got it out, passing it to Muller who looked at it—a dragon symbol on the bottom of the paper.

"So for the moment we're none the wiser on our other little venture."

"You're right, we're not."

As they drank their beers, Graf said, "Did you assemble the bits?"

"Yes, they're in the car in the car park."

"*Wunderbar!*"

"We'd better go if you want your curry hot."

They got up and made their way down to Muller's Renault Scenic that was parked in the underground car park.

Reaching it, Graf said, "Can I check the boot, Klaus, in case you've forgotten something? We don't want to come back, do we?"

Muller opened it and Graf rummaged through, satisfying himself everything was in order.

"Yes, it's good," he said. "Okay, let's go."

Reversing out of the bay, Muller drove up to a rope that was hanging down, opened his window and pulled it. The garage door opened and he drove up a steep slope onto the road, heading for the curry house.

As they did so, Meyer started his engine. He was about to leave when his mobile rang. "It's Andre Ernie. Listen; stay where you are. They've only gone for a takeaway. They'll be back in about ten minutes."

"It makes me feel hungry thinking about it," Meyer replied. "Okay, thanks Andre."

"What's happening?" asked Gendarme Henckels.

"We're advised to stay here as they've gone for a takeaway. However, when they return and leave again, that's when the next stage of Andre's plan kicks in."

CHAPTER 24

▼

Time seemed to pass by in the tunnels at Fort Nieder-Grünewald as the three men worked in the dimness of the gas lamps that guided them.

Once the barrow was full of earth, Monsieur Barthel wheeled it round to a nearby side tunnel. There was a continued smell of sweat from them as they worked in the confined space, their efforts hampered by the low ceiling of the tunnel.

As they dug the men talked, each finding out about each other. A mutual bond was forming between them.

After a while Jason said, "God, I'm knackered. I didn't realise we'd be digging for gold today!"

"Jason, I don't think any of us did," replied Monsieur Barthel.

"I have not had as much fun in years," said Roland.

Jason walked down the passageway and collected his water bottle. Taking a swig, he offered it to the others who gulped down a few mouthfuls to quench their thirst.

"I think we should concentrate our effort on the end of the tunnel," said Roland. "If you use the pickaxe to break up the soil, Jason, I'll use the spade to dig it out."

They resumed work. Monsieur Barthel took away another barrow of earth. When he returned, they discussed various theories of why Muller Senior had never been back. During this, Jason was curious and asked, "Why do you think Muller senior didn't discuss all this with his son before?"

"Do you know anything about the SS?"

"Only what I've read and seen in the movies."

Roland Halsdorf laughed as he dug. "Well, I'll tell you. When an SS officer took his oath, he had to honour and defend the Fatherland for life. Remember, the Third Reich was meant to last for a thousand years. Therefore his pledge to the Fuhrer didn't end when the war ended. Many SS soldiers secretly kept their vows. Those that did kept many secrets from the allies. Some things remain secret even today. Whilst many old Nazis are now dead through old age, Muller's father is still alive and on realising he was getting too old to retrieve the gold has possibly had to tell his son his secret, thus breaking his SS oath. However, if he didn't, the secret would be lost forever. Now Muller junior is actively searching for the gold, but doing it in a way that no one will think he's acting suspiciously."

"But what's that got to do with a girl committing suicide?"

"That's a good question that for the moment, Jason, none of us know. The two could be linked, or they might not. Both could be a coincidence—only time will tell. Now are we digging or what?"

"Sorry," said Jason who had stopped for a breather. He picked up his spade and continued.

"The other odd thing about this is the Jenisch connection," said Roland Halsdorf.

"What do you mean?" said Jason.

"Well, you said you spoke to the old man in Pfaffenthal who spoke Jenisch. He helped you translate the letter you found, right?"

"Yes, and?"

"Well, how did Muller learn Jenisch?"

"I don't know."

"Well, someone must have taught him."

"Maybe."

"Jenisch is not a language or dialect that many people know."

"Yes, we know that."

"Well the chances are he learnt it from his mother. After all, don't most offspring learn a language from their parents?"

"Well, I learnt my French at school."

"Yes, everyone learns a language in school. Nevertheless, you're missing the point, Jason. Muller grew up in East Germany where he would have learnt Russian. Jenisch wasn't spoken that I'm aware of in East Germany."

"You've got a point there," said Jason.

Roland Halsdorf continued: "Muller's mother would have learnt her Jenisch from her mother and family, the language having being passed on from generation to generation. She would also have learnt it at the local school. Of course, if she spoke Jenisch, it meant her origins weren't truly Luxembourgish, so the family would have found life hard."

"What do you mean?"

"Well, to be Luxembourgish until fairly recently you had to prove you could trace your roots backwards by four generations."

"Really!"

"Oh yes, the local Jenisch population like many others were discriminated against by the state, as they weren't regarded as true Luxembourgers. These days the European Union has changed this."

"Am I missing something here?" said Jason.

"Look, Jenisch is special."

"I know that," added Jason patiently.

"It's a dying language. Not many people speak it, and those who do are a rare breed. Look, most Luxembourgers haven't even heard of it. By learning Jenisch in East Germany, Muller had an advantage others didn't have. In everyday life he wouldn't need it, but as we know he did use it and to his advantage in whatever he is up to at the moment to cover his tracks."

While the two diggers rested, Monsieur Barthel took another barrow of earth into the adjacent tunnel.

They were all beginning to feel a bit despondent as the time ticked by. Nothing had been uncovered and it was hard to tell in the area they had been digging whether the earth had been dug previously.

Roland and Jason continued their efforts excavating the extreme end of the tunnel.

"We're tunnelling, Jason!" said Roland.

As they dug, Jason noticed something unusual. "This earth is coming away easier than I thought."

"You're right," replied Roland.

At that moment all felt tired, hungry and on the verge of calling it a day, their enthusiasm draining rapidly. Monsieur Barthel was beginning to wonder if Jason was wasting everyone's time.

Thirty seconds later Jason's spade hit something harder than earth. As he dug more soil out he said, "I've got something here."

The others watched as he used his trowel to probe and dig, scooping the earth up with his hands to put in the barrow.

Monsieur Barthel shone two of the torches at the area Jason was digging.

"There's definitely something there," said Jason excitedly.

As Volkert Graf finished his Indian at Klaus von Muller's flat in Limpertsberg, he said, "That was delicious, Klaus. I do like a good curry. It's so English."

"Yes, me too. We have some good Indian restaurants in Luxembourg." Drinking his beer, Muller added, "When you're ready, Volkert, we'll make tracks."

"Give me five minutes to get changed, Klaus."

"Yes, no problem."

Once they had finished their drinks, Graf put on a pair of old jeans and sweatshirt after which they went down to Muller's car.

Driving out of the basement car park, they turned left down the road towards the city and Fort Thüngen.

As they did so, Detective Meyer rang a number on his mobile. "Muller's just departed, Andre. I'll see you at the rendezvous."

"Okay, Ernie."

"Let's go, Tammy."

Meyer started the black VW Golf and drove off.

There was excitement in the tunnels at Fort Nieder-Grünewald as Monsieur Barthel shone the torches where Jason had made a discovery. Roland assisted Jason dig out the earth with the trowel. Suddenly all three could see something gleaming in the torchlight.

"Look," said Jason. "Is that what I think it is?"

He and Roland now dug carefully around the object.

None of them could believe what they saw. Never in their wildest dreams did they actually expect to find anything, yet at that moment, staring them in the face was the edge of a piece of gold.

"We've struck gold, boys!" yelled an ecstatic Jason Evans.

"I can't believe it!" said an elated Monsieur Barthel.

"Let me use my trowel, Jason," said Roland.

"Hang on, I want to take a photo of the moment," added Jason.

He pulled out his small digital camera and took a couple of photos before putting the camera to one side. Then he scooped carefully around the area.

"It's a huge piece of gold," said Roland, "and if I'm not mistaken it looks like the edge of a gold bar."

They continued to scrape away the soil.

"Let's try to pull it out," said Jason.

Slowly Roland and Jason edged the gold out from its hideaway. As they could now see, it was indeed a gold bar. Gradually they pulled it out.

"This is incredible," said Monsieur Barthel. "Congratulations, gentlemen. This is a moment to remember."

They all looked at the bar, taking it in turns to hold it like a child with a new toy. On top of it was something unusual.

"Look at that!" said an amazed Jason.

"It's the crest of the Third Reich," added Monsieur Barthel.

"It's a swastika," replied Jason. "A genuine Nazi swastika! This is real Nazi gold!"

"It must be worth a fortune," added Roland.

Jason picked up the camera and took a few more shots before Monsieur Barthel said, "Well, don't just stand there—let's see if there's any more."

"I'm amazed," said Jason. "My brother and the girls won't believe me when I tell them."

"Yes, if your girlfriend hadn't overheard Muller's conversation about him trying to find the treasure, none of this would have happened. You've got to thank her, Jason."

"Yes, and I might take her to McDonalds to celebrate!"

Everyone laughed before Jason placed the camera in a safe place and set to work again, using the spade and trowel to resume the excavation.

Roland said jubilantly, "There's more—I've hit something."

"Yes, and I have as well," said Jason.

The two men used their trowels and hands to probe further. The earth was removed by hand and as Monsieur Barthel held the torches they could all see the shine of yet more gold.

Working in silence and with bated breath, Roland and Jason edged the second gold bar out of the earth, then a third.

Jason said, "This is incredible! We've definitely hit gold! Can you take a few pictures of all this, Roland?"

He showed him how to use the camera and Roland took a couple of shots.

"My wife won't believe me when I tell her," said Monsieur Barthel. "Like you said originally, Jason, this is real treasure!"

"What a moment, eh!" added Roland.

Jason and Roland continued to dig while Monsieur Barthel held the torches. The gold was placed on one side of the passageway to allow the soil to be put in the barrow.

As Jason dug, he hit more resistance.

"I feel I've hit more than I did before."

He used his trowel. Roland assisted him. Suddenly a gleam of gold was detected in several places. As the earth was removed, a wall of gold revealed itself.

"Wow, look at that!" said an excited Jason. "This is what you dream of!"

"It's truly incredible," Monsieur Barthel said. "You know, a little earlier I was beginning to have doubts, but now I don't know what to say."

As Jason grabbed the camera from the floor and took more photos of the moment, Monsieur Barthel said, "Muller will kick himself when he discovers you've found his father's gold."

Jason replied, "He'll do more than that, he'll go ballistic! Still, now we'll need to find where the gold came from and anything else we can about it."

Klaus von Muller drove his black Renault Scenic up the rue Milliounewée and parked it next to two cars that were in the car parking area of Fort Thüngen.

"I thought you said this place was deserted at night?" said Graf.

"It is normally, but I forgot about the restaurant up here."

Getting out of the car, they went round to the boot and unloaded a barrow, spades, trowels, torches, gas lamps and some red hats they would need for the digging ahead.

As they did so, one of the undercover team was watching their every move. From the darkness of the forest, he phoned his boss.

"Andre, it's JD. Muller's arrived at Fort Thüngen car park."

"Okay, thanks JD."

Back at Muller's car, Graf asked, "Where did you get these?" pointing at the hats.

"I borrowed them from a Portuguese friend who works on a building site."

"Good idea, Klaus. I would never have thought about it."

Once everything was prepared the two men set off towards the clearing in the forest with Muller pushing the barrow and Graf walking beside him.

As Detective Meyer drove the Golf under the railway bridge and up the hill of rue des Trois Glands, the car headlights lit up some police officers and parked police cars ahead of them. Swinging into the car park bay, he and Gendarme Henckels got out of the car.

"Hello, Andre."

"Good evening Ernie, Tammy."

"Everything set?"

"Yes, we're all ready to go. Graham's phoned to say the Englishman and two Luxembourgers are still in the tunnel. JD has phoned saying Muller has pulled up next to the Luxembourgers' cars."

"So the stage is set," said Meyer.

"Do you want to know the other big news, Ernie?"

"Surprise me, Andre."

He spoke in a hushed tone. "The Englishman's found the gold."

Meyer looked at Andre in disbelief.

"Blood Hell, has he really! And?"

"According to Graham, you were right. So far that's all we know. We'll find the rest out shortly."

"I have to say I'm amazed what the Englishman's discovered. He has a knack of finding the answers."

"Yes, he's certainly assisted your enquiries."

"What about your guy? I take it he wasn't discovered?"

"Who, Graham? No, he did a bit of scouting down the tunnels, getting as far as he could without being discovered. Listening in the dark is not as glamorous as it might sound."

"I never said it was glamorous, Andre."

"No, I'm not saying you did. Still, he managed to find his way out following a trail he laid. He's just informed me."

"This exercise should be fun. Shall we go?"

"Okay."

Addressing his officers, Andre said, "Are you ready to leave?"

"Yes sir," they replied.

Leading the way, Andre and Meyer set off shining their torches with everyone else following.

Walking up the dark winding wooded path, Meyer said, "Where's Bruno?"

"He's on his way with his friend as we speak."

Underground at Fort Nieder-Grünewald Messieurs Barthel, Halsdorf and Evans had dug out fifty gold bars. Jason recorded the moment on film.

After further digging, Roland said, "There doesn't appear to be any more."

"I think you could be right," added Jason.

"Well, what a haul!" Monsieur Barthel laughed.

"We'll have to celebrate this, gentlemen," said Jason. "I could do with a beer!"

"A beer!" Roland exclaimed. "More like champagne for a find like this!"

They stopped digging and passed around the water bottle that Roland had thoughtfully brought with him.

"It's the nearest thing to champagne in the circumstances," said Roland. "Cheers, and thanks for making this a terrific day for me."

"Cheers!" said the others, drinking the remaining water.

At the clearing in the forest, Volkert Graf shone his torch as Klaus von Muller wheeled the barrow up to the opening of the secret tunnel. Putting it down, Muller said, "That's funny, the grate is open. I'm sure it's normally locked. Maybe the tour guide forgot to lock it on Sunday?"

"No—I remember him locking it."

Graf handed Muller a torch. Shining his torch down the steps, he said, "I don't want to worry you, Klaus, but the tunnel door is slightly open."

They walked down the steps and could see in the torchlight that it was slightly ajar.

"What have you got to say about that?"

"I must admit it's odd. I can't believe anyone like Monsieur Barthel would forget to lock up."

"Maybe someone is down there, Klaus?"

"Who would be here at this time of night? These tunnels are visited during the day. Of that I'm sure."

"Perhaps someone else ran a tour down here and they forgot to lock up?"

"It's possible Volkert. I've yet to meet everyone in the organisation. Anyway, let's not worry about it now. At least you don't have to pick the lock!"

"Pity, I was looking forward to it."

They walked up to the surface, carrying the barrow down the steps. They opened the secret door and went into the tunnel system.

Underground at Fort Nieder-Grünewald, Monsieur Barthel returned to the side tunnel, having emptied a barrow of earth. "You realise we can't keep the gold, Jason? We'll have to hand it over to the authorities."

"Yes, I discovered that yesterday from someone I met in a café. But do they give rewards?" asked Jason.

"I doubt it, but it depends on the significance of the find. Quite frankly, this discovery will have to be investigated further."

"Let's not worry about that now," Roland said. "Shall we load the barrow and take it to your car, Jerry? We might have to do several trips. I'm not sure how heavy the gold is. Might I suggest we deposit it at your flat? Then we can show it to your wife before handing it in tomorrow. What do you say?"

"It's fine with me. What about you, Jason?"

"Yeah, no problem. I'd like to show the girls and Shaun, if that's okay."

"Why not? But let's do that later."

"On a serious note, what do you think will happen?"

"We'll probably have to show the police down here and there'll be a few questions," replied Monsieur Barthel. "But we've done the state a favour, so have no worries. Shall we go?"

They gathered some bars and put them carefully in the barrow. Jason took a few shots before handing the camera to Roland.

"Can you do the honours and get some of me holding the gold?"

"My pleasure," he smiled.

As he did so, they heard sounds emanating from further up the main tunnel. Each froze, listening in silence; each could hear someone or something coming closer.

Whispering, Jason said, "Someone's coming."

The others nodded. Roland passed the camera back to Jason who put it in his pocket. They stood there waiting, saying nothing.

Muller and Graf heard voices as they manoeuvred their barrow along the tunnel system. As they approached the place with markers, there was no sound, only a gaslight shining.

Looking at each other in horror, both realised someone was at the location of the gold. Leaving the barrow with the tools inside, each picked up a spade and continued along the main tunnel, shining their torches as they arrived at the side passageway.

Suddenly in the gaslight that lit the end of the tunnel Jason, Roland and Monsieur Barthel saw the silhouettes of two people, their appearance masked by the poor light and their torchlight. The figures started walking towards them.

Jason shone his torch first, followed by the others who had picked theirs up from the floor. Dropping his jaw in astonishment, Jason saw the face of one of them.

"Klaus von Muller?" he said.

On hearing his name, Muller stopped and stared in disbelief. He could see the gold neatly stacked in the barrow in front of him and on the floor on the right of the tunnel, as well as the dimly lit features of three men standing behind it shining their torches on him. Shining his torch onto Jason's face, he immediately recognised him as one of the people on the previous Sunday's tunnel tour. Moving the torch onto the other faces, he saw Roland Halsdorf and the tour guide.

"Herr Barthel," he said in astonishment.

"Herr Muller," replied Monsieur Barthel.

All at once Muller's mind was awash with Sunday's trip, the couple in the passageway kissing, the couples with them, the cowboy couple and the undercover police officer with the dog.

"Who are you?" he asked Jason in German.

"Do you speak English?" asked Jason.

Switching languages, Muller repeated the question.

"I'm Jason Evans."

Muller wasn't sure what to say.

Jason continued, "As you can see, we've found your father's gold."

Muller couldn't believe what he was hearing. For a moment, he stood there, dumbfounded.

Finally, he said, "Yes, I can see that. How did you discover it?"

"Oh, that was easy; my girlfriend overheard you discussing it with your friend on Sunday. You were speaking Jenisch."

"How do you know that?"

"You're not the only person who speaks it. You communicate with your friend using it."

Jason shone the torch on Graf's face and continued with a smirk on his face. "You run a porn operation in Frankfurt which is where one of your flats is. You have another in Spain for filming."

Graf couldn't believe a complete stranger could know so much about their business.

Muller said, "How do you know all this?"

Jason paused. "I watched one of your movies, the one staring Nadia Ponomariov. I was the one who saw her jump from the bridge."

Muller remembered the police officer telling him an Englishman had witnessed the event. Realising it was obviously him, he said, "What's she got to do with this?"

"She left a phone number on the bridge when she jumped. I picked it up and followed it from there. As for the gold—well, dustbins are not the best place to leave discarded letters."

Muller remembered the letter he had put in the dustbin in Frankfurt, not believing for a moment that anyone, especially from Luxembourg, would have picked it up.

He had had enough. Putting his spade down he walked towards the loaded barrow, picked it up and wheeled it backwards into the main tunnel.

"Oh no, you don't!" Jason rushed round the barrow, attempting to stop him taking it.

Suddenly there was action. Graf, who had moved to the corner of the tunnel intersection to let Muller by with the barrow, leapt to his defence. Dropping his spade, he pulled Jason from behind away from Muller, punching him in the face. Jason fell backwards onto the floor.

"You bastard!" yelled Jason.

The two old men looked on but realised they would have to get involved if Muller wasn't to steal the gold from right under their noses. Roland moved round and rushed at Muller who dropped the barrow awkwardly. It overturned, spilling the gold bars across one side of the tunnel floor. Roland lashed out at Muller but he retaliated with his fist and Roland fell awkwardly onto some of the spilled gold.

Jason rapidly recovered and rose to lunge at Muller. The two men fought in the gaslight, which projected the flickering silhouettes of the action against the tunnel wall. Muller retaliated and aimed another punch at Jason, who fell badly onto one of the torches that lay strewn on the tunnel floor, shining out in the chaos of the moment.

At the same time, Monsieur Barthel grabbed a spade and moved forward to tackle Graf. But Graf swerved and lashed out with his fist, dropping his torch in the process. He picked up his spade and the two fought like swordsmen, Monsieur Barthel with all his might until Graf's spade whacked him painfully on the leg, causing him to falter, yell in pain and fall.

Standing up, Jason grabbed Muller and punched him in the face. Muller was knocked against the side of the tunnel but was quick to retaliate. Jason fell against the other side of the tunnel wall but grabbed Muller. Both fell to the floor where they rolled over and over, wrestling with each other, throwing cascades of dust into the air.

The two old men wrestled with Graf who threw Roland hard against the tunnel wall. From the side, Monsieur Barthel swore in Luxembourgish. The two of them used all their strength, grabbed Graf and pushed him into the central tunnel where he knocked the gas lamp flying. The two old men managed to throw Graf to the ground where, using their combined weight, they sat on him as he struggled in the dust and mayhem.

At that moment from the darkness of the tunnel of the opposite direction to where everyone had come in came a familiar voice.

"Police, Stop!"

Detective Meyer stepped out of the shadow of darkness, dressed in uniform, into the confused scene. "Well, well, well!" he exclaimed. "What have we got here?"

The five men looked up in amazement.

Behind him was Gendarme Henckels in uniform and behind her was Andre in casual gear and an armed uniformed police officer.

At the same moment, two uniformed officers carrying guns, along with the two undercover agents, appeared from the direction of the main tunnel the five men had entered. They each shone their torches on the scene. Behind them, the sound of barking dogs could be heard rapidly approaching. Two other officers arrived with Bruno and Bessie on their leads. The noise in the tunnels of the dogs barking was deafening.

The five men got up, looking in awe. Everyone except Roland recognised Andre and Tammy as the cowboy couple from Sunday's tunnel trip.

In order to make himself heard, Meyer yelled: "Can you take the dogs out and wait by the grate!" As they were led back along the tunnels, Meyer continued: "So, Herr Muller, you finally came to dig for the gold your father requested you to find? I must say it took you long enough, and when you did, you discovered someone else had found it, eh! Trying to steal someone's gold discovery is not a good idea." Looking at Jason, he said, "I have to congratulate the Englishman for doing such a magnificent job in beating you to your father's gold."

Jason kept his mouth shut, wondering what the hell would happen next.

Meyer continued: "We've been keeping an eye on events so know the Englishman and his two Luxembourg friends weren't going to run off with it. You won't have to deliver it to any police station—we'll be delighted to recover it tonight." He turned to Muller and Graf. "Herr Muller and Graf, I would suggest you come with us—there's one or two questions I'd like you to answer at the station. You can come voluntarily or we'll arrest you and take you down there in handcuffs. It's up to you."

"We'll go voluntarily," said Muller sourly.

"Fine. My officers will collect the gold using the barrows you've very kindly left us. You can collect your torches. Everything else must remain so we can check the site thoroughly. Shall we all take a walk outside? I don't know about you, but it's rather hot down here."

The five men collected their torches and followed the police towards the exit of the fortress tunnel system.

Everyone gathered in the forest clearing. Detective Meyer spoke in Luxembourgish to the assembled police officers with the dogs: "Take Muller and Graf to headquarters. I'll be there shortly."

They duly complied and set off with them, the dogs on either side, along a path that headed through the forest and down to the car park in the rue des Trois Glands.

Meyer took out his mobile, dialled a number and said in French, "Pierre, can you bring the cars down, please?"

Turning to the others, he said in English, "Messieurs Barthel, Halsdorf and Evans, you are free to go, but I will need you to come down to headquarters tomorrow morning at ten."

"No problem," Monsieur Barthel said. "Will I need to lock the tunnel up?"

Meyer replied, "As you can see, Herr Barthel, we have our own keys, so leave it with us, eh?"

Monsieur Barthel got the message. "We'll be off then. *Äddi.*"

The three left the forest clearing and, shining their torches, made their way along the forest track towards the car park.

Once they had departed, Meyer said to Andre, "That's a job well done. Thanks for your help."

"Yes, it was an interesting assignment. It did make a change from the normal run of the mill operations we do."

The two officers who were collecting the gold surfaced and Detective Meyer and Andre helped lift the barrows up the steps.

A minute later car headlights approached the forest clearing. Two police cars pulled up and from one of them a woman in her late sixties appeared.

Rushing up to Meyer, she said, "Have I missed the action?"

Laughing, he replied, "I think you have, Milly."

"You always spoil the fun, Ernie Meyer."

"I'm only doing my job," he replied, laughing.

Looking round, she added, "So where are my lovelies?"

"Oh, they're on their way to headquarters escorting some new friends they've met. You can pick them up on your way back with us."

During this conversation, the officers who had collected the gold loaded it into the boot of the police cars.

Meyer turned to Andre. "I'll let you and the boys lock up for the night."

"Yes, no problem. We'll go back and double-check the tunnel to see if we can see any more gold. We'll seal the tunnel and check it fully tomorrow."

"Okay, let's clear the area." Meyer turned to the woman. "Come on Milly, it's time to go."

She was busy looking round the clearing but dashed back to the police car where she sat next to Gendarme Henckels in the back seat.

As Meyer got in the passenger seat of the first police car, he closed the door, wound down the window and said, "That was a bloody good idea of yours to come in the back way, Andre."

"Yes, Sunday's tour proved its worth in the end. Of course, having special keys made it easy, but that's part of our job. Listen, I'd better go and finish up." Andre signalled to Graham and JD to come over from the steps of the tunnel entrance. "Right, see you, Ernie."

"Yes."

"If I get anything I'll call you."

"Yes, that's good," Meyer said.

Andre nodded.

Meyer signalled the police cars to depart. Soon they disappeared up the narrow forest track.

Turning to Graham and JD, Andre said, "Right, let's complete this operation. If you lock and seal this entrance JD, Graham and I will check inside and meet you at the rendezvous point. After that we'll head back to the tower."

"Okay," said JD.

They descended into the tunnel. JD duly locked and sealed the door and grate before walking out of the clearing.

CHAPTER 25

▼

Standing by Monsieur Barthel's car at Fort Thüngen, Jason Evans yelled with joy: "Yes! We did it!"

Roland Halsdorf and Jerry Barthel also let off steam and everyone shook hands.

Jason looked at his watch. "Is that the time? Shaun will be wondering where the hell I am. He'll have thought I've left the country."

"Well, with that lot you could have!" Roland laughed.

"My friends won't believe me when I tell them what's been going on," said Jason.

"Nor will my wife!" Monsieur Barthel chuckled. "Okay, Jason, you come with me. Roland can follow. See you at my flat, Roland."

Monsieur Barthel parked his car outside his flat. Jason pulled out his mobile and said, "I must ring Shaun. He'll think something's happened. I was meant to be having dinner with him, Carmen and Maria. They won't believe it when I tell them…"

"Why don't you invite them round to my flat?" said Monsieur Barthel, and added, "Only don't tell them everything. Let it be a surprise, if you know what I mean."

Jason nodded as he turned on his phone. Some messages beeped through. "Shaun's been trying to reach me," he said as he read them.

He rang his brother.

"Shaun, its Jason. Where've I been? Oh, don't ask! Where are you? Amundsens Bar in the Grund. Great! No, I'm not coming. Yes, I know Maria's there. Listen, I've got a big surprise for all of you. No, I'm not winding you up. Listen Shaun…no, no, listen; can you drive over to where I am? Its really important, bruv! Can you come straight away? You'll thank me for it…Yeah, really! Bring the girls. Yeah, yeah. Where am I? Just a minute."

Jason looked over to Monsieur Barthel. "What's your address?"

Monsieur Barthel told him and Jason told his brother.

"How do you get there?"

Handing the phone to Monsieur Barthel, he said, "Can you give him directions, please?"

"Hello Shaun, it's Monsieur Barthel. How are you? Good. Fine thanks. The directions you need are…"

After everything was sorted he passed the phone back to Jason who ended the call by saying, "See you in half an hour or so." He hung up.

They got out of the car and went into the entrance hall of the flats where a jubilant Monsieur Barthel said, "Josephine won't believe me when I tell her."

Taking the lift up to the fourth floor Monsieur Barthel opened his flat door with his key and walked in.

Josephine appeared from the lounge and said in Luxembourgish, "Jerry, where've you been? I've been worried sick about you."

In English he said jokingly, "Ah, there speaks a typical wife, Jason. She wants to know where I've been. Never get married! You see what happens?"

He didn't mean a word of it, as Jason was well aware. Monsieur Barthel went up to his wife and kissed her.

"I'm sorry for not having phoned earlier, Josephine, but this Englishman delayed me. Let me introduce you to Jason Evans."

"Good Evening—um, how do you do?" said Jason a little shyly.

"Hello Jason," Josephine smiled. "Ah, I see you've been keeping my husband out late. I hope there's good reason!"

"Oh there is, Madame Barthel." Jason realised Jerry and his wife enjoyed an amicable relationship and got on well.

"We've got a surprise for you, Josephine," Monsieur Barthel winked.

"Oh, I like surprises," she beamed.

"Unfortunately it's not here. We're not actually able to show you."

"Have you been drinking, Jerry?" his wife laughed.

"No, it's not like that, you'll see. Wait in the lounge and we'll come in shortly."

Josephine returned to watching TV, wondering what he was playing at.

As Jason and Monsieur Barthel went into the kitchen, the door buzzer went. Monsieur Barthel went to the intercom, picked it up and, on hearing it was Roland, let him in before returning to the kitchen to find a few bottles of Crémant.

As the doorbell went, he said, "I'll get it Josephine."

"Sorry, I had to park the car round the corner," Roland said as he walked in. "You know what the parking is like round here!"

"I told my wife I had a surprise for her. Go and say hello, Roland, and she'll think *you're* the surprise! But don't say a word about the gold, if you know what I mean."

Roland went into the lounge where Josephine was watching TV.

"Surprise!" he said.

Josephine looked up. "Oh, hello Roland." She was a little per-plexed. "*You're* the surprise?"

"Yes, I'm the surprise, Josephine. What do you think?" he laughed. "Shall we run away now or later?"

"Roland, you're hardly a surprise—you're round here most weeks. As for running away, we'll leave that for another day, eh!"

"Actually, Josephine, you'll be sorry to hear I'm not the surprise."

Josephine looked quizzically at him. "Is it my new sofa? Jerry keeps talking about getting one."

"Oh, it's better than that. Wait a second."

Returning to the kitchen he saw a tray had been prepared.

Monsieur Barthel said, "Jason can you take the glasses in—and Roland, can you take those bottles? Thanks."

This they did as Monsieur Barthel found some biscuits. He put them on a plate and followed them into the lounge.

"Goodness, what's going on, Jerry?"

"Well, I should warn you to be prepared for a shock."

"Oh my God, Jerry, what have you done?"

"Well, Josephine, let me surprise you."

He sat down next to her and said calmly, "This evening, my friends and I found some Nazi gold."

Josephine wrinkled her nose as she screwed her eyes up at him. "Are you *sure* you haven't been drinking?"

"No, I'm telling you the truth, dear."

The others nodded.

Raising her hands to her mouth, she said, "How much gold?"

"Fifty gold bars."

"How much! Oh my God, Jerry, have you robbed a bank?"

The three men burst out laughing.

"Rob a bank. *Moi*! Come on, Josephine. You know I'd never do that."

"Well, where did you get them?"

"We found them in the tunnels. You know I had a tour this afternoon? Well, afterwards I went with young Jason here to search for this gold."

"Jerry, you just don't go tunnelling and find fifty gold bars."

"Of course not, but thanks to his girlfriend, his friends and their detective work, we've discovered one of the largest finds ever found in Luxembourg in recent times. I can only describe it as…" He was lost for words.

Jason stepped in. "One of the last secrets of the Third Reich."

"Are you kidding me?" Josephine said in disbelief.

"No, he's telling the truth," Jason smiled. "Unfortunately, the police arrived…"

"The police! Jerry, are you in trouble?"

"No dear, let Jason finish."

Jason briefly explained the extraordinary events of the day, after which Monsieur Barthel said, "That's why we've celebrating with the bubbly."

"I see," said an unconvinced Josephine.

"Shall we celebrate?" added Monsieur Barthel who started to uncork a bottle.

"Hang on a minute," said Jason.

As everyone looked at him, he added, "I think your wife needs a bit of convincing. We forgot to mention the camera."

As he got it out, Roland said, "I thought you'd have to get the photos developed?"

"No, this is digital. You can view every shot."

Jason passed it over to Roland who passed it to Josephine.

"Take a look at that," he said, showing her the last shot.

Josephine looked and was shattered.

"You see, dear, I was telling the truth," Monsieur Barthel smiled.

There was a moment of silence before Jason said, "Let me show you all the photos we took—then you'll get a clearer picture."

Taking the camera, he played with it for a moment, setting up a mini-slideshow. He passed it over to Josephine who watched with the others looking on. As she did so, she gasped with wonder.

When it had ended, she passed the camera back to Jason who reset it. Josephine said, "I don't know what to say."

"I know," said Roland. "Let's have that drink."

"Good idea," said Jason.

Monsieur Barthel finished uncorking the bottle and poured it into the four glasses. Handing them out he raised his glass and said, "Cheers, everyone. Let's toast the occasion, even if the gold is now with the police."

"Cheers," said Roland. "This doesn't happen every day, does it?"

After the drink Josephine asked, "But Jerry, what happens next?"

"Don't worry, it's all in hand. Tomorrow we have to go down to the police station at ten o' clock to answer a few questions. We're the good guys—we found the gold."

"But will you be in any trouble?" asked a concerned wife.

"Technically, yes, but in fact, no. If we hadn't dug it up Muller would have, so we've done the state a favour."

The doorbell rang.

"Maybe its Shaun?" said Jason.

Monsieur Barthel went over to the intercom and answered it.

"Hello Shaun, come up to the fourth floor, will you?"

He walked over to the front door and opened it. Thirty seconds later Shaun, Carmen and Maria walked in.

Jason greeted them, kissing the girls.

"Thanks for coming over—sorry about earlier. I promised you something special, so follow me."

They walked into the lounge.

"Let me introduce you to Monsieur Barthel, his wife Josephine, and this is Roland Halsdorf."

As they greeted one another, Shaun said, "When you passed your phone over to Monsieur Barthel I knew something was up. The question is, what?"

"Shall I tell them?" said Jason jokingly.

"Show them the photos," added Roland.

Jason passed the camera over to Shaun and said, "As you will see, we found the gold."

"Did you really!" said an enthralled Carmen.

Shaun re-ran the slideshow and they watched it. When it was over Maria went over to Jason, kissed him smugly on the lips then sat on his lap, saying, "Well done, Jason."

Josephine took her cue.

"Well, don't just sit there, Jerry, get another couple of bottles out, oh and some glasses. Let's celebrate this moment with our guests."

Monsieur Barthel did what he was told. The Crémant was poured and passed around.

"Here's to the new Indiana Jones and his team," said Monsieur Barthel smiling.

The story of the day's dramatic events was retold once again…

Some time later Shaun said, "Jason, it's been a great surprise and has certainly made our day, but some of us have to get up in the morning, so if it's all right with you, can we go?"

"No problem. Actually, I'm pretty knackered and I need a shower," replied Jason. Turning to Monsieur Barthel, he said, "What's happening tomorrow?"

"May I suggest I pick you up around ten in the morning? I'll pick Roland up as well. We can go in together, eh?"

"That sounds fine," replied Roland.

"Until tomorrow," said Jason. "Thanks, everyone, it's been a great day."

The others thanked their hosts and the four of them departed, Shaun dropping the girls off en route to his flat.

At Shaun's flat, Jason indulged in a long hot shower. Afterwards, as he left the bathroom, he said, "I wish you had a bath, Shaun, I could have done with a long soak after all that digging."

Shaun turned from watching TV. "Yeah, I miss a bath, but you get used to it. Anyway, it's healthier to have a shower—but I know what you mean."

As Jason lay on the sofa bed he said, "It's not everyday you uncover a pile of Nazi gold, is it?"

"That's true," Shaun nodded.

"The thing is, I wonder what Muller thinks of it all."

"His father will be mad with him."

"Maria's brilliant. Her language skills are what did it."

"You're right there. But listen, Jason, let's call it a night—I've had a hard day at work."

"Yes, I suppose even I've had a hard day's night!"

The lads both crashed out and slept heavily.

CHAPTER 26

▼

At Police Grand-Ducale headquarters the door to one of the interview rooms opened and two armed police officers walked in. They crossed the room going over to a cell on the right of the room.

"You've got fifteen minutes to use the toilet," one officer said as he unlocked the cell door.

There was a proper toilet area beyond the cell. Muller and Graf made use of the opportunity before returning to the cell.

The door was relocked and the officers stood in silence outside.

At eight, Detective Meyer and Gendarme Henckels walked in.

"Good morning, gentlemen. Did you manage to get a good night's sleep?"

They ignored him.

Signalling to the guard the cell door was opened.

Speaking in German, Meyer said, "Please take a seat."

Muller and Graf came out of the cell and sat down at the interview table where Gendarme Henckels was seated with her large notepad and tape recorder.

Meyer took a seat at the head of the table and said to a guard, "Could you give everyone a glass of water?"

The guard complied.

Meyer continued: "There's a few questions I'd like to ask you. You don't have to answer but it's in your interests if you don't want a few more nights behind bars."

Muller and Graf looked at each other but said nothing.

"Herr Muller, we know all about your father's past, and as you are aware, I'm investigating the suicide of your girlfriend Nadia Ponomariov. Nevertheless, there are a few points I need to tie up. I would ask for your cooperation."

There was a moment's silence, after which Muller said, "Very well."

Meyer commenced. "Can you explain the reason why your father hid the gold?"

"During the war my father was an SS officer."

"Yes, I'm aware of that, but go on."

"As you probably know, he was assigned to Luxembourg and worked at the SS Villa. He had access to plans of the tunnel systems in the city and subsequently got to know their layouts. He married a local girl from Pfaffenthal and had a house there, but in 1943 was transferred to Paris, coming home once a month to see his wife, daughter and friends. Erich liked the place, so in August 1944, when the allies were closing in on Paris, he took the opportunity to get out and come back to Luxembourg."

"What's that got to do with the gold?"

"Some high ranking Nazis decided to loot several Parisian banks and art galleries and send the contents to Berlin and Switzerland. They used Luxembourg as the mid point."

"Mid point, what do you mean?" asked Meyer.

"The wagons were split in Luxembourg with the art going to Berlin and the gold to Switzerland. It's a trick the Nazis used to fool the allies. The Germans did the same sort of thing in The Great War using armaments. My father's mission was to escort the consignment to Luxembourg.

From here, other Gestapo officers took over. The idea being, once in the Grand Duchy, he would continue his old job. The thing is, my father wasn't stupid. En route from Paris he went into one wagon and transferred a quantity of gold into his own trunks. No one would question or search his luggage, as he was Gestapo. He had it delivered to his house in Pfaffenthal where shortly after he had it moved into the tunnels. Under armed guard, some French workers were forced to extend the tunnel and conceal the gold. Mallets and spades were used to seal and smooth the surface so it would look the same as any other tunnel. They were taken into the forest and shot dead, not by my father but by another member of the Gestapo who my father ordered to do the deed. He marked an area in the tunnel with yellow and black paint and nailed a small piece of wood in the wall."

"How many gold bars did he conceal?" asked Meyer.

"Fifty"

Meyer nodded and Muller continued: "My father worked in Luxembourg for a month before transferring back to Berlin to work from Gestapo headquarters. He took his wife with him, as it seemed the best option with the allies rapidly closing in on Luxembourg. He departed at the end of August 1944 days before the allies arrived on the 9th September, remaining in Berlin until the Russians captured him. Enrich was held in a prisoner of war camp and sentenced to ten years hard labour, which he survived. Many others didn't. On his return to Berlin, he was reunited with his wife where he started a new life. As a result of his return, nine months later I arrived."

"I see, but why didn't your father come back to Luxembourg?"

"The Russians wouldn't let him. You have to remember it was a different world from the west, especially in those days."

"And when the wall came down?"

"He was involved in a hit and run car accident in the late nineteen-eighties. He was nearly killed, but instead was confined to a wheelchair and had little enthusiasm for living. Poetic justice, you might say."

"That doesn't really answer the question."

"He couldn't travel."

"So where do you come into this?"

"My father was an SS officer who swore an oath to Hitler. You know what that means."

"Yes, I do," Meyer nodded.

"He didn't tell a soul until last year when he finally realised that unless he did, the gold would be lost into time. He broke the oath and told me, as financially it would have set me up for life. Those bars are worth a small fortune."

"Maybe," said Meyer.

"There's an old saying, 'nothing ventured, nothing gained.' Yes, it would have been good to have the gold. However, the Englishman beat me to it. Me and my big mouth, eh Volkert!" Muller gave a hollow laugh.

"I'm curious on a couple more points," continued Meyer.

"Yes?"

"Your girlfriend, Nadia Ponomariov—she knew about this, didn't she?"

"She did."

"But you tried to stop her from telling anyone."

"Yes, it's true."

"You beat her up to keep her quiet."

"Detective Meyer, you know I cannot answer that fully."

"But she knew the importance of it?"

"She did, but I couldn't let her discuss it."

"When did Nadia find out?"

"She heard me discussing it with Volkert in Spain. When we returned to Luxembourg, Nadia found my father's map and copied the inscription down. She was a spiteful girl and got her own back when she had the tattoo done."

"I'd like to return to what it means?"

"I didn't tell you before for obvious reasons. The inscription *UB44138JS* was something my father made up. If it fell into the wrong hands, it could be thought of as a bank account. Whilst the date was easy to work out, it being the date my father hid the gold, the rest could be a problem. Tell me, Herr Meyer, what did you make of it?"

Detective Meyer smiled and said slowly, "At first we did think it was a bank account."

"Most people might think the Union Bank of Switzerland, UBS. Nevertheless, the letters are not what you think. U is for Unter or Under, B is for Bunker as in tunnel, S is for Schweigen or Secret. Finally, the J is for Jenisch—or Jéinesch, in its own language.

"Jenisch?"

"Sure, the Jenisch connection."

"The Jenisch connection? What do you mean?"

"It has several meanings. Firstly, my father's link to Luxembourg was when he married a Jenisch girl from Pfaffenthal. He hid the gold in the tunnel so after the war they would have a nest egg. Unfortunately, as we know, that didn't happen. The phrase, you could also say, is because my mother taught me the language. In East Germany it wasn't called for, but it had its uses and still does."

"We know all about that."

"Lastly, because the tunnels were practically on his doorstep in Pfaffenthal, where they spoke Jenisch."

"That's very interesting."

"It's funny, because I am working at the embassy, yet my father used to work up the road. Don't you find that ironic, given the circumstances, especially as I was unaware of the gold until recently."

"Herr Graf. How did you learn Jenisch?"

"I was taught by my mother. I'm from a gypsy family where Jenisch was spoken."

"I see," said Meyer. "Tell me, Herr Muller, what happened to your mother?"

Muller paused before replying. "She died in the car accident my father was involved in and he never recovered, which is why for many years he lost the will to live."

"I'm sorry to hear that," Meyer replied in a softer tone. "Is the dragon symbol anything to do with the Jenisch connection?"

Muller laughed. "You're funny, Herr Meyer. I think you're aware they are not connected. If I read between the lines, you haven't worked that one out yet, have you?"

Detective Meyer ignored the comment. "You are the connection between Nadia, her suicide, the Nazi gold, and the dragon. We are aware that Nadia's death has something to do with the dragon to the point where you stopped her telling anyone."

Muller ignored the comment. "As you know, Detective Meyer, I didn't kill her."

"But you pressurised her into a corner where she had no escape."

"Yes, I pressurised her, for her own sake, otherwise she would have been dealt with. Do you get what I'm saying?"

"I do, Herr Muller. She must have realised that knowing what she did put her life in grave danger."

"Exactly! She was young and foolish, but as for taking her own life, even I think it was unnecessary and crazy. Keeping her mouth shut would have been easier, but in the circumstances we'll never know."

Meyer paused and sipped some water. "You've been most helpful. Apart from a public order offence, which will be dealt with in the usual way, I have no reason to detain you further, especially in the light of your frank discussion. You are both free to go."

"Thank you," replied Muller.

As they stood up to leave, Meyer said, "Two things, gentlemen. There will be a press conference tonight to publicise the discovery of the gold. If I were you I'd consider a few days holiday outside Luxembourg."

Muller got the hint.

"Secondly, we shall be watching you, so bear that in mind."

"We will," Muller nodded.

Muller and Graf departed and walked briskly out of the police station.

Meyer stood up and said to the guards, "You can go now. Thanks for your assistance."

As they departed he added, "Come on, Tammy—let's have a break before the next lot arrive. I don't know about you but I fancy a coffee and some breakfast."

"Good idea, Ernie."

She grabbed her notepad and tape recorder and they went to the canteen.

In Shaun's flat, Jason Evans had drifted back to sleep after his brother had departed for work. A sudden slam of another flat's door woke him.

"Is that the time?" he said to himself aloud.

It was nine-forty. He got ready quickly. Just before ten he picked up his keys and left the flat.

Thirty seconds later Monsieur Barthel's car pulled up. Leaning out of the rolled down window, he said, "Good morning Jason, jump in."

"Good morning, gentlemen. That was good timing. I only just made it!"

Roland Halsdorf sat in the front passenger seat. Turning his head, he said, "Have you recovered yet, Jason?"

"Actually, I slept like a log."

The other two laughed as the car drove down the street.

Having parked in a police parking space, Monsieur Barthel, Jason Evans and Roland Halsdorf walked into Police Grand-Ducale headquarters to the reception area where Monsieur Barthel pressed the bell for service.

The police officer operating the desk appeared and Monsieur Barthel said in Luxembourgish, "Good morning, we have an appointment at ten o' clock with Detective Meyer."

"Could you give me your name?"

"Monsieur Barthel."

"Just a minute." The police officer picked up a phone and dialled a number. "Detective Meyer, it's the reception desk. There's a Monsieur Barthel and two other men to see you." The officer replaced the receiver. "He'll be with you shortly. Could you go up to the waiting room on the second floor?"

Turning to Jason, Monsieur Barthel translated the request, to which Jason replied, "This way, gentlemen!" He led them up to the waiting room where he took a seat. "This is where I came on the night of Nadia's suicide. I never thought I'd be back here so soon, especially to sort out a discovery of Nazi gold!"

"Life is full of surprises, Jason. It will be interesting to see what happens this morning, eh!" Roland winked at him.

After a few minutes' wait, Detective Meyer and Gendarme Henckels walked in. Jason thought it felt like old times.

Speaking in English, Meyer said, "Good morning gentlemen, will you follow me please?"

They got up and followed him into an interview room where he continued, "Please take a seat." Once everyone had, he commenced. "Thank you for coming this morning. It was an interesting night, don't you think?"

"Very," Roland nodded.

"What happened to Muller and his friend?" asked Jason.

"They had a night in the cells to calm down. However, this morning they were released."

"Released!" said Jason.

"Have you charged them?" asked Roland.

"They will be charged with public disorder, but that's all. Technically neither has done anything wrong."

"They were stealing the gold!" said Monsieur Barthel.

"Yes, but they hadn't actually stolen it, so we can't charge them." Meyer moved on: "There are a few questions I'd like to ask you. Mr Evans, to begin with—how did you meet Olga Yeltsin?"

"When I was on the bridge—and this is something I forgot to mention in the interview: I found a crumpled up pink piece of paper with a telephone number on. I found it moments after the girl jumped. Something made me put it in my pocket. However, with all the events that followed I didn't realise its significance and completely forgot it until much later. Eventually, I rang the number and discovered it was hers. We met up, as she was curious about me having it. To cut a long story short, it led me to the gold."

"What do you mean, it led you to the gold?"

Jason gave Meyer a précis of events, adding at the end, "As you probably know, I have also been investigating this case and would be interested to hear what Muller had to say."

"All in good time, sir."

Jason nodded and Meyer continued, "Herr Evans, I am aware of your visit to Frankfurt."

Jason looked a tad surprised but the detective continued, "Was there a reason for going, or was it a day out?"

"Actually, it was a bit of both, but more a day out. However, I struck lucky when I saw Muller discard a letter in a dustbin."

"A letter? Can you explain?"

Jason paused before answering. "At the time I didn't understand its meaning, but in a roundabout way it told me about the Jenisch connection."

Meyer couldn't believe he was hearing the same phrase again. "The Jenisch connection?"

"I met an old man in Pfaffenthal who translated it for me. That's when I discovered more about the Jenisch language Muller was using. I also found out about his father and mother."

Jason realised he knew a bit more but decided for the moment to keep it to himself.

"When did you hear about the gold?"

"My girlfriend heard Muller and his friend discuss it in the tunnels when we went on the fortress trip on Sunday. Actually, I believe you were there with your dog?"

Meyer laughed. "Yes, I was out for a Sunday afternoon stroll."

"Yeah, right! We did see your colleague dressed as a cowgirl." Jason looked straight at Gendarme Henckels who blushed. He continued, "Anyway, we checked out the tunnel and found the markers Muller had left. On the Monday I bumped into Herr Barthel and told him, didn't I?"

"You did," said Monsieur Barthel.

"And to cut a long story short, we found the gold," concluded Jason.

"Monsieur Barthel, you are aware it is technically illegal to do what you did?"

"Of course, but in the circumstances, Detective Meyer, you would have done the same, would you not?"

The detective didn't comment and Monsieur Barthel continued.

"As you know, I run many tours down those tunnels. I am also fully aware of Luxembourg state procedures, so know that any gold found automatically goes to the state. Considering the magnitude of this find you should be thanking us, not scolding us."

"My apologies, Herr Barthel, if I am giving you the wrong impression. You are quite right, your discovery is simply staggering and I'm hoping later today to hold a press conference with yourselves to publicise it. It is news the press will love, but you must appreciate this meeting is merely finalising a few points before we go public. I'm sure the press will have a thousand questions to ask you later." Continuing in a lighter tone, he said, "We are to hold a press conference at the town hall in Place d'Armes so we can display the gold to the press. If it's possible, we'd like you to attend."

"What time?" asked Roland.

"I propose six o' clock. How does that sound?"

"Is it just for the press or can we invite a few friends?" asked Jason.

"You can invite whom you like," replied Meyer. "I'm sure it will be fun."

After Monsieur Barthel conferred with Roland and Jason, he said, "We are happy with your suggestion. What time should we arrive?"

"About a quarter to six."

"No problem."

"Good. Well, that's it, gentlemen. Thank you for coming in. See you tonight."

The three men got up and said '*äddi*' as they walked out.

Detective Meyer and Gendarme Henckels grabbed themselves a coffee and called in at Inspector Bruns' office.

On seeing them, Bruns said, "Detective Meyer, Gendarme Henckels, come in, have a seat." After they were seated he added: "I hear there's good news."

"Yes sir."

"Actually, whilst you've been interviewing I heard all about it from everyone else. Well done, both of you."

"Thank you, sir."

"Perhaps you can recap before we move forward?"

Detective Meyer and Gendarme Henckels went through all the events again. When they had finished Inspector Bruns said, "Your assignment has proved to be interesting. Are you publicising the find?"

"We have arranged a press conference in the town hall in Place d'Armes tonight at six. I hope you can make it, sir."

"I'll clear my schedule for you, Ernie."

"Thank you, sir."

"I shall look forward to it, but if we can come back to the case in question for the moment, there's still some unfinished business to sort out."

"Yes, whilst we've solved one side of the case there is the unsolved question of the dragon."

"Well, you know what to do…"

"To solve it, sir."

"You took the words right out of my mouth. Of course, it may not happen straight away, but I'd say the two of you can handle it in-between everything else."

"Thank you sir," Gendarme Henckels replied.

"Well, I'm sure you've lots to sort for tonight, so I'll see you there."

Detective Meyer and Gendarme Henckels got up and walked out. As they went up the corridor he said, "Come on Tammy, we'll have to get our skates on if we're going to deliver this press conference."

"Ernie," she smiled, "I do believe you're panicking…"

CHAPTER 27

▼

On the first floor at the City Hall, Place d'Armes, everyone had gathered inside the grand ballroom. The room had two sections of seats laid out with a walkway down the middle. The press were seated in the front rows with everyone else behind. Above them stood two glass chandeliers. The local television station had cameras positioned on each side.

At the front of the room was a long table with a row of chairs behind it. On the right on the opposite side from a window stood another table, either side of which stood two armed guards. On the left was a projector screen.

As the town hall clock struck six, the door opened and Detective Meyer and Gendarme Henckels walked into the room, past the two-armed guards stationed at the door. Behind them followed Jason Evans, Monsieur Barthel and Roland Halsdorf.

They sat down behind the long table. After a moment Meyer stood up and said, "Good evening ladies and gentlemen. Thank you all for coming to this press conference. I'm Detective Meyer and this is my colleague Gendarme Henckels. Last night a major haul of Nazi gold was discovered here in Luxembourg. Tonight, we'd like to show it to you and introduce everyone to the people who found it. For those of you in the press, there will be plenty of time for questions in a moment. To the friends and families gathered, thank you for coming. As it is a hot evening, drinks are available at the bar. After the press conference, may I suggest a social gathering? But first, let me introduce you to…" as he spoke, he pointed to, "Monsieur Jason Evans, an Englishman, Monsieur Jerry Barthel and Monsieur Roland Halsdorf. Last night they discovered in the tunnels of Fort Nieder-Grünewald a quantity of Nazi gold that has been hidden from the world for nearly sixty years. If it were not for these men, it could have disappeared from Luxembourg without trace. I'll let them explain their story, as I'm sure they'll tell it better than I can. Before they do, let me show you the discovery."

Meyer walked over to the table with the gold and pulled back a cloth covering it. There was a moment of astonishment from the people in the room before a round of applause took place.

Taking one of the bars to the centre table, Meyer remarked, "As you can see, this is real Nazi gold with the swastika emblem on the side." He went over to a projector, turned it on and added, "Just to prove the point, here's a remarkable set of photographs that capture the moment." He ran the slide show after which there was another round of applause. Detective Meyer added, "Enough of me talking—the floor is yours. Perhaps you have some questions?"

The press started their questions and during the next thirty minutes, the story was retold…

Afterwards, at the back of the hall, everyone gathered to have a drink and talk about the find.

Maria and Carmen had come straight from work after Shaun had phoned them. Carmen went up to Jason, who stood there a little perplexed, and said, "Well done, you were great."

Maria grabbed Jason and kissed him. As she did, a few flashlights went off as the press caught the moment. She added, "Yes, he was good, wasn't he? A real Inspector Clouseau, or is it Morse…"

They laughed. Jason loved her accent.

"Well done, bruv," said Shaun, shaking his hand.

Monsieur Barthel was hovering next to the tray of white wine.

"May I have one of those, please?"

"Of course, Jerry, you deserve a few tonight," said his wife who was serving the drinks.

Roland Halsdorf stood next to Monsieur Barthel and said, "Well Jerry, what an amazing few days. This certainly is the icing on the cake. What an adventure, eh! Cheers, I'll have another!" He knocked back one drink and picked up another.

Inspector Bruns stood with a glass of wine in his hand, sipping it whilst talking with colleagues. On seeing Meyer, he walked up to him and said, "Ernie, I must congratulate you on a well organised press conference."

"Thank you, sir."

At that moment Milly appeared.

"Ernie Meyer, my hero! What can I say, adventure last night, party tonight! What next?"

Meyer laughed, "I don't know, Milly, but I'll let you know."

Gendarme Henckels had walked over with her drink to join them.

"Quite a gathering, Ernie."

"Yes, I'm pleased. By the way, Tammy, I forgot to say something to you."

"Oh, what's that?"

"Thanks for your help."

"No problem," she blushed. "But we've still got quite a bit to do, Ernie."

"Oh yes, but that's for another day."

Out of the corner of his eye, Meyer saw a familiar figure standing next to the exit door with two colleagues. Wandering over, he said, "Andre, fancy seeing you here!"

"It's hardly a surprise, Ernie."

"No, of course not, but thanks for your help."

"Well, it's not only me, there's Graham and JD for starters."

"Of course; well, thanks, lads, and enjoy the moment!"

Turning to his right, Meyer walked over to where a man and woman stood drinking some wine and said, "Doctor Jennings, what's this!"

Everyone laughed and the Doctor replied, "Medicinal purposes. Ernie, how are you? You remember my receptionist, Severine?" They shook hands. "Good to see you and the Englishman found the first part of the puzzle on the girl's back. I look forward to the rest!"

Standing by a pillar was a party of girls. Jason walked over to them, smiled and said, "Hello, Olga."

On seeing him, her eyes lit up. Kissing him on his cheeks, she said, "Hello Jason. Well done! This is great; I can't believe it after everything that's happened."

"Tell me about it…"

Olga introduced her girlfriends, some of whom Jason recognised from the Eastern Delight nightclub.

"And this is my boss," she said, pulling Boris Tarovsky over to her side.

"Good evening," he said with his strong Russian accent.

They chatted for a while before Jason said, "Sorry, got to circulate, see you later."

He went over to his brother and said, "You know Shaun, I'm thinking about going back to England."

"What, after all this? Well, it's up to you. You're welcome to stay."

At that moment, Meyer walked over to where the brothers were talking and asked Jason, "How's it going?"

"Fine, fine, but you know what, there's two people missing from here."

"Who's that?"

"Who do you think? I'm talking about Muller and his friend."

"Oh, don't worry about them. Mark my words, they'll be back. Let's just say right now they've taken a small vacation from Luxembourg!"

The three of them laughed and moved on, circulating. Jason saw some of Shaun's friends standing there.

"Hello Liam," he said.

"Top of the morning to you, my old son!" He clinked Jason's by now empty glass. "You never mentioned anything about all this."

"Ah well, some things are best left till the end."

"You remember John and Judith?"

"Oh yes. Well, thanks for coming."

Maria arrived with another two glasses of wine. Giving one to Jason, she pulled him away and kissed him.

"I love you Jason Evans," she said.

"I love you too!" he replied.

Two men walked over and joined them. One was an old man with a stick. On seeing them, Jason said, "*Bonsoir messieurs.* Maria, let me introduce you to the two men who translated the letter. This is Jean-Claude Kremer and his father René."

"*Bonsoir*, delighted to meet you," said Maria.

"Hello," said Jean-Claude.

"*Moïen*," said his father, his stiff jaw still fascinating Jason.

Everyone shook hands before Maria held Jason's hand.

"So Jason, you solved the mystery of the Jenisch Connection," said Jean-Claude.

"Yes, but I couldn't have done it without your help, so thanks a lot."

"Ah, no problem! You know this is very exciting for all of us. My father is delighted for you. This kind of thing doesn't happen very often in Luxembourg, and for you as a foreigner to help us—well, we Luxembourgers appreciate that."

"It's my pleasure."

"I told you, you made him feel twenty years younger."

"You did and I'm delighted, but I must tell you I don't think the game's over yet."

"What do you mean?" said Jean Claude.

"Well, part of that letter is still unsolved and I've not said anything to anyone, yet. Also, I've been doing my own bit of ear wigging and, according to what everyone is saying, one thing is very clear. There's the mystery of the dragon to solve…"

The story continues….

About the Author

David Robinson, 44, worked for Lloyds TSB in England until being made redundant in 2001. Seizing the opportunity, he moved to Luxembourg for three and a half years, moving at the end of October 2004 to Bratislava, Slovakia. Currently he is teaching English whilst writing his second reality book—about Bratislava.

More information available at **www.diadembooks. com/robinson.htm**

By the same author:

An Expat's Life, Luxembourg & The White Rose
ISBN: 0-595-31485-6
See **www.diadembooks.com/luxembourg.htm**

0-595-34840-8

Printed in the United States
29373LVS00001B/58

9 780595 348404